Lisa Marie Rice

Midnight Run

ELLORA'S CAVE
ROMANTICA PUBLISHING

An Ellora's Cave Romantica Publication

www.ellorascave.com

Midnight Run

ISBN 1419951068, 9781419951060
ALL RIGHTS RESERVED.
Midnight Run © 2002 Lisa Marie Rice
Cover art by Syneca.

This book printed in the U.S.A. by Jasmine-Jade Enterprises, LLC.

Trade paperback Publication December 2004

Excerpt from *Woman on the Run* Copyright © Lisa Marie Rice, 2004

Also by Lisa Marie Rice

ഇ

Port of Paradise
Christmas Angel
Midnight Angel
Midnight Man
Woman on the Run

About the Author

જ

Lisa Marie Rice is eternally 30 years old and will never age. She is tall and willowy and beautiful. Men drop at her feet like ripe pears. She has won every major book prize in the world. She is a black belt with advanced degrees in archeology, nuclear physics and Tibetan literature. She is a concert pianist. Did I mention the Nobel?

Of course, Lisa Marie Rice is a virtual woman and exists only at the keyboard when writing erotic romance. She disappears when the monitor winks off.

Lisa welcomes comments from readers. You can find her website and email address on her author bio page at www.ellorascave.com.

Tell Us What You Think

We appreciate hearing reader opinions about our books. You can email us at Comments@EllorasCave.com.

MIDNIGHT RUN

෯

Chapter One
Saturday, December 12th
The Warehouse
Portland, Oregon
Midnight

ဢ

She looked like a Princess, lost in the forest, trying to find her way back to the castle.

So what the fuck was she doing at The Warehouse?

Lieutenant Tyler 'Bud' Morrison, Portland Homicide, sucked down the beer he didn't want and raised his eyes to look over to his right. To the Princess he'd been watching all evening.

She was on the other side of the U-shaped counter, in profile, watching the dancers and talking to a girlfriend with wild red hair.

Bud had the redheaded girlfriend all figured out. He'd been observing her for three nights now. The Warehouse, Portland's wildest dance club, had a mix of trendy corporate types and lowlifes, enjoying each other's company. Getting off on the dance floor and getting high in the bathrooms. The Princess's friend worked in some high-rise somewhere and came to The Warehouse to shed the stress and to get her rocks off.

He knew the type and the Princess wasn't it. The Princess belonged somewhere else.

Bud belonged somewhere else, too, but he was here on business, being the resident expert on international organized crime. IOC and murder. Made for a volatile and interesting mix.

He'd been coming to The Warehouse for three nights in a row, waiting for Yevgeny Belusov, a snitch who hadn't showed. Belusov was the brother-in-law of Viktor Kuzin, the reputed head of the Siberian mafia, who'd relocated to Portland and was setting up business on the West Coast. Belusov's sister, Tatiana, was married to Kuzin. A week ago she'd landed up at Portland General with multiple contusions. On a hunch, Bud had gone over all the hospital records in a 100-mile radius and came up with a Russian woman matching Tatiana's description being treated repeatedly for injuries. Besides being a major international criminal, Kuzin was a fucking wife beater.

Belusov had promised to give up information on Viktor Kuzin and his US spearhead, Paul Carson, in exchange for the Witness Protection Program for himself and his sister. Meeting-place for negotiations, The Warehouse, where no one would pay them any attention.

Bud hadn't worked undercover in years, but he'd taken this on because Kuzin was a suspect in the murder of three informers. Kuzin and Carson, the Russian Mafiya's Mr.-Fix-it on the West Coast, were at the top of his list of scumbags to be nailed. He was pursuing every lead to track them down and finally bag them.

He'd first come across the name Carson in connection with the death of a prostitute in Beaverton. She'd been found dead in a windowless room with the door nailed shut, starved to death. She'd had whip lash marks on her back, some of them years old, the coroner had said. The woman had painstakingly carved the name Paul Carson on her arm with a rusty nail head while dying.

Bud had gone to visit Paul Carson, one of the wealthiest men in Portland, in his 40th floor penthouse office and had come away convinced of the man's guilt without a shred of evidence to prove it. Bagging Kuzin and Carson was what got him up in the morning. This was why he'd spent the past three nights listening to bad loud music and drinking watered beer. A small sacrifice to land two very big fish.

But Belusov hadn't shown for the past three nights.

Well, maybe it was understandable. Dropping a dime on Viktor Kuzin was dangerous business. Kuzin had a habit of hanging traitors to his organization on a meat hook and watching them bleed out. Belusov was either cowering in fear somewhere or dangling from a hook. Either way, he wasn't going to show. Not tonight. Not ever, maybe.

Time to go.

Bud had an overnight case in the trunk of the car. He'd head out to the coast for the weekend, maybe Astoria. Book into a motel. Have himself some sex. Probably with the waitress who worked at a diner he'd found one weekend. Nancy. Nancy…something.

Nice girl, hot in bed, not much going on upstairs. Luckily, she rarely wanted to talk. The three times he'd been to see her, they'd fucked like minks, ate to make up the calories lost, then fucked some more.

Yeah, that's what he'd do. Drive to Astoria and fuck the weekend away.

But he didn't move, just looked over again. Bud watched her, wondering what she was thinking. Her attention was caught by a couple at the edge of the Pit.

Bud could see the exact instant in which she realized that the couple was fucking openly on the floor. Her pretty, full lips formed an O and she turned her head, averting her eyes.

Jesus, the Princess was beautiful. She had dark shiny hair tumbled on top of her head, held there by funny sticks poking out from her head, pale perfect skin, a delicate profile, no makeup that he could see.

He remembered a picture he'd seen once in the library. Growing up, he'd spent a lot of time in the library, where he spent long afternoons instead of going home to his stepfather's drunken fists. He wasn't much of a reader so he'd leafed through picture books instead. There'd been one on turn-of-the-century New York and showed a beautiful young woman with delicate features and dark hair piled high on her head. A Gibson Girl, the caption had read.

So what was a Gibson Girl doing at The Warehouse?

The past three nights, he'd watched the Princess's girlfriend, snorting in the bathrooms and leaving with a different man every night. He knew her type well. So what was the Princess doing with her?

The Princess. He snorted at the thoughts going on in his own mind. He shook his head, had another sip of beer and unwillingly looked back at her.

She was in profile, the long slender neck arched as she people-watched. She'd only taken a few sips from the glass of white wine. She looked so innocent, so achingly impossibly young...

Too young.

Bud caught the bartender's eye and the bartender sauntered over. Teddy, he called himself. Big guy, more gut than muscle, more attitude than street cred. Spiked gelled hair, Hawaiian shirt, stovepipe pants, bored expression. He was dealing out back and Bud had already notified the drug squad. This time next week, good ole Teddy'd be in the Box, singing like a tenor.

Bud didn't give a shit. The drug squad took care of drugs, he took care of homicide. Right now, for example, he was hot on the trail of the fuckers who'd kidnapped ten little girls from their families in Moldova and shipped them halfway around the world to be sold for $100,000 each as virgins to the highest bidder, then farmed out as prostitutes. They'd earn their owners a cool million a year each. The girls were destined to be used hard and to die young. Most would be dead by 18, from disease or despair or at the hands of a client who got off on violence.

As it happened, the shipment of girls had died right away, suffocated to death in the hold of a ship flying a Panamanian flag for a company Carson owned, though the paperwork running through five countries was almost impossible to follow and would require forensic accountants to testify to ownership in court.

Drugs were bad. Kidnapping, raping and killing little girls was worse, in Bud's book.

Bud remembered every second as the police came on board in a midnight raid. The stench the captain was trying to hide, the sick feeling of pity as he and his officers looked down upon ten little girls, tragically young faces livid and desperate, hands out in claws, trying to find an air hole. Bud had stared hard at each little girl's face, memorizing it, letting the anger burn deep inside. He'd make sure each family would know what had happened to its little girl. And he vowed to take down the men responsible.

Paul Carson and Viktor Kuzin, traffickers in human lives and human misery. Kuzin, a Russian citizen, was mainly the INS's business. But Carson was red-white-and-blue and his. All his. Carson was going down. Hard. Bud would see to it personally.

"Yeah?" Teddy leaned on one elbow, close in so his voice could carry above the music. He glanced at Bud's half-empty glass. "What's your pleasure, big guy?"

Bud hooked a long forefinger in the collar of the Hawaiian shirt and tugged Teddy and his hibiscus flowers closer. "Brunette, other side of the counter, blue dress, very pretty, next to the redhead."

Teddy looked behind him then back to Bud. Mr. Bored. "Yeah? Wanna buy her a drink? Ask her to dance? Fuck her?"

"Card her."

Poor Teddy was confused.

Bud had been undercover these past nights. He had the cover down pat. Loser, drifter, user. He knew he looked the part. Teddy had bought it, hook, line and sinker.

"Listen up." Bud pulled on Teddy's shirt and yanked him down until his nose met Bud's Portland PD badge with the nice shiny eagle. Teddy's eyes widened. "Card the girl. *Now.*" He stared straight into the bartender's eyes. "And I might forget about the shit that's being dealt in the back room."

He'd just broken cover, but what the fuck. Bud released good ole Teddy's shirt.

"Whoa. Sure." Teddy straightened his shirt, trying for dignified and failing. "Sure thing, ah, Detective." He crossed over to the other side of the horseshoe shaped pit. Bud saw him talk to the Princess. Saw her frown and reach into a small velvet purse and pull a laminated card out. A minute later Teddy was back.

"She's 25 and legit," Teddy said, scowling.

Bud was astonished. Twenty-five? The Princess was *twenty-five*? He'd put her at seventeen…eighteen, tops.

What color eyes did she have? He couldn't tell; she was in profile, lashes down as she pretended to be absorbed by the glass of white wine she wasn't drinking.

She was on her own. The girlfriend had taken a powder and wouldn't be back, though the Princess didn't seem to realize it, lifting her head at regular intervals and looking around. Some jerk with a hundred bucks' worth of snow up his nose had pulled the redhead off her seat and they had disappeared into the maw of the Pit—the writhing dance floor.

The instant the girlfriend left, men started coming on to the Princess. She was pretty good, able to deflect attention with a smile and a shake of her head. Damn, why wasn't she turning her head this way? What the hell was the color of her eyes, anyway? Brown? She was a brunette, after all. But her skin was so pale, porcelain white. That kind of Black Irish coloring often went with blue eyes and it was a devastating combination.

Shit. Bud looked down into his beer. This was crazy. What the hell did he care what color the Princess's eyes were? What the hell did he care about *her*? She was in The Warehouse, after all, not your usual Princess hang-out. And she was in the company of the redhead, who'd definitely been around the block a few times. So had the Princess, he was sure, even if she didn't look it.

That air of innocence? Good genes, fabulous skin, delicate bones, nothing more.

A piece of shit dressed like Eurotrash in a $3,000 suit and no shirt detached itself from the writhing mass on the dance floor and sauntered over to her. He bent down close and the Princess pulled away. He said something and she shook her head, frowning. Instead of taking the hint, the fucker smiled, moved in closer and grabbed her shoulder.

The Princess looked around and Bud caught his breath. He'd wanted to know the color of her eyes and now he knew. Her eyes were a stunning electric blue, framed by long lush lashes. Gorgeous eyes. Eyes to break a man's heart.

Eyes full of fear.

Bud was up and moving before his next heartbeat.

Good Lord!

Claire Parks, through no fault of her own Portland's oldest living virgin, looked out over the dance floor. Actually, *down* on the dance floor, since it was in a pit called…the Pit.

Some time over the past twelve years while she had been busy dying, the most amazing styles had come into fashion. She could hardly believe her eyes. Everyone had short spiky hair like medieval helmets, the spikes colored wildly improbable hues like fuchsia and neon green. Either that or dreadlocks falling messily over faces and shoulders.

Belly-buttons were in. Or, to be precise, out. Certainly visible, not all of them attractive, but most of them bejeweled with flashy studs.

Claire watched a couple dancing in a corner, gyrating to a heavy funky beat. It was impossible to tell which was the man and which was the woman. Assuming they weren't the same sex.

Well, she'd wanted to fling herself into life and here she was. People-watching, as she'd done all her life. Only these people were a little more, er, colorful than usual.

"Gr...lace...it?"

"What?" she shouted. The noise from the speakers booming around the dance floor was deafening.

Lucy Savage grinned and placed her lips next to Claire's ear. "Great place, isn't it?"

They'd only recently met, during Claire's first week at her new job, starting her new life. Lucy lived up to her name—she was wild. It hadn't seemed that way in the office, though. Lucy had been friendly and efficient, showing Claire the ropes as the newest secretary at Semantika, a successful ad agency, while getting an enormous amount of work done herself. She'd been funny, helpful and friendly. When Lucy had asked Claire to go clubbing with her Saturday night, Claire had accepted eagerly. She'd never been to a club before, and it was high time she did.

She'd barely recognized the woman who showed up on her doorstep, glittery body gel over a lot of bare body. Much of it pierced, including her belly button, nose and left nipple, clearly visible through the black net top. A 'beeper', one of the partners had called her, because she set off metal detector alarms.

Lucy had disappeared several times into the bathroom and each time she came out, her smile had been a little wider and her pupils a little smaller. She'd also managed to down four margaritas and two shots of whiskey to Claire's single glass of white wine.

Claire swiveled around again to observe the dance floor. She watched a thin bare-chested man with rings hanging from his nipples dance. He was a good dancer, sinuous and lithe, but his baggy jeans were cut so low they looked as if they were going to fall off any second and...Claire blinked.

His chest was hairless, but so was his groin. His pants had dipped so low she could clearly see the root of his penis, surrounded by smooth pink skin.

Men had hair down there, she knew they did. Didn't they? Even her favorite statue, the David, had thick curly white marble hair. How come Mr. Hairless didn't?

Lucy's head was swaying to the beat, eyes half-closed as she smiled dreamily. "See that guy over there?" she asked, putting her mouth close to Claire's ear. She was pointing at Mr. Hairless, who had turned his back to them. Claire could see the crack of his backside.

"Yes," Claire said.

Lucy's smile widened. "Guy's got a Prince Albert. Really hot, know what I mean? God, they feel good."

Claire didn't have a clue what Lucy was talking about, but hated to admit it. "Oh yeah?" She nodded, trying to look with it, then gave it up. Why pretend to be cool? She shook her head. "Actually no, I don't know what you're talking about. What's a Prince Albert?"

"Oh baby, where've you been? A Prince Albert is a pierced cock. Makes a guy really exciting to fuck. Felt divine when we fucked last week. Last week? No," Lucy's head tilted to the side, thinking. "Two weeks ago. The metal really increases the friction." She licked her lips. "Jesus, I came like crazy."

Claire had to force herself to move her facial muscles, which had gone numb from shock. She said the first thing that

17

came to her mind. "Why doesn't he have any hair around his, um…"

"Cock?" Lucy's laugh rose above the din of the music. "Lots of guys shave. Their chests and around the cock. I like that. Keeps you from picking hairs out of your teeth, know what I mean?"

Claire thought about it, and then turned red.

Lucy put her mouth close to Claire's ear again. "I got a piercing myself."

Claire nodded. Besides the nipple ring, Lucy had little silver earrings all around the rim of her right ear, a diamond in her nose and a curved metal stud with a red stone in her belly button. "Yes, I know."

Lucy laughed. "Not just there." She was swaying in her chair to the beat. "I got myself a Queen Kristina—a clit piercing—last month. Mmm. I loved it after the swelling went down. Drives the guys crazy. Drives *me* crazy. You ought to try it, Claire. You don't even have pierced ears. Piercings are soooo sexy."

Claire was used to hiding her feelings behind a bland facade and her face smoothed out as she gave an expressionless smile, as fake as a doll's.

There had been a time in her life when she had received fifty shots a day. Every single one of them had hurt. She would break the arm of anyone who came within five feet of her with a needle.

"I'll think about it," she said, noncommittally, and went back to her people-watching.

There was a lot of very strange behavior on display, all of it fascinating, some of it disquieting. The men and the women seemed to skip all the mating rituals and go straight to simulating sex. Some not even simulating.

Her eye was caught by a couple at the edge of the Pit. The strobe lights on the ceiling illuminated them, and then cast them in shadow, flickering. They were fused at the hips, moving in time with the beat. The woman's skirt rode up to expose a bare hip. Surely she was wearing — what did they call them? Thong panties? Surely…no…*good heavens!*

 Claire tried not to peer and felt her face flush as she looked away. But she'd seen. The woman was naked under her skirt and those gyrations were…they were actually — oh my goodness — they were making love. Having sex, she corrected herself. On the *dance floor!*

She'd lived so long with illness, encased in a sex-free zone, that it was as if all those things she'd missed growing up — little-girl flirting with round-faced beardless harmless boys, those first closed-mouth kisses, holding hands in the movies, making out on the family couch, the first timid sexual encounters with a boy as breathless and scared as she was — all those steps on the way to becoming a woman were concentrated tonight in a fog of hormones and sweat and music.

It was all a little overwhelming, but this is what she wanted. What she'd quit her job as librarian at the family foundation for. What she'd argued with her father to have. This was Life. Something else she'd fought so fiercely to have.

She was officially healthy. She'd done it. She'd survived. She was never going to be sick again, she could feel it. Life pulsed in her veins, tingled in her fingertips. Tonight for the first time in years, she could see the road ahead. Or rather, *a* road ahead, something more than bleak, pain-filled days and anguished, solitary nights. She was going to catch up on time lost and live every second to the fullest.

Today she'd moved out of her father's house and out of his over-protective embrace. Today she was going to start snatching back all those years that had been stolen from her.

Mr. Hairless weaved his way over to them, eyes half slitted shut, thin torso writhing, belly so flat it was almost concave. The music had turned hip hop and the decibel level went up a notch. He hooked an arm around Lucy's neck.

"Hey baby," he crooned. He nuzzled Lucy's neck, dancing in place. "Wanna fuck?" Claire wouldn't have heard it above the music, but the DJ was suddenly between songs and she heard him clearly.

Claire opened her mouth, indignant, to tell the creep off when Lucy laughed. She rubbed against Mr. Hairless's chest. "We already did, honey. Two weeks ago, 'member? I might be up for another round if you ask nicely, but let's dance first."

The music started up again and Lucy and her romantic suitor drifted off to the dance floor, that Lucy called the Pit. Apt name for it, Claire thought. It was indeed a pit, at least ten feet below the bar area. The flashing lights picked out writhing limbs. The people were closely packed, features indistinct in the pulsing strobe lights. Arms writhing about the dancers heads made it look like a den of snakes.

Lucy and Mr. Hairless had already disappeared from view. The Pit was enormous. If Claire wanted to contact Lucy, she'd have to wade into it—she shuddered at the thought.

"Wanna...?" a man shouted in her ear.

"What?" She whipped her head around and met a grinning fatuous face. The man had gelled slicked-back hair and a tiny little beardlet under his lower lip. She could smell hair gel, deodorant, a strong aftershave and, rising above those, the acrid smell of body odor. Surely he hadn't just said—"—dance?" he shouted again.

Claire slumped in relief. She had no idea what to answer a man who asked her to fuck. She knew exactly what to say to a man who asked her to dance.

The idea of descending into the Pit made her skin crawl. It was one thing to people-watch; it was another thing entirely to be trapped in a crush of writhing bodies. She forced herself to smile. "Thanks, but I think I'll sit this one out."

There.

That was a nice reply, one she'd read in a novel. Of course the novel had been set in the Regency period, when presumably there were discrete dances, one after another, instead of the constant pounding noise issuing from the speakers. But her nice reply was lost on the man.

He leaned in close. Much too close. "What...say?" A generous amount of spittle came out on the 's' and Claire's smile slipped a notch.

"No!" she shouted. Then, because politeness had been drummed into her, she added, "Thank you!"

The man shrugged and moved five seats down to ask another woman.

Three men approached her, one after another, moving away when she shook her head.

The fourth man was very handsome and he knew it. Dark, well-cut hair, dressed in an elegant narrow-cut suit with no shirt. What was going on? Had men's shirts suddenly gone out of fashion while she'd been ill?

His clean-cut features were smiling but the hair on Claire's forearms stood up. She'd spent many years—too many years—sick and vulnerable. She was fine, now—just *fine*, thank you—but life looks different when you're flat on your back and all you can see is the ceiling.

You can't see trouble coming when you're on your back.

Claire had learned, very early, which nurses could be counted on to take care not to cause pain and which secretly liked hurting a little girl who couldn't defend herself. Which doctors took care to warm the stethoscope first and which treated her like an interesting piece of meat, fodder for another scientific paper.

Consequently, she had a very sophisticated and accurate Creepometer and right now the Creepometer's arrow was vibrating wildly in the Red Alarm Zone and buzzers were going off.

Claire could sense—could almost *smell*—cruelty and craziness and that smell was coming now off the man asking her if she wanted to dance.

He was good-looking and elegant, clearly well-to-do and successful. But his eyes glittered. His teeth were too white and his lips too red. He licked his lips with a sharp, pointed tongue. He was biting his back teeth so hard his jaw muscles were jumping. Everything about him was tightly wound, muscles so tense she could see the grain.

He gave her an air kiss and everything inside Claire recoiled.

"Hey, pretty lady." Confident smile, what he thought was charm oozing from every pore. "All alone? We can fix that. Come on and dance with me."

He leaned down to her, red mouth open, and Claire tried not to panic. Inside her head she was wind-milling her arms to get away from him, screaming her head off. Outwardly, she gave a tight smile and shrugged.

"I'm not alone," she protested. He tugged at her arm as if he hadn't heard her, and she raised her voice, trying to keep alarm out of it.

"I'm with a friend. She's…ah…" Claire craned her neck to peer down into the Pit, but Lucy was nowhere to be seen. Claire pretended to catch someone's eye and waved. "…down there, dancing. She'll be back in a minute. I'm fine, thank you."

Now get lost. Fast.

"I don't think so." The creep's eyes were heavy-lidded, drooping further as he leaned in close, whiskey fumes and bad breath making her turn her head sharply. Claire's very cells scrambled to get away from him. "I don't think you're with a friend, babe. I think you *need* a friend. I think you need me."

His fingers closed on her shoulder. His hand was strong and when he pulled, she had to close her fingers on the counter to resist his pull. He tugged harder.

Her heart was beating wildly now. She looked around desperately. There must have been five hundred people in The Warehouse, though no one was paying attention to them.

Surely he couldn't just—just *abduct* her here, amidst a thousand people?

And yet that was exactly what Rory Gavett had done. Kidnapped her out from under the noses of the hospital nurses.

Her head swam and she fought tears. She tried to pull away, but it only made his fingers dig more deeply into her arm. His smile widened and she suddenly knew. He liked inflicting pain. He got off on cruelty. Claire bit her lips to keep from screaming.

She glanced around wildly for help, but everyone was watching the action in the Pit. Her eyes caught those of a man on the other side of the U-shaped bar. A big man, totally untrendy—short sandy unstyled ungelled hair, sipping an unfashionable beer. His shoulders strained against a black tee shirt, which cupped large, hard biceps. Could he help? His eyes met hers. He certainly looked strong enough to deal with her tormentor.

She closed her eyes against the pain. Mr. Cruel and Creepy was digging his fingers into her shoulder. Horribly, he'd come up close to her and was rubbing against her. She could actually feel his erect penis. She tried to pull away, but he was holding on to her tightly.

Claire looked around again. The big man was nowhere to be seen, his seat vacant. Well, of course. He'd left or gone off to dance. It was crazy to feel so bereft.

"Come on, babe, no use being shy." Creepy's breath was hot in her ear. Claire felt nauseous. He tugged again, sharply and she bit her lips to keep from crying out. An expression of pain would only excite him more.

"Get lost. The lady's with me," a deep voice said from high above her head.

It happened all at once. The pressure in her shoulder eased and then was removed altogether. Her tormentor turned pale. His mouth was open but no sound came out except for a high-pitched wheezing noise. He backed away, mouth pinched, face deathly white, then disappeared.

Something large—*very large*—moved into her line of vision. The big man she'd seen at the other end of the bar had chased off Creepy and had sat down in the seat next to hers.

Claire tensed. She'd just traded one potential danger for another. Creepy had freaked her out and had proved hard to shake but he hadn't been physically overwhelming like the man now sitting next to her. Scaring off *this* man could prove to be impossible.

This was getting worse and worse. Claire stared into the Pit, frantically searching for Lucy. She had to get out of here, she was way too freaked, this was way too weird, she felt way too…what?

She stilled. Actually, she felt…okay.

Amazing.

She looked down at the wine glass and her hands clasped around it. Her hands had stopped trembling. Her Creepometer was silent, the arrow having gone right back around the dial to the blue Everything's Cool Zone.

Everything in her quieted, calmed. She was encased in a bubble of protection. Nothing could hurt her here.

It was the man sitting next to her. The *very big* man sitting next to her. He was the one responsible for the feeling of being looked after. Of sitting on the banks of a gently murmuring river on a warm spring day.

Claire chanced a glance. Gosh, he was big. Tall, even sitting down, with massive muscles on show. A lot of the men in The Warehouse were prancing around, parading physiques bought in some gym. This man didn't look like that at all. He looked like he'd been born tall and strong and had used his body well ever since. He was clearly in some kind of labor-intensive job. A stevedore, maybe, or a lumberjack.

His limbs were long and heavily muscled. Claire tried not to stare in fascination at the snake tattoo curving around the right forearm. She'd never actually seen a tattoo up close and this one was gorgeous, lifelike and artistic. A cobra, the hooded head depicted in lifelike detail on the back of the hand, the body curling around a hard, powerful forearm. Whenever the man's hands moved, the ripple effect made the snake twist sensuously. As an artistic effect, it was riveting.

The man's hands were extraordinarily beautiful—long-fingered, elegant, sinuous. Powerful without being meaty. He might be a lumberjack, but the fingernails were clean and cut short.

Claire cleared her throat and turned to look him straight in the eye. "I'd like to thank you," she said, "for taking care of that guy." The music was at a lower decibel for just an instant and people's voices could be heard without shouting.

"Don't mention it." The man's voice was clear and deep, a pleasant bass that reverberated in her stomach.

Close-up he was compelling. Clean, stern features. Strong, straight nose, square jaw, full lips. She held her breath when she met his eyes. They were a light brown, as piercing and keen as those of a hawk. There was strength and compassion in that gaze. She felt as if she could fall forward into him and be caught, and held.

She took a deep breath. She trusted her instincts. She wanted to fall forward. And be caught.

"My name's Claire. Claire…Schuyler." It wasn't entirely a lie. She was Claire Schuyler Parks. Schuyler was her mother's maiden name, and the name she used in her new job. Tonight she didn't want to be Claire Parks, scion of one of Portland's oldest families. She wanted to be Claire Schuyler, anonymous secretary.

Not to mention the fact that ten years ago, the name Claire Parks had been plastered all over the headlines in *The Oregonian*. Claire Parks belonged to the past.

"Bud," the big man said. "Bud Morrison." He held out a large hand and, after a second's hesitation, Claire took it and nearly had a heart attack at the electric jolt.

The feeling of well-being, of protection, intensified. And something else, something she was totally unprepared for, something she'd never felt in her life, flooded through her. As his huge hand curled around hers and squeezed gently, her entire arm tingled and she felt a huge warm rush of sexual excitement surge through her body. Every nerve in her body jangled and the hair on the nape of her neck stood up.

The sight of their clasped hands was riveting. His skin was tanned, much darker than hers, his hand sinewy and muscular. Their two hands entwined were almost a poster for Man and Woman, strength and delicacy together.

The only men who had ever touched her had been doctors, and her father. The doctors had all had soft, delicate, almost feminine hands. And her father, bless him, had the soft, mottled hands of an old man.

Her hand was half the size of this man's, totally surrounded by the hard and warm male flesh of his. Not soft, not delicate, but powerful and sinewy. The raised veins of an athlete coursed over the back of his hands, covered in old scars and new nicks. Hands that were used a lot.

She felt encased in something immensely powerful, yet gentle. And more.

Nothing—*nothing*—could have prepared her for the powerful surge of sexuality leaping through her body.

Sex surrounded her. The whole Warehouse was one big testosterone and estrogen pump, but it had left her totally unmoved. Now sexuality coursed through her veins, and she felt as if someone had suddenly plunged her into a socket and turned her on.

Bud Morrison was, in all senses of the term, a man. He was simply, even cheaply, dressed. Nothing trendy about him at all, from his simple short haircut to the clean, unbuffed and unmanicured fingernails. He wasn't looking around, trying to troll for women. He wasn't preening, hoping for attention.

He made every other man at The Warehouse look like a puppy.

With a start, Claire realized that her hand was still in his. That they were, in effect, holding hands. She tugged gently and his hand immediately opened to release hers. She missed the warmth and the connection.

This was nuts. Sure, her Creepometer was signaling safety — though it might have suddenly gone on the blink for all she knew — but that didn't mean she should go all moony over a perfect stranger.

"Freshen your drinks."

She looked up at the bartender's tone and was surprised to see a sour, forbidding expression on his face. It wasn't a request, it was an order. She'd been occupying a bar stool for over two hours, and had only consumed half a glass of white wine. They probably frowned on that, expecting customers to order overpriced drink after overpriced drink. The thought of ordering more alcohol made her stomach curdle. Okay, if she had to have a drink — "I'll have ginger ale with a twist of lime."

The bartender leaned forward on one elbow and frowned belligerently. "Look lady, this isn't kindergarten — "

"The lady wants a ginger ale and you'll bring her exactly what she wants. And I'll have another beer. Domestic." He didn't raise his deep voice, but it penetrated the din of the music. Coupled with a piercing gaze, it got results. The bartender's jaw muscles jumped as he bit back an answer. He nodded, disappeared and a minute later slammed two drinks in front of them, the liquid sloshing over his hands. Beer and ginger ale.

Her rescuer dug into his jeans for money and Claire gasped.

"Oh no!" She put her hand on Bud's hard forearm, the one with the snake, and again felt the sizzle of electricity. She pulled back immediately but it was enough to get his attention. He'd saved her from Creepy and had clearly appointed himself her watchdog. No one had come up in the last ten minutes asking her to dance. He'd glared hard at any approaching men—he gave great glare—and they'd all skittered away immediately…for which she was grateful. And now he wanted to buy her a drink.

The Warehouse was expensive. The gate was $40 and drinks went for $10 a pop. Claire had more money than she knew what to do with. Her rescuer was clearly a working man. Ten dollars meant nothing to her but it was probably what he earned for an hour of hard labor. She couldn't allow him to pay for her drink.

"Please, Bud," she said, looking up into those clear light eyes. She leaned forward and pitched her voice above the music. "You don't need to buy me a drink. If anything I should pay for yours."

She might as well have not spoken for all the good it did her. By the time she closed her mouth, he'd slid the money for the drinks and a tip across the counter and had started sipping his beer. Sighing, she sipped at her ginger ale. It was cold and tart and familiar. For many years of her life, too many years, it had been one of the few things her stomach could tolerate.

Bud wasn't making any attempt at conversation. The music was too deafening. Any words had to be almost shouted, making any exchange feel silly and artificial.

But his body was talking to her, loud and clear, and it was telling her she had his protection for as long as she wanted it. He was aware of everything and everyone and seemed to stave off trouble before it arrived.

Trouble would have come her way, or danced her way, before long. It was well past midnight and it was as if someone had thrown a hormone bomb into the cavernous room.

The gyrations down in the Pit were becoming wilder and items of clothing were coming off. Claire could see one bare-breasted woman, then two more. The dancers' movements were suggestive, pumping hips and bouncing breasts. A lot of bodily fluids were being exchanged.

Not all the cigarette smoke wafting her way smelled like tobacco. The music was so loud it was almost painful, the rhythmic beat making her head pound. She could feel the vibrations in the countertop.

Damn, where was Lucy? Claire anxiously watched the Pit, looking for wild red hair and a naked male torso to appear. Sooner or later, Lucy was bound to pop up. Wasn't she?

Should she go looking for Lucy? The idea of leaving the protective presence of Bud made her stomach clench with anxiety. As long as he was there, large and reassuring beside her, she felt safe. If she plunged into the Pit in search of Lucy, she'd have to fend off the men who were getting wilder and bolder.

This wasn't fun any more. Her eyes stung from the cigarette smoke and the wine sloshed acidly in her stomach, threatening to come up. The pounding beat of the music reverberated in her stomach. She couldn't think with the noise and confusion and she wanted to go home *now*.

She was without a car. Lucy had insisted on picking her up and at the time Claire had been grateful. Particularly when it turned out that The Warehouse was on the outskirts, in a tough part of town. Claire had been glad she hadn't had to drive around alone, looking for the club. But now she wished, fiercely, that she had her car so she could go home.

She had a brand-new house that her friend Suzanne Barron had decorated for her. It was soft and warm and welcoming. She hadn't even slept there yet. Now she yearned to be home, curled up on the pretty yellow chintz-covered sofa Suzanne had found.

Bud leaned down, not to crowd her, but so he could communicate without shouting. His mouth was close to her ear and his deep voice carried easily above the din. She could feel the puffs of air as he spoke and a shiver ran down her spine.

"If you're looking for your redheaded friend, she left about half an hour ago with the guy she was dancing with. I saw them go and she had her coat on."

Claire turned her head in alarm, her nose bumping against his. This close, she could see the golden flecks in his light brown eyes which made them look almost amber at a distance. There was strength there and, oddly, kindness.

"She-she'll be coming back!" she shouted. Claire didn't believe her own words and he didn't either. He didn't answer, just watched her steadily.

What was she going to do if Lucy didn't come back? Not panic, that was for sure. Her first outing and she was damned if she'd lose it. No, there was bound to be a solution, a way—a taxi! Of course! She'd call a taxi.

Claire finally caught the attention of the bartender, busy pulling beer spigots and mixing drinks. The alcohol level was rising together with the decibels. He served a drink to a man on her right who definitely didn't need another one, then came over. "Yeah?" he shouted. "You ready for a real drink now?"

Claire leaned forward over the counter. "I want a taxi!" she yelled. "Please, can you call one?"

"No way. You crazy or something, lady?" the bartender shouted back, rolling his eyes. "No taxi's coming out here after midnight, too dangerous. Find your own ride home." He was gone before she could answer.

Oh God, oh God. Now what? Lucy wasn't coming back. Claire knew it, she could feel it in her bones. Lucy was a lot of fun, but she wasn't reliable. Claire hadn't wanted reliable tonight, she'd wanted fun, and look at what it had gotten her.

She should have come with Suzanne. Suzanne was totally reliable. She would never have left Claire all on her own. On the other hand, Suzanne would never have accompanied her to a place like The Warehouse.

Beside her, Bud rose. And rose. And rose.

He was overwhelmingly tall and broad, almost a giant of a man. He held out his hand and, hesitatingly, Claire placed hers in it. His hard callused hand closed gently around hers, the grip warm and reassuring. He lifted her out of the barstool and lightly touched her waist, turning her toward the Pit. The top of Claire's head barely reached his chin and she was wearing heels. She'd reach his shoulder in bare feet.

"Let's go," he said.

Oh, God, he wanted to dance. The last thing Claire wanted was to descend into the Pit. She was feeling battered enough as it was without being jostled and pushed in the crush. But Bud had been kind. If he wanted a last dance, perhaps she owed him. And something told her he'd make sure nobody jostled her too hard.

But he wasn't taking her down into the Pit, after all. He was skirting it. Even off the dance floor the place was packed, but people magically parted for Bud as he escorted her carefully around the walls. He touched her briefly, just enough to guide her, pull her gently out of people's way, help her up steps. That protective bubble still surrounded her.

He bent down to her. "Do you have your coat check stub?"

"Yes," she said puzzled.

He gestured with his hand. "Let me have it."

She dug into her black beaded purse and handed it to him. "Why?"

He was standing with his back to the room, broad shoulders blocking everything out. Even, somehow, the noise. He kept his deep voice low, but she heard him clearly. Those magical hawk's eyes stared into hers.

"Because I'm driving you home."

Chapter Two

ജ

Bud ushered the Princess—*Claire*—outside.

The Warehouse's big steel fire doors closed behind them and suddenly the world fell silent. No music penetrated the door. All that was left of the clatter and chaos inside was a deep beat, more a vibration than a noise. It was exactly that time of night when it was too late for new customers to come to The Warehouse, and too early for the clients to be going home. They were alone in the large loading apron that now served as a parking lot.

It was snowing. Two feet from the door and they were in their own private, white world, pristine, silent and clean.

Claire's coat was a long cloak with a hood framing her face. She tipped her head up and closed her eyes in delight. She drew in a deep breath. The corners of her mouth curled up. "Oh," she breathed. "I love the snow." Her head turned and her eyes opened. "Thank you," she murmured. "For rescuing me and for offering to drive me home."

The hooded cloak, the dark night, the heartbreakingly beautiful young woman, the snow. It was harder than ever for Bud to shake off the feeling that he was caught in a fairy tale. The woodsman, maybe, escorting the Princess back to the palace after rescuing her from the dragon. Or the knight, coming to claim his fated bride.

She wasn't a Princess. He had to keep reminding himself of that. She was a perfectly ordinary Portland girl named Claire. Claire Schuyler. She spoke in a normal American accent and was wearing ordinary clothes. And yet, if she threw back her cloak to reveal a ball gown instead of a blue sweater dress and she'd said in a foreign accent that she was the Princess

Esmeralda of a far-off kingdom, he wouldn't have been surprised.

"No need to thank me," he said and took her elbow. It had been really hard, back in The Warehouse, to keep his touch light as he guided her through the teeming pack of people. What he'd wanted to do—what he'd had to clench his teeth to keep from doing—was to lift her in his arms and carry her away. Find some quiet room somewhere and strip her clothes off. Find out if her skin was as soft as it looked, trace the shape of her breasts with his hands, pull out those sticks in her hair and watch it tumble over bare shoulders, curl around her breasts and hard little nipples.

His cock stirred in his pants.

Whoa.

This was definitely not what she'd want. Her rescuer coming on to her. She was taking a big chance, getting in a car with him, a total stranger. Granted, she didn't have much of a choice. The redheaded bitch had abandoned Claire outright, off to fuck the latest boy-friend. And the bartender was right— the taxis wouldn't come out here. No, she'd been stuck.

"Here we are," he said quietly, a hand on the passenger handle. The snow was falling in light drifts, big fat snowflakes, fairy tale snowflakes. Claire pushed her hood back and lifted her face to him, lips upturned. He found himself foolishly smiling back, though he wasn't much of a smiler. The flakes kissed her skin and melted at the warmth. He knew exactly how they felt.

He opened the passenger door and took in a deep breath. She was getting into a car with a man she didn't know. A man who outweighed her by at least 90 pounds and who was a foot taller than she was. Time to break the enchantment and tell her who he was.

Why was he hesitating? He'd be breaking cover, but he'd already done that with the bartender. That wasn't it.

Bud was used to being brutally honest with himself about himself and he knew the real reason he didn't want to say who he was.

Women had one of two reactions when they found out he was a homicide detective. They were either turned off or turned on. He didn't want either one from her. He didn't want her to shy away in disgust and he didn't want her to be morbidly curious about what it was like to fuck an armed man who investigates dead bodies for a living.

For a little while longer, he wanted her to be The Princess and he wanted to be her knight.

She was looking up at him as he hesitated in the vee of the open car door and he sighed. Time to break the spell.

"I want you to know you'll be safe with me," he said quietly. "I'm a—"

"I know," she interrupted, her voice just as quiet as his, as if both of them had been battered by the noise of The Warehouse. "I know I'm safe with you. I can feel it." Her eyes searched his for a long moment, luminous gorgeous blue eyes, full of trust. She smiled, bent and got into the passenger seat. He was left holding the door open, feeling like an idiot.

Okay.

He got in and started the engine, letting it warm up. They turned to each other and he had to grip the steering wheel hard not to pull her in his arms.

She was wearing some kind of light perfume that had been drowned out in the sharp smells of The Warehouse. Now the delicate scent all but reached out with insidious tendrils to grab hold of his brain and play havoc with the cells. The perfume, coupled with the stunning eyes and delicately uptilted mouth smiling at him, also made its way into his pants. He started getting a hard-on. Good thing his sheepskin jacket reached his knees.

This was crazy. He was crazy. He was going to escort her home, go back to his place, take a cold shower, fall into bed, then leave early tomorrow morning for Astoria where he'd fuck Nancy non-stop until Sunday night. Get the Princess out of his head.

"Okay." The engine was warm. "Where do I take you?"

She gave him the address. It was on the other side of the city, about eight blocks from his apartment complex. "I'm afraid I'm going to make you cross town," she apologized. "In the snow."

In the din of The Warehouse, when they'd had to shout to communicate, he hadn't had a chance to hear her speaking voice. It was just his damned luck that it was soft, light, feminine, seductive and sexy as hell.

Shit.

"No, that's okay." Bud pulled out of The Warehouse's parking lot. "I've got a lot of experience driving in the snow and I have snow tires. And chains, if necessary." He peered up out of the windshield at the fat, wet, lazy flakes. "This kind of snow won't stick to the ground anyway."

"It's so pretty, though," she said softly, smiling. She was looking out the window, as delighted as a child at Christmas.

"Mmm." Bud could hardly breathe. *She* was so pretty. So pretty it almost hurt. Her skin glowed like palest ivory in the lights from the dashboard. She was turned away from him, looking out the window and watching the snow so he could watch her—a much nicer view than the snow.

There was very little traffic but he was driving slowly so he could sneak frequent glances at her without running into a lamppost. She was in profile, a pale cameo against the dark window. Perfectly curved eyebrow, long lashes, straight nose with finely arched nostrils, the corner of her mouth uptilted in an unconscious smile. That must be her default expression. A smile.

She looked pretty and innocent and he shouldn't have this massive hard-on he'd developed. She wasn't his type at all.

He didn't like pretty and innocent. He liked women who knew what they were doing in bed and who knew what the score was.

He'd had a hard life and he had one of those jobs where you put on rubber boots and waded through the muck and filth of the worst humanity has to offer.

He'd seen it all—wife-beaters and hopheads and drunks. The lowest of the low. And the highest of the high. Respectable businessmen who hired a hit man to take out a business rival. Society matrons who smothered their newborn children because the baby interfered with their social life. Rich youngsters who beat their parents to death because they wanted a bigger allowance.

Yeah, he'd seen it all. Twice. The last thing he needed was some innocent young miss who'd be stiff in bed and cling to him afterwards.

Nope, he was going to drive pretty little Miss Schuyler safely to her door, say goodnight politely like the gentleman he wasn't, go home, get some shut eye, then take off for his weekend of hot sex. Yup, that's what he'd do.

His cock wasn't listening to a word his head was saying.

His cock didn't give a shit about home or sleep. It didn't want Nancy Whosis, it wanted *her*, the Princess, and it wasn't taking no for an answer. He had a boner in his pants so hard he could knock on doors with it. She shifted a little in her seat and a little whiff of that perfume wafted his way and he nearly came in his pants.

Jesus, what was this? He hadn't come in his pants since he was 13 and Molly Everson took off her bra behind the Rexall. He'd always had a lot of sexual stamina and coming once had just primed the pump. Molly had left smiling. But that was a long time ago, a lot of women ago, and the Princess not only hadn't taken her bra off, she wasn't giving off any sex signals whatsoever.

Any other woman who wanted it would have had her hand on his thigh by now, would have been sighing and crossing her legs and giving him long meaningful glances. Pretending it was too hot in the car and unbuttoning. That's what Nancy had done two weeks ago when they'd taken a drive down the coast and she'd ended up giving him a blow job in the car.

Claire was just sitting there, a faint smile on her lips, watching the snow, buttoned up to the neck in her cloak, slim pretty hands still and folded in her lap. No come on at all.

But he remembered, and above all his cock remembered, how she'd filled the sweater dress she had on. She was slender, almost slight, but curvy with surprisingly full breasts. Round and full and high.

Walking behind her as they made their way around the Pit he'd had to clench his fists not to clasp her around her tiny waist. He had big hands and he'd bet he could almost span her waist. Hold her there as he kneed her legs apart from behind, slip right into her. She'd be tight, he'd bet anything on that. Tight and wet and…

Oh God. He nearly groaned aloud. This was torture. How much longer?

He tried to peer through the snow that was falling more thickly now and caught a glimpse of the white and blue street sign on the corner. Another three blocks to go and he could dump her on her doorstep and go home and jerk off. He was as hard as a rock. He wasn't going to let Nancy up for air this weekend, that's for sure. He felt like he could fuck for 48 hours straight.

But not Nancy.

Jesus, where had *that* thought come from? Since when was there a reasonably attractive woman — and Nancy was more than okay if a little on the clueless side — he couldn't fuck?

He needed to get rid of the Princess, right *now*, she was messing with his head.

He stepped on the gas a little and the wheels spun. The whole universe was conspiring against him, he thought, as he slowed the car back down. He could feel sweat breaking out. Come on, come on, let's get her home, hurry this *up*.

But the road was slippery and he was making lousy time.

"Turn to the right here," she said, scanning the street and even her voice in the dark turned him on. No, he was already turned on, the voice was just icing on the cake.

It was another tortuous ten minutes before he pulled up to a house that looked just like her—small, charming, nicely built and pretty. Jesus, this gentleman thing was deadly stuff because to keep in character he'd have to walk her to her door. With a hard-on. The knee-length coat would cover it but it was there and it fucking *hurt*.

He killed the engine, grimly determined to play the part of the gentleman to the bitter end, for the first and definitely the last time in his life. It would take two minutes, tops. Walk her up to her door, shake hands maybe, though just touching that smooth skin would be like lighting a detonator, then walk away—hobble away—with his hard-on. That's what he'd do.

"Here we are." His voice was hoarse. He cleared his throat. "I'll walk you—"

"Would you like to come in for some coffee?" she asked in a rush, the words tumbling over themselves. *Wouldyouliketocomeinforsomecoffee?* As if she'd been rehearsing it.

She'd turned to him fully, but wasn't meeting his eyes, asking his chin if he wanted to come in for coffee. Her breathing was slightly speeded up and the hand holding her cloak together was trembling. She was asking him in for more than coffee. She might not even be aware of it herself, but he was.

Coffee was a synonym for sex.

Absolutely not.

No sex, no. Not with her.

She was trouble with a capital T which rhymed with C which stood for Claire.

It wouldn't be happily vigorous sex for a couple of hours, then a handshake and goodbye, which was all he was looking for, all he wanted from a woman. He liked sex that was hard and long and uncomplicated. He didn't want sex with her. She had complication written all over that gorgeous face of hers. No sex with Claire Schuyler. No, no, no.

His head was clear on that and he opened his mouth to say no, but his cock got there first.

"Yeah, love to."

Chapter Three

There, Claire thought. *I've done it.*

She was so proud of herself. She'd been thinking furiously as Bud Morrison drove them all across town. Driving her home was kind of him; *he* was kind, instinctively so. He was kind and strong and definitely straight. Good-looking and clean—that was important. Some of the men who'd asked her to dance could have done with a shower. Not Bud.

He was also electrifyingly sexy, with all those muscles, that deep, rough voice, that tough-guy demeanor and, wow, the snake tattoo, cherry on the icing.

So he was a lumberjack with a tattoo. Who cared? Her father would be appalled—one more good reason to ask Bud to take her to bed.

Sleeping with a man you'd just met was risky behavior, she knew that, but she felt safe with Bud and she knew she was right to feel safe. She trusted her feelings.

Claire knew she was young and inexperienced in some ways—certainly in sexual affairs—but not in the things that counted. She'd faced death twice and won.

While other young girls her age were eyeing the boys at the mall, buying their first lipstick and experimenting with sex, she'd been hooked up to heart monitors, in constant pain and fighting for every breath she took.

She knew more than most people about life and death, danger and safety.

She knew her heart and she knew she wasn't wrong to want this man. She wasn't wrong about him. He wasn't insane or cruel or kinky. He wasn't going to hurt her or make her feel dirty. She found him incredibly sexy, the first man in her life she'd had these feelings for.

Bud was definitely the right man for this job.

He was at her car door, opening it and extending a big hand to her before she finished her thoughts. Another thing she liked about him—his totally untrendy, politically incorrect chivalry. He'd defended her in The Warehouse, protected her from the crush and had gone way out of his way to make sure she got home safely.

So this was It.

Now that she'd made up her mind, the mechanics of it—how to get from being fully clothed on a snowy evening to naked in bed—seemed almost daunting. She fretted all the way up to the door, as Bud held her elbow and made sure she didn't slip in the snow.

How on earth did this work? Had he understood that she was asking him to make love to her? Or would she have to make the first move—and if so, how do you make a first move? She'd probably have to make coffee first, since she'd offered, but then what? Bring the conversation around to lovemaking and make some suggestive comment?

That didn't sound like her at all.

Stand up and start stripping? No way.

And besides, she didn't even know if she had any coffee. She wasn't much of a coffee drinker and she didn't know how to run the brand-new amazingly complicated Italian coffee machine Suzanne had installed.

Why hadn't she asked Bud in for *tea*? She definitely knew how to make tea. Only he hadn't looked like a tea sort of man.

Oh, dear. Maybe this was a bad idea.

No. She sneaked a glance up at the big, good-looking man by her side, holding her arm so carefully, steering her over the slippery spots.

It was a great idea, a fabulous one. Bud Morrison was definitely the one. He was big and strong and kind and so exciting she found it hard to breathe around him. She found him extremely attractive. He looked like he'd know exactly what to do with a woman.

When was the last time she'd met someone like that? Never. Maybe she'd have to wait another 25 years to meet another Bud Morrison.

No, she thought with renewed determination. This was her 'window of opportunity'. That was the phrase her father's business manager used, only it referred to dumping Microsoft shares and buying Slovenian bonds, not finding a man to bed her, but the principle was the same. It was now or never.

Maybe she wouldn't have to do much of anything at all, let him take the lead. Maybe it would be simple and natural. They'd kiss and go to the bedroom and then her life as a woman would finally start.

Except for one thing.

She didn't know how to kiss.

It all had to start with a kiss, didn't it? Surely that was the prelude to lovemaking? So if she flubbed it right at the start, how could she get to Stage Two? She'd flunk the kissing test, she knew she would.

It was insane that she'd never kissed a man, but it wasn't her fault. Not entirely. Or was it? Surely somewhere along the way, in these past ten years, there'd been *someone* she could have practiced on, if she'd just been paying attention?

Nope. Thinking back on it, her only contact with men had been with amazingly unattractive doctors, surly male nurses, the wimps at the Parks Foundation—most of whom would rather have kissed the backside of a chimpanzee than a woman's mouth—and her elderly father, who'd always given her pecks on the cheek.

She'd received her share of pecks on the cheek but no soul kissing. French kissing. Whatever it was called. Full frontal, in the arms of the man, open-mouthed, tongue-in-throat kissing. The tongue-in-throat thing had always given her pause because though she knew it was supposed to be sexy and thrilling—all the books said so—it actually sounded kind of awful. Someone's *tongue* in your *mouth*. Ugh. But if that was what it took to get rid of her virginity...

So how did it work? Did you just open your mouth and press it against the man's? And how were you supposed to know the right moment? Suppose you opened your mouth and his was puckered and closed? Wouldn't that be embarrassing? Or the other way around. You puckered and he opened?

Oh God, this wasn't going to work, not at all, she thought frantically as she dug in her bag for the keys. Her hands were shaking and her mind was racing.

She dropped her bag and almost burst into tears on the spot.

"Sorry," she gasped, throwing Bud an appalled, apologetic look, and started to bend down.

"Let me," he murmured. He gracefully bent, picked up her keys and magically opened the door in a second. Another second and they were through it and she was planning what she would say next and—her brain shorted.

Complete, total static.

She was kissing. *Kissing.* Just like that.

She hadn't had to think about it, hadn't had to plan it or fret about it because Bud had taken care of everything. He'd just closed the door, taken her in his arms and bent down to her.

Her mouth seemed to know what to do all by itself. He'd opened her lips with a twist of his own and stroked his tongue into her mouth, sliding his tongue over hers and oh God, a bolt of electricity shot straight through her, so intense her breath stopped. This was so delicious. How had she missed out on this all these years?

The tongue was a penis. Why hadn't she realized that when she'd read about kissing? A part of the man's body in the woman's body, stroking rhythmically. Pure sex.

Did it work the other way around? She couldn't put her penis in his body, but she could...Claire lifted herself on tiptoe for a better angle and licked his tongue, stroking hers into his mouth. Oh boy, that worked! Bud shuddered, groaned in her mouth and tightened his arms around her.

She was bombarded by sensations, all of them new, all of them mind-blowingly exciting. Pure explosively hot pleasure.

A shake and her purse fell to the floor with a bump and her cloak slithered off. Now she could lift her arms around his strong neck, rise on tiptoe as he placed one big hand on her backside, pulling her up into his groin, hard. Hard. Lord, he was hard, hard all over, but especially *there*. He pressed again with his hand and through the layers of clothing she could feel his penis. Erect penis.

She had spent her entire life not entirely certain that the male penis wasn't just a myth, and here in the space of one evening she'd actually felt two of them. Erect, if you please. Creepy's and Bud's.

Bud's penis wasn't anything like Mr. Creepy's. It was larger, for one thing. Much, much larger. And it didn't freak her out, it turned her on.

Yes, she, Claire Parks, who by all rights should have been dead these many years, her bleached bones rotting in the cold ground, was turned on. Waves of heat rolled through her body in liquid surges. The heat became almost incandescent in her breasts and in her loins, but her entire body burned and tingled with heat and life.

She moved her hips against him and felt him swell even larger, felt him shudder and groan into her mouth. All three at once and it took her dazzled brain a few seconds to realize that *she* had done that to him. He was so big and so strong and yet she had the power to actually change his body. Make him shake. Make his heart beat faster and his penis swell.

A surge of electricity ran through her body as she felt the power of womanhood for the first time. She had been right to cling to life so desperately because this — *this* — was the essence of life itself.

And kissing — how on earth had she managed without kisses? Such sweet, hot excitement. A man's tongue in your mouth was the most intense experience she could imagine. Bud's tongue was soft, insistent, rubbing against hers. And just as her movements had created exciting changes in his body, his tongue tangling with hers made her breasts swell and caused heat to flutter in her loins.

No, wait…he held her more tightly, slanted his mouth over hers, licked his tongue deep into her and she felt…she felt a flutter in her *vagina*!

There was no mistaking it and for the very first time in her life she was aware of her vagina as a separate entity. She fluttered again and liquid heat filled it, as if a small sun had suddenly bloomed there. Oh my God, was she having an orgasm? Her knees buckled and she would have fallen if she hadn't been plastered up against Bud's big strong body, held tightly there by his arms around her.

His arms loosened slightly. She didn't fall but she felt the world tilt on its axis. He had picked her up and was carrying her somewhere. Where? It didn't matter. Her own arms were still twined around his neck and she could feel the fascinating play of shoulder muscles as he lifted her up.

His mouth left hers for a second, far enough to speak but close enough for her to feel his hot breath wash over her.

"Bedroom," he said, his voice harsh.

"Yes," she breathed. Oh yes, bedroom sounded wonderful.

He made a rumbling noise that sounded like a choked laugh. "Where?"

She rained kisses on his face, nuzzling his chin. What wonderful textures this man had. He had a *beard*. He was close-shaven but she could still feel the roughness of his beard against her face as she rubbed her cheek against him. The skin was rough to half-way up his cheek, then became softer where the beard stopped. Fascinating, the difference between the two. She licked him along that line of demarcation and his breath left his lungs in a rush. He breathed in deeply after a second or two.

"Where?" he said again and the word just glanced off her heat-dazzled brain without sinking in.

"Where what?" she murmured. Lord, he was fascinating. She breathed in deeply and could smell soap and musk and the lingering smell of tobacco and the other stuff from The Warehouse.

Again, that rough rumbling sound. Laughter?

"Where. Is. The. Bedroom?"

Claire sighed and nuzzled and licked, his words just bumping around inside her head. She pressed her open mouth against his and was in perfect alignment, their lips together in exactly the right way, as if she'd been practicing kissing for fifty years.

Claire just knew she was going to be very good at sex.

Bud lifted his mouth and her lips felt wet and cold and swollen. Why wasn't he kissing her back?

"Claire," he whispered, "honey, I need to know where your bedroom is before I run us smack into a wall. Either that or we make love in the kitchen or the bathroom or the closet or right here on the floor. Your choice. But make it now."

"Bedroom," she sighed and kissed him again. She spoke against his mouth, lifting her right hand from his neck, pointing. "There, second door right."

As directions went, it wasn't going to earn her brownie points any time soon, but Bud managed without any difficulties. He moved unerringly in the right direction and in an instant they were in her bedroom.

Claire hated darkness and always left small lights on. The one in her bedroom was a bronze flower holding up a small globe of pale yellow light. It was just enough to see Bud in a golden haze, not enough light to ruin the atmosphere.

Bud didn't spare her bedroom a glance, though Suzanne had outdone herself here. It was pretty and feminine, with vases of fresh flowers and scented candles. Claire didn't spare a glance at her surroundings either, though it was going to be her first night in the house.

How could she look at a four-poster bed and Shaker dresser drawer when she could look at Bud, watching her with such heat in his golden eyes she thought she could melt from that alone?

He put her down gently, still kissing her, and reached up to pull the kabuki sticks from her hair. He pulled back to watch her hair cascade over her shoulders, running his fingers through it.

"Clothes," he growled and she agreed—they had on way too many of them. Bud reached down to gather the soft folds of her cashmere Valentino sweater dress. A swift tug and it was flying over her head. She started to drop her arms but he caught her wrists with one big hand and just looked at her, his heated gaze moving over her, breath harsh in his lungs.

Claire knew what he was seeing so she watched his eyes instead, to understand what he thought of it. He was seeing someone fashionably slender, yet with a few curves.

Curves were something new and had taken hard work to acquire. She'd once been so underweight her kidney had slipped. Her weight loss had been so severe she'd stopped menstruating and had had to be put on the pill.

But she was okay now; she ate like a horse to ensure it. More than okay, actually, judging from Bud's expression. She looked down at herself. The dress had a wide neck so she'd worn a strapless bra and high-cut panties not to create a panty line. Black. And black thigh highs because she hated panty hose.

"Christ," he breathed, "you're sexy."

Her underwear, which she'd chosen purely out of practicality, was actually...sexy? Apparently. The look in Bud's eyes made her feel like a sex goddess. Power surged in her, tingled in her fingertips as she twisted in Bud's strong, painless grip.

He'd been studying her breasts, probably noticing that her nipples had turned hard. He seemed like the kind of man who'd notice something like that. His gaze lingered on her body, traveling slowly upwards until he met her eyes again.

Bud reached around her and unfastened her bra, letting it drop to the floor. Still holding her hands above her head, he slid his hand around her hip to her backside, fingers sliding under the elastic of her panties, tugging downwards until they cleared her hips and slid to her ankles, leaving her only in her black lace thigh highs and heels. Bud released her hands. She stepped out of the shoes, rolled her stockings down and was naked.

Claire had been naked with a man before, of course. Doctors had seen—and prodded and poked—her naked body when it had been weak and emaciated. But this was the first time she was naked with a man who looked at her with burning hot desire in his eyes.

Bud bent, but instead of kissing her mouth, he kissed—oh God!—her breast. He kissed and licked, his tongue warm over her heated skin. He wrapped his free arm around her back, bending her over his arm. He opened his mouth over her nipple and started sucking, hard.

It was inflaming, as if a hot wire were drawn straight from her nipple to deep in her vagina and electricity surged along that wire in time with the movements of his mouth.

Bud lifted his head suddenly, as if she'd spoken, though no words could come out of her tight throat. He had her tightly drawn, like a bow, her wrists in one big hand, bent over his other arm. She should have felt weak and powerless, trapped in the arms of such a powerfully strong man, but she didn't. She felt big and powerful and strong herself.

"It's gotta be fast the first time and probably the second, but I swear I'll slow down by the third." His voice was thick, the words slurred and she didn't understand them. But whatever it was he was saying, there was only one answer.

"Okay," she sighed.

In seconds, Claire was stretched out on the bed and a naked Bud was mounting her, kneeing her legs apart and settling heavily onto her. She hadn't even had a chance to really see his body. He'd whisked off his tee shirt and shucked shoes, socks, underpants and pants in one blur of motion, with a crackling sound as he fished in the pockets for something.

But she could feel and he felt wonderful. Heavy and warm and furry and muscular, thick penis prodding her thigh like a rod of warm steel.

This was happening so fast, she couldn't sort out her sensations, her feelings. He reached down and caressed her briefly between her legs, rubbing the folds of her sex. Then he used his index and middle fingers to open her up, fitting the head of his penis right there, at her opening.

When Claire had thought about losing her virginity—and she'd thought about it a lot—she'd imagined something slower. But this had a powerful beauty all its own. She was caught up in a wild whirlwind and knew she had to ride it out. Whatever it took.

Bud's penis was very…large. Well, he was a large man. His heavily muscled body and long limbs were part of the attraction. For the first time it occurred to her that of course a man as large as he was, with huge hands and enormous feet, would have to have a big penis.

It was going to hurt. She knew that, knew that there was a membrane that had to be ruptured and was prepared. Feeling the size of the enormous bulbous head barely inside her entrance, she realized it was going to hurt more than she'd thought. It burned already, her inner muscles stretched to their maximum limit.

That was okay. Claire knew pain, knew how to deal with it, and knew all the tricks of the mind to cope with it. He was pressing forward slowly and some of her excitement left her as she felt the burn. She let her mind float, high above her body, distancing herself from what was happening...

The jolt of Bud's large body brought her back to earth.

His face inches above hers registered shock. He levered himself up on his arms, biceps bulging, and stared down at her, sandy brows drawn together in a frown.

"You're a virgin," he said and it wasn't a question.

Oh no. He couldn't back out now, he simply couldn't.

Claire wrapped her legs around his, pulled his face down to hers and stared fiercely into his eyes. "Yes, I'm a virgin, but not for long. Not if you do this right."

Chapter Four

ဆ

Bud had spent 36 years on this Earth without fucking a virgin and he had no intention of starting now. This was much more trouble than he was willing to put up with. A woman's first time should be special and he wasn't anyone special. Besides, he knew he was big. Sometimes it was hard even for women who fucked a lot to take him. He'd hurt her and she'd start crying and he'd feel rotten. He didn't need this.

A virgin...*shit*. Nope, no way, wasn't going to happen.

And even if it did happen, what then? She'd get all moony-eyed over him, maybe be imprinted with him, follow him around like those ducks followed that scientist. No, he didn't want entanglements, didn't want pretty Claire Schuyler following him around like a little duckling.

So he made his apologies, got back into his clothes and was out the door in record time. He went back to his apartment for a few hours' sleep then headed out for the coast. Nancy was free that weekend and he fucked her until she was sore. Hell, he fucked her until *he* was sore.

Monday morning he was back at work, his hormones back in balance and a wide-eyed Princess completely forgotten.

That's what happened in that alternate universe, the one where he thought with his head instead of his dick.

In *this* universe, what happened was that his heart squeezed tight and his breath left his lungs with a whoosh.

Claire's slender legs were twined around his as if she were strong enough to hold him down. Maybe she was, because he had no intention of going anywhere.

"Bud?" she whispered. That fierce look had left her face and now she was looking lost, impossibly young as she searched his eyes. Innocent and heartstoppingly beautiful. "You won't leave me?"

"No." His voice was thick in his throat and he had to wait a second before continuing. Leave her? Not even if someone pointed a Sig at his head. "I'm right here, not going anywhere. We need to do this differently now."

Her eyes opened wide, sky blue surprise. "We were doing it *wrong*?" she breathed.

"Not wrong, exactly, just—" He shook his head. "Never mind, let me show you."

Her legs had relaxed enough for him to slide off her. He perched on the side of the bed and put his hand on her belly. It almost spanned her hipbones. He sat there a moment, looking at her, really looking at her. The slenderness, the delicacy, the near fragility of her had been enticing before, but now they worried him a bit.

He wasn't delicate at all when he fucked. He wasn't even that good at foreplay. He usually just shoved it in. The kind of women he dated wanted straight, meat and potatoes, cock in cunt sex, heavy and vigorous and for hours. That was his specialty. He had no friggin' clue how to deflower a delicate princess.

Well, looked like he was going to have to learn on the job.

She was watching him steadily out of those big blue eyes.

"Look, Claire," Bud said gently. He barely recognized his own voice. His hand turned and cupped her mound and he nearly groaned. The dark hair was soft, not crinkly, a delight to the touch. He stroked her there a moment, then moved his hand down further, sliding his fingers through the folds of her sex. She was slippery and definitely turned-on, but not enough.

"That feels good, doesn't it?"

"Yes," she breathed.

He turned his hand so he could insert a finger into her. Just one, just barely in, and she winced. "Feels less good, doesn't it? And that's just my finger. Look at my..." Bud stopped himself in time. He'd been about to say cock and with any other woman he would have. But it wasn't the right word. Not right now. "Look at me."

She sensed what he meant and they both dropped their gaze to his lap, where his hard-on twitched and lengthened under her gaze. The condom made his cock shiny, as if a spotlight were turned on it.

Everyone made such a fuss about size but it hadn't gotten Bud anything special. He wasn't the kind to linger in locker rooms, comparing dick sizes so he could feel important. He was a big guy, always had been, and having a big cock went with the territory. The only thing it meant to him was that sometimes he had to be a bit more careful with the ladies.

Very careful now. For the first time in his life, he wished he were a little smaller.

Bud stroked Claire, feeling the moisture well up as his hand moved. He could insert his finger a little further in now. "I don't want to hurt you, honey. We'll take this slow and easy, okay?"

She nodded, big-eyed. "It will—" she stopped, embarrassed, and pulled her luscious lower lip between two rows of small perfectly white teeth.

"It will what, honey?" he asked, keeping his voice low. He continued stroking, pushing his finger in a little deeper with each stroke.

Claire's eyes dropped to his cock then rose to his face. "It will work, won't it? I mean—"she turned slightly pink, "we'll fit, won't we?"

Bud knew better than to smile. "Yeah," he said softly, "we'll fit. It's just that we'll have to do this only when you're ready. Open your legs for me more, Claire."

She obeyed immediately, sliding her legs apart, and his heart gave another hard squeeze in his chest. She was trying so hard to please him, watching his eyes carefully to see what he wanted, as if this was about him and not her.

She wasn't scared of him; that was good, but he didn't want her anxious, either. *He* didn't need pleasuring, that's for sure. He was hard as a rock and had to consciously think about not coming by tightening his groin muscles. He probed further with his finger, watching her eyes, gauging her breathing. When it speeded up, he speeded his strokes. In and out in a slow steady rhythm.

Her mouth opened a little, so she could get more air in her lungs. Good.

He pushed his finger in further, then stopped. He felt it and a big ball of emotion filled his chest. Her maidenhead. My God.

For the very first time in his life he understood the premium some men put on virginity. The fact that no man had had her, that no man had touched her, no other man's cock had entered this tight little cunt...it was mind blowing.

Even under the condom, he could feel moisture seeping out of the head of his cock, he was so excited. He'd hurt her, otherwise he'd jump on her immediately and start pumping hard. He felt like he could stay in her until next week.

His life hadn't been easy and he'd had to make his own breaks along the way. What was happening now seemed almost like a miracle, as if someone up there was making up for all those years of hard times by dumping this amazingly beautiful untouched woman practically in his lap.

It was up to him to do this right.

First things first. She needed calming down. So did he.

Bud wished he were more of a ladies' man, someone used to sweet-talking. He wasn't. He lived in a man's world. Hell, in the cop shop, even the women were men. They were hard and cynical and foul-mouthed, just like the other cops. He'd never courted a woman. All his relationships had been based on sex. He wished he had the words, the right words, for this. But since he didn't, he'd have to use the words he did have.

"You're beautiful," he said quietly, watching his hand move in and out of her, slicker by the second. He could feel the walls of the little cunt warming and softening. "Beautiful everywhere, and so soft. I can't keep my hands off you." His other hand smoothed over her left breast, carefully touching that smooth ivory skin, stroking until he could actually feel the skin of her breast heat up. She sighed as his thumb brushed over her nipple. It had turned deep rose in color and stiffened under his hand. "I want to do this right. You're going to have to tell me what you like, honey."

She gave a half smile. "I don't really know myself what I like. I know I like what you're doing now."

"This?" Fingers deep inside her, his thumb brushed her clitoris and he saw the muscles in her belly contract. His hips moved involuntarily and his cock surged, as if it had a mind of its own. It wanted to be in her *now*. It wanted to start fucking *now*. He took a moment to control his breathing. "You like this?"

"Yes." She whispered the word.

He bent and took the little nipple in his mouth again and suckled, moving his middle finger in her gently, rubbing the tight walls. She was much, much wetter now and his finger slipped in and out with ease.

He lifted his mouth. "And this?" He slipped another finger in.

"Bud," Claire breathed, bringing her hands up to caress his head, his neck, his shoulders. The touch was light and delicate but he felt it all the way to his cock. It swelled and he nearly lost it. Damn, he almost came when she arched her back and opened her legs even further for him.

He wanted to stroke her for hours but it wasn't going to happen. If he were a gentleman, he'd finish himself off right now with his hand and continue with the foreplay, but he wasn't. He was sweating with the effort of not ramming into her.

She needed to come first and he knew the quickest way for that to happen. "You'll like this, too," he whispered against the soft scented skin of her neck and started kissing his way down her body.

He tugged until her buttocks were on the edge of the bed and knelt on the floor, settling her legs on his shoulders. For a moment, he just stopped and stared. She was so beautiful here, too. Ivory and rose folds, glistening and tender, small and soft, ringed with silky black hair. His gaze traveled up her body and he caught his breath. She was watching him with heat in her eyes, like the sky on a hot summer's day. No fear at all, no anxiety.

There was complete silence in the room. The snow outside dampened all noise from the city and it was as if they were the only human beings alive on earth, just the two of them in the silent shadowy room.

Bud bent and let his breath out slowly against that soft little cunt. Her legs shifted on his shoulders. He opened her with his fingers and thought of a flower unfurling.

Clearly Claire had cast a spell on him—that must be it.

He rarely gave head and when he did he wasn't thinking in terms of rose petals and unfurling flowers, that's for sure. He was doing what he had to do to soften the woman up, wet her to make sure she could take him. Sometimes as a little thank you for going down on him. He didn't particularly like it. It was a chore, part of the price of getting laid.

Now he couldn't imagine anything he wanted more than to taste her.

He brought his mouth to her and kissed her, exactly as if he were kissing the lips of her mouth. He felt more than heard the sharp intake of breath and he knew it wasn't from pain.

She tasted wonderful, fresh and delicately spicy, all at once. Why hadn't he ever liked going down on a woman before? It was deliciously intimate, feeling all that softness with his lips and tongue. He could gauge her arousal more clearly with his tongue than with his cock and could make her even wetter so she could take him more easily.

If it weren't for the fact that his hard-on, which he'd had forever now it seemed, was driving him crazy, he could do this for hours, kissing her, sliding his tongue in and out of all that softness and spicy warmth. Just the two of them, the outside world forgotten, her staked out on the bed, gleaming hair around her, looking like a pagan sacrifice, and him kneeling at her feet, loving her with his mouth. The only sounds were her sharp breathing and the deliciously sexy wet sounds his mouth was making against her cunt.

He held her apart with his fingers as he stroked his tongue in and out of her. Amazing. He could see and feel exactly what he was doing to her. The folds of her sex were turning a deeper pink and were glistening wet.

The muscle walls contracted and his cock twitched in sympathy. He stroked his tongue further, rubbing against the walls and Claire's legs trembled on his shoulders.

She moaned softly and he nearly lost it right there, pulling the muscles around his cock tight, having to concentrate fiercely not to come. His tongue probed more deeply. Claire cried out and then he felt it, felt her climax against his mouth, sharp little tugs. He could *see* it, too. Pulling back a little he could actually see the rhythmic contractions of the dusky pink tissue and it was the most mind-blowingly exciting thing he'd ever seen.

But he couldn't watch for long because now was the moment. Now now *now*.

Moving fast, Bud pulled her up on the bed as he mounted her, shaking with excitement. He needed to put his cock in her while she was still coming so the pain of losing her virginity would be lost in the climax, but it was so hard to keep his focus. So hard not to get drunk on the smells and textures of her. He wanted to suck her breasts, touch her all over, linger over all the tender places, bury his face in that glorious hair, but there wasn't time.

He cupped her head with his hands and looked down at her. His cock was so hard he didn't need to position it. It knew what to do all on its own. He entered her slowly as he watched her face. He wanted to kiss her but he needed to watch her reaction more.

Jaws clenched against his own climax rushing along his spine in a hot trail of excitement, Bud tightened his ass and pressed forward. She was still coming and he could feel her tight wet walls milking him. Every muscle in his body was tense, shaking, tight with control. Beads of sweat broke out on his forehead. He pressed forward.

Claire was watching him, watching his eyes and they both breathed in sharply as he reached her maidenhead, the sound loud in the quiet room.

"Now," she whispered.

"Yes," he answered, tightening his ass and thrusting forward. The membrane stretched slightly, then broke and he was in her, pressing against her womb. Claire closed her eyes and wrapped her arms around him as he buried his face in her neck.

It was too much. Bud was dying from sensory overload. That cloud of fragrant hair—Christ, she had enough hair for six people—providing a soft pillow for his head, the soft, slender figure beneath him, the tight little cunt just now finishing its climax in slowing contractions. Every system in his body went into overdrive. All on its own, his body started thrusting, two, three, four times and—*ohmyGod*—it was all over. Just like that.

Yup.

Mr. Stamina himself, the guy whose one claim to fame in bed was the ability to fuck for hours, had all of a sudden morphed into Quick Draw McGraw.

He jerked inside her, breathing hard with the mind-blowing pleasure. His head was blowing up, and he felt like screaming but he managed to bite the pillow instead, aware with the three brain cells left to him that he was lucky he wasn't biting *her*.

He was dimly aware that her pleasure was over, absorbed by the pain of losing her virginity. It wouldn't be polite to show just how explosive his own pleasure was. Some things he simply couldn't control, however. His toes dug into the mattress and his hands clutched her hips as he tried to push himself even further into her. He clenched his teeth, trying not to shout, but nothing could stop the air bellowing in and out of his lungs.

The hard-on had lasted way too long, he was too revved, nothing could hold him back. He just came and came and came. His hips jerked reflexively; he couldn't stop it. He wasn't pumping in her, fucking her with controlled movements. No, it was more like jerking off inside her, nothing smooth and controlled about it at all. Just the grinding movements of a body out of control. He twitched and moaned and groaned his way through his explosive orgasm, nearly mindless with pleasure.

Finally, he sank completely onto Claire, panting, totally wiped out. Every once in a while he'd shudder, an electric shock running through him, an overload of the nervous system.

Slowly, slowly, his senses returned. One by one, as if he were coming back from the dead.

When he could put a thought together again, he took stock, and it wasn't pretty.

He was flattened on top of Claire, probably crushing her. His hands were clutching the soft skin of her hips and he had to tell his fingers to let go, one by one. They didn't want to do it. He wanted to keep clutching her ass, holding her still, trying to crawl further inside her by pushing with his toes. He had to let go. Had to. He had strong hands and he was probably leaving bruises.

He was still hard as a rock inside her with not even a hint of softening. He wanted to stay in her forever but he had to pull out, now, or the rubber would start leaking. He'd done enough damage as it was.

He could feel his brain sending out the message. *Pull out of her, relax that death grip on her, get off her.*

The message wasn't getting through. Like a lone rider trying to deliver a message to the general in battle and falling with a bullet to the chest. He was completely ambushed by the softness of her skin, the small breasts against his chest, the tight feel of her cunt, the floral scent mixing with the smell of sex. He simply couldn't move.

Maybe he should take it in stages. Kiss her, maybe. That wouldn't take too much muscle control. He shifted to brush his mouth over her cheekbone and felt wetness.

He froze.

She was crying.

Jesus, of course she was crying. What did he expect?

Well, that solved the problem of letting her go. He opened his hands and braced himself against the mattress, pulling out of her. She was so tight, he was half-way expecting his cock to make a 'pop' sound as it emerged. He lifted his head, thumb wiping a tear from her pale, perfect cheekbone.

"Don't cry, honey." He wanted his voice to be firm, reassuring, but it came out hoarse and cracked. "Please."

She turned her head to meet his eyes and smiled. Amazingly, she smiled. "Oh, they're tears of joy. Because it was so wonderful," she said. She ran a slender finger down his cheek.

It was?

"I've never felt anything as exciting as that before." Caressing his chin.

She hadn't?

"You're magnificent." Moving over his lips.

He was?

He was smiling back down at her. He simply couldn't help it. He dropped a quick kiss on her lips, then lingered. Ah, Jesus, she tasted so good, warm welcoming softness...

His cock was blindly trying to enter her again and he had to jerk himself back to awareness.

He lifted his head and put his finger on her chin, right there, on the charming little dent. "We've got to get you cleaned up," he whispered. "Then we'll talk."

Her narrow rib cage expanded on a sigh. "Okay." She smiled, her hand caressing his shoulder as he lifted himself away.

Bud found the bathroom with no trouble and switched on the light, catching a reflection of himself in the pretty oval mirror with wrought-iron flowers around the frame.

He looked incredibly smug and pleased with himself. Usually he was wiped out after sex, sweaty and disheveled, like he'd just finished a hard game of one-on-one basketball. He wasn't happy or sad after sex, just tired. Well, he had the sweaty and disheveled part down pat but he looked like the cat who'd found a whole barrel of cream.

He started to remove the condom, then took a good look. It was smeared with blood. Her blood. The blood of her virginity. He should have been appalled, but it was all he could do not to prance with pride in the pretty little perfumed bathroom.

Hot damn.

He'd read somewhere that in the Middle Ages men used to hang the bloody sheets out the window after the wedding night.

Shit, yeah. Absolutely. No flies on medieval men, no, sir. Staking their claim and proving to the world who the woman belonged to. It was totally barbaric and primitive, but who ever said men were civilized?

He glanced down quickly at his hands to make sure no hairs had sprouted on the backs of them, then bared his teeth at the mirror to make sure his incisors hadn't suddenly grown. He felt like an animal and wouldn't have been at all surprised to see that he'd turned into one.

Bud pulled the condom off his cock and washed up. His cock was still as hard as the iron towel railing, even with cold water. It wasn't going to go down any time soon. No chance of another round, though. She'd be too sore.

Oh, yeah? the animal in him asked, and the human answered, *yeah, you asshole*.

How long until he could fuck her again?

Well, how the hell should he know? And how could he find out? It's not as if he could call a colleague at the cop shop.

Hey, how's it hanging? Business slowed down any 'cause of the snow? Anyone making any progress on the Lorenzetti case? And oh — by the way, how long do you have to wait after fucking a virgin to do it again?

Nope. Asking advice was out of the question.

Walking in the door of the house, he'd been dimly aware that she had a gazillion books in her living room, but he doubted any of them would yield the information he needed. He couldn't exactly find a medical text and look up 'cherry, elimination of', could he?

Well, tonight no second round. He looked down at himself, his cock happily upright, swollen and ready, weeping to fuck her. *Hear that?* he told his cock. *Not tonight. Tomorrow.*

Maybe.

It was still at full salute, but tough shit.

In a little wooden chest of drawers he found stacked washcloths and chose the first one, a pretty pale rose pink. He ran the water in the tap until it was warm, wet the cloth and went back into the bedroom to clean up his Princess.

Chapter Five

ഔ

Oh my, Claire thought, watching Bud as he entered the bedroom. Never in her wildest dreams would she have imagined lying in bed, watching a man like this walk through the door to her bedroom.

How many nights had she lain in bed late at night, just like now, only in pain and despair? Gritting her teeth, hoping she would make it through the darkest, loneliest hours of the night? Feeling a soul-deep weariness?

Watching Bud walk to the bed like a Viking stalking prey was definitely her reward for hanging in there. For not giving up and dying.

He was so gorgeous, all rippling muscles and masculine grace and...

Oh my my my!

He was still erect. And how. All the books said that men detumesced after orgasm. So why hadn't he?

And why did people think that hairlessness in men was sexy? Lucy had said that most of the men at The Warehouse shaved their chests, and the guy she'd run off with had actually shaved his groin.

That was stupid of them. It made them look like boys.

Bud looked like a man. Straight broad shoulders a yard wide, large hard biceps with the raised veins of an athlete coursing over them, a thick mat of blond hair a shade darker than the hair on his head covering his pectorals, narrowing down to the groin, the hair growing darker still and framing...

Lord, he was big. Her vagina twitched in sympathy, a little sore. She couldn't possibly tonight, tempting though the idea was.

It was a miracle they'd managed to make love at all. His penis nearly touched his navel. She was almost certain that her hand wouldn't reach around it, but she wanted to test that...first-hand. She wanted to touch him all over, pet him, feel all those hard muscles. Sink her nose into him, smell him, taste him, bite him.

He sat on the side of the bed, watching her. Did he think she was having regrets? That she wished it hadn't happened? Nothing could be farther from the truth. Tonight was the best night of her life.

Claire smiled up at him. "Are you okay?"

She'd shocked him. His face went blank for a moment, then he slowly smiled.

"That's my line, isn't it?" He pushed her legs gently apart.

"It is? Well, then the answer is—absolutely. Couldn't be better."

He was wiping her between her legs, in long swipes of the warm wet cloth. Claire levered herself up on her elbows and watched him. It was terribly intimate, there in the quiet room. This huge naked and aroused man, ministering to her, cleaning her gently. She'd been cleaned before, of course, when she was sick, but not like this. Definitely not like this.

He seemed fascinated by what he was doing, watching his hand closely as the washcloth moved around the folds of her sex. Yes, fascinated and—turned on. Definitely.

It wasn't just the erect penis, though that was a dead giveaway, of course. His breathing speeded up and his nostrils flared, as if to take in more of her scent. The skin over his cheekbones was red, pulled taut. A muscle in his jaw was jumping. It seemed impossible, but his penis lengthened. What a waste of perfectly good manhood, but...

"Bud," she murmured, "I don't think I can..."

"Not tonight, no, I know that," he replied absently, all his attention focused on his hand moving around her sex. Her own attention was focused there, too, at the feel of his hand encased in the soft warm washcloth, slow and languid, caressing her, in and out, in long lingering wet swipes.

"Tomorrow," she whispered and his eyes whipped up to hers. She nearly recoiled to see the heat there, turning the light brown to molten gold.

"Tomorrow," he whispered back. "All day if you can manage it."

It took her a moment to catch her breath. "It's a date."

Sex all day. Wow. It beat trying to put up the laundry room shelves and finishing her Elmore Leonard, which had been her original plan for the weekend.

He was smiling now. A little of that predatory expression, the one that said — get ready because we're having sex *now* — was gone. She missed it, but knew that sex *now* would hurt.

Bud placed the washcloth carefully on the back of a bentwood chair and Claire nearly sighed at what Suzanne would say. Suzanne would go ballistic at the idea of a wet cloth on an original Thonet.

Claire didn't care. Bud could do what he wanted with her furniture as long as he stayed close to her with that amazing erection which she had every intention of putting to good use. Tomorrow.

Bud's expression had turned serious. *We'll talk*, he'd said before disappearing into the bathroom. Looked like he was ready for that talk. "Honey, how is it that you—" He hesitated a moment.

Uh oh. The one question she didn't want asked.

How is it that a woman your age is still a virgin? Any way you turned it, it was pathetic. It was either have him think no man had ever desired her, or tell him the truth.

The truth—no, no way. *I've been very sick*, was the last thing she wanted him to know. He'd get...*that* expression on his face. The one her father always had, the one Rosa, the cook who'd been with the Parks family forever, had. The one Suzanne often had. Watching Claire carefully for signs of sickness, when she felt fine.

Are you too hot? Too cold? Should you be doing that? Eating that? How *are* you?

Claire was fine, just *fine*.

Having sex with Bud wasn't about sickness at all. Having sex with Bud was about joy and delight and pulsing life in every cell of her body.

"Come here," she commanded. She patted the other half of the bed. "Lie down."

Bud raised sandy eyebrows at her tone, but he shut up and obeyed. Good. She wanted action, not questions about her lack of a sex life.

And anyway, she *had* a sex life now. Big time. It was stretched out on her bed, all six feet two inches of male, sporting mouth-watering muscles and a real live penis, fully erect, if you please. And every inch of him was all hers.

Claire was about to make up for lost time. *Look out, Bud.*

Claire looked Bud up and down. He was like a feast laid out for her, a thousand delicacies. Should she start with the caviar or the chocolate?

A man's body was a fascinating thing, but she knew absolutely nothing about it. What to do first?

She was kneeling beside him, watching him watching her. His gaze was riveted on her breasts, which felt swollen and hot. She felt a rush of warmth between her thighs when he looked lower.

Aha.

Claire opened her legs a little and it was as if someone touched him with an electric prod. He stiffened, eyes locked on her sex and his penis moved as if it had a mind of its own.

This was so delicious she nearly laughed aloud.

She opened her thighs a little more, knowing he could now see the folds of her sex, probably glistening, because she could feel her own moisture welling up at the expression on his face.

Bud was breathing hard, almost panting. Very slowly, lingering on her breasts for a long time, he brought his gaze back up to meet hers.

His eyes were heavy-lidded and that golden predatory look was back. "You're going to torture me tonight, aren't you?" he growled. "You know I can't make love to you, so you're going to dangle it just out of my reach."

Torture. Now *that* was an exciting thought.

"Mmm." Claire bent forward to lay a hand on his thigh. It was furry with thick blond hairs a lighter color than the skin, the powerful muscles visible under the tanned skin in long striated bands. His quadriceps clenched beneath her hand. His penis was only a few inches away, but she didn't touch him there. Time enough for that later.

Torture, indeed.

Touching his thigh like that, Claire was reminded all over again how powerful this man was, how well-muscled that tall frame was. She was no match at all for him in that department. And yet, just as it had at The Warehouse, his body spoke to her loud and clear. She could do anything she wanted with him and had nothing at all to fear from him.

She smiled. "I think—I think I'll make you my love slave."

His eyes widened. He was trying not to smile, but his lips twitched. "Your...love slave?"

"Yes." Claire's voice was definite because as she spoke, she realized that this was exactly what she wanted. All that maleness, stretched out beside her, hers to command. Power where once she'd been so helpless. A superb body stretched out for her, whose body had once been so weak and ill.

Her prize for not dying.

She'd won it, fair and square.

Bracing her arms on his shoulders, she lifted a leg over him, straddling his chest. It was so broad her legs were stretched wide open. The chest hairs tickled sensitive flesh and her open sex kissed his chest. She rotated her hips tentatively, relishing the feel of the hairs and hard muscle underneath her, against her open labia. It was almost as exciting as when he'd kissed her there and she'd experienced her first orgasm.

What now?

She'd felt so delicious when he'd held her arms up above her head, as if she were powerless to stop the pleasure coursing through her. Okay, she thought. Let's make Bud powerless.

Ridiculous, of course. The man was the essence of physical power. But she had power of her own—he was the one who had given it to her.

"Put your arms above your head." Her voice didn't ring with command. It was soft and breathless because her lungs seemed to be filled with more heat than air. But it got effects, just the same. Bud stretched his arms up and she nearly climaxed as the chest muscles rippled along her open, wet sex. His eyes burned pure gold at the helpless sound of pleasure that escaped from her.

"What are you going to do to me now?" he asked, his voice a low growl.

"Tie you up so you can't move." She ignored raised sandy brows and stretched out to catch his wrists in her left hand. It was ridiculous. His wrists were thick and hard. She could barely span them both with her hand, let alone encircle them. Still, she pressed down on his wrists and he stayed put as obediently as if she'd put a metal shackle around his wrists.

"Stay," she whispered.

"Okay," he whispered back.

O-kay. Yes, indeedy.

Claire all but licked her lips at the sight of the powerful man between her thighs. All those hard, honed muscles, all that hair-roughened honey-dark skin...all hers.

She ran her hands over his outstretched arms, drunk on the feel of him. The skin on the underside of his arms was unexpectedly smooth, almost silky. Such a contrast with the rough textures of the rest of him. The hair of his armpits was lighter in color, long and straight and soft. The hair on his chest was darker, rough and crinkly. Both textures were enticing. She could spend days exploring him with her hands, her mouth.

She bent and kissed his eyelids closed. Here, too, the skin was soft, such a contrast with his beard-roughened cheeks. She kissed and nuzzled and licked her way over his face. Tracing the sandy eyebrows with her tongue, licking his lips, biting his cheekbone. He shuddered when she explored his ear with her tongue. Claire sat up, enormously pleased with herself and looked down at Bud, stretched out under her.

The skin over his cheekbones was flushed, as were his lips. Shards of golden light glittered between nearly closed eyelids. His veins stood out. Every muscle he had — and he had a lot of them, all honed — was corded.

Extreme rage could look like that, she supposed. But it wasn't rage.

"Ride my cock," he growled.

She must have looked startled because he shook his head sharply. "Don't put it in you, you can't take me. We won't fuck, that's for tomorrow, but I have to feel you on me. Sit on it, let me feel you."

"Okay," she whispered.

Claire shifted to slide down his body. He gave a sharp gasp when her sex passed over the huge bulbous head of his penis. It was wet. So was she.

She slid further down until the folds of her sex opened over the base of his penis. It was almost as exciting as having him inside her. His penis was almost unbearably hot, velvety skin over iron. She slid back and forth in tiny movements and watched, fascinated, as a big drop of liquid formed on the head of his penis, jutting out past her dark pubic hair.

Claire sat up, cupping her hands over the strong muscles of his shoulder. Such strength, such power. There was no give to him at all, the skin over the muscles was like leather over steel. What must it feel like to be so strong? To know that you could do just about anything?

He might be unusually strong, but he hadn't led a charmed life, her lumberjack. He was covered in scars. She hadn't noticed before, but now she could see them, under the chest hair. A long, jagged welted scar along the rib cage. Another one, a white straight scar along the biceps, and the worst one: a big puckered puncture wound on his left side, just over his heart. He was lucky to be alive.

Claire touched the scar over his heart. "You've been hurt," she murmured.

"Mmm." A muscle jerked in his jaw. "Not as bad as you're hurting me now. If you don't move I might die."

Claire laughed and bent down to nip the skin of his shoulder.

He didn't want to talk about his scars.

Fair enough.

She had scars of her own and she didn't want to talk about hers, either. Surgical incisions along the small of her back where she'd had two bone marrow transplants, the first one having failed. A knife scar over her kidney where Rory Gavett had held her hostage at knifepoint.

No talking about scars, no talking about pain, no talking about the past or the future. No talking at all.

His breath was short now, coming in pants, as if he'd been running. She touched her mouth to his, briefly, enough to lick his tongue and make him moan, then she bent lower, biting his neck and chest muscles in short, light nips.

She'd loved it when he'd suckled her nipples. So did he, she found out when she explored through the thick chest hair with the tip of her tongue and found his nipple. It was smaller than hers, hard as a rock. The areole around it was copper-colored, unlike hers, which was light pink. Such intriguing differences.

She swirled her tongue around his nipple and sweat broke out on his forehead. He arched, a low moan coming from deep within his chest. Whenever he moved, the hair-roughened muscles of his chest brushed hard against her nipples, the friction sending liquid waves of heat rolling through her.

"Breast," he muttered, his voice low, guttural, hardly recognizable. Just the one word, as if he were so far gone with lust he couldn't form whole sentences. Maybe he couldn't, because she could barely speak herself. They didn't need words, anyway.

An odd notion, not needing words. Words were Claire's coin, the only thing she'd had to express herself with, defend herself with, for many years. She'd had words instead of a life.

She didn't need words now.

She and Bud understood each other perfectly without words. Their bodies understood each other.

She cupped her breast and bent down to him, her hair falling down over her shoulders and around his head in shiny waves.

They made a pagan picture, her sitting naked on this huge man's groin, sex open over his penis, offering her breast to him, her hair forming a wild dark curtain over them both.

She jumped when his mouth clamped over her breast. His eyes were closed tight, arms still locked over his head, muscles bulging and corded with the effort not to move. She watched his mouth working as he sucked at her breast, feeling the sharp, almost violent tugs in her vagina, keeping time.

Bud released her breast for a moment and opened his eyes. She almost recoiled at the heat that was there, twin golden suns. His hips ground under her in short stabbing movements, the movements of sex. They stared at each other. The sandy hair had turned dark with sweat and his features were strained, as if he were in pain.

"Breast," he muttered, sentences still beyond him. "Again."

For a sex slave, he seemed to be calling all the shots.

Smiling, Claire cupped her breast again and bent down to him, the smile instantly wiped out by the heat generated by his mouth. He was pulling hard at her breast, harder than a child ever could, the pulls echoing deep in her body, golden waves of heat roiling through her and, just like that, she slipped over the edge into climax.

This time his mouth followed her rhythms. He must have felt the clasp of her vagina against his penis as he sucked even harder, in time with her, groans coming from deep in his chest. Claire's thighs shook as heat rolled through her in waves, her labia contracting tightly over his penis.

Instinctively, his hips rose as he ground against her, clenched tightly over him. It went on forever, the heat and the waves, the groans, her heart seemingly stopped. For the first time in her life, Claire lost all connection with her body out of pleasure, not pain. Grinding, blinding pleasure that went on and on as she overheated, lungs heaving for air.

Beneath her, Bud's hips were bucking, sliding back and forth under her, prolonging the pleasure. She was so wet, he slid with ease. He bit her nipple lightly, and Claire cried out again, another orgasm rolling through her, like catching a wave out to sea.

He released her breast and fell back against the pillow, gasping, watching her through half-shut eyes as the climax vibrated through her. At the end, Claire was shaking, sweating, able to keep her grip on his chest only because the chest hair afforded friction.

Liquid was pouring out of her, from her vagina, all over her body in the form of sweat, leaking from her eyes. His gaze froze on her face, tawny eyes glittering.

"You okay?"

She nodded and bit her lip as she looked down at him. He was trying so hard to keep control of himself. Every hard muscle was so contracted she could see the bands and long sinews, his hands in their imaginary shackles closed in tense fists, the snake coiling as he flexed the muscles of his forearms. His lungs bellowed so much her thighs had to open with each intake of his breath.

Her knight in shining armor, letting her have her control.

"Yeah," she whispered.

She was more than okay. She was *fine*. The contractions were easing off and that slippery sliding feeling was subsiding, leaving a new person behind. Something important had shifted in her. She was a completely different woman. In the past hour she'd crossed some invisible divide.

She had always felt disconnected from everyone, even as a little girl, the only child of elderly parents, playing alone in the gardens of the Parks mansion. During her illness, she'd been encased, imprisoned in a sick body, alone on a hospital bed, separate from everyone in the world.

She'd only met Bud a few hours ago, yet she felt so…so *connected* to him, heart and mind and soul and sex. This big man, trying so hard to let her call the shots, understanding instinctively she needed that. This man who'd sheltered her and protected her. This man who was shaking with sexual desire, but wouldn't allow himself to penetrate her.

He watched her carefully, eyes golden pools of fire. "What are you thinking?"

What was she thinking? Not much. She was feeling, more than anything else. Feeling suffused with pleasure, soft and womanly. Feeling powerful and sexy.

Alive.

The angel of death had hung over her for so *long*. Bud had somehow chased the stench of death away forever.

He needed to know. He needed to understand what he'd done for her. He deserved it.

She watched his eyes as her chest lifted on a sigh. She tried to smile, but it wouldn't form. What she was feeling was too solemn for a smile. Too important.

"I'm thinking," she said, and her voice cracked. She waited a moment to get control over her voice again, and a lone tear tracked down her face. When she finally mastered her feelings, her voice came out an intense whisper, past the tightness in her throat. "I'm thinking that I'm so glad it was *you*, Bud."

Bud's eyes flared. His penis swelled between the lips of her sex and just like that, he climaxed, hips arching off the bed, taking her with him, semen spurting over his stomach in fierce white jets. He'd clung to control until now, but her words had set him off.

He groaned as if in pain, hips straining under her, not in regular movements but in uncontrolled jerks. It went on and on as Claire watched, fascinated, the white jets of sperm spurting out of the big red bulbous head of his penis. After her own climax, her flesh was supersensitive and she felt every movement keenly as he shook and groaned his way through the orgasm. They were both panting by the time he finally stilled.

Bud was sweating, chest hairs pearled with sweat, stomach slick with semen. Who knew that sex would be so…*slippery*?

"Man." His closed eyes finally opened. He was watching her eyes and she felt that he was trying to gauge her feelings. "Can I use my hands?" he asked finally.

Claire was sweating herself, still trembling with the aftermath of her own orgasm. There was no energy to talk. She nodded, her long hair kissing his shoulders.

Immediately, Bud's arms came down, came around her, easing her down onto his chest. She felt the slickness of his semen on her stomach, gluing them together. His big hands tunneled through her hair, easing her way down, holding her head still for his kiss. It was hard to remember she'd just learned how tonight. They meshed, mouths melding perfectly. His tongue was deep in her mouth, stroking.

Bud lifted her head away from his mouth for a moment. "That was Goddamned amazing," he whispered.

Claire nodded, exhausted. Her forehead fell onto his chest. He wrapped his arms around her as she slid down. There was no energy for talk, not even for more kisses. She was completely wiped out, sliding quickly into sleep.

"I hope you recover by tomorrow morning," Bud said. She was lying with her ear to his chest and the deep voice reverberated in her head. "Because we're going to spend the whole day fucking."

She sighed with pleasure at the idea.

"Okay," she said before slipping into sleep.

Chapter Six
December 13th

৪৩

Claire woke up late, aware of Bud's body before she was aware of her own.

An old trick of the mind.

Mornings had always been the hardest. Waking to another day in the hospital.

While sick, she had often had intense dreams of sunshine and laughter, the mind making up for what the body was missing. She'd be running through fields or playing skip rope or dancing. She'd loved her dance lessons as a little girl, before the sickness.

The dreams were all of lightness, of running and playing and laughing. In her dreams she'd always been healthy. Whole.

Waking up had always been so horrible, the difference between her happy dreams and the crushing weight of reality threatening to sap her of what little strength she had.

Until she'd trained herself not to, she'd woken up crying every morning. So she'd learned to wake up at a far remove from her body, allowing her mind to slowly realize that she wasn't in a field of flowers or on a wooden stage in her tutu and ballerina slippers. She was chained to a hospital bed by IV lines, in fierce pain and close to death.

Training her mind to be out of body for those first few moments of wakefulness allowed her to make the transition from her dreams to reality. It was a habit she hadn't managed to break now that she was healthy again.

So Claire was aware of Bud first, at her back, before she was aware of herself. He was so heavy the mattress dipped deeply and she'd have slept close to him even if he hadn't had his arms around her. She was sleeping on one brawny arm. As pillows went, it wasn't soft, but she wasn't about to complain. The other arm was draped over her hip, large hand spanning her belly. She was completely surrounded by warm, hairy male.

She'd slept in the arms of a man.

Something so simple, so basic. Something millions of women the world over did, every night. Something she'd never done. Never dreamed she'd live long enough to do.

How did that old song go?

Someone to watch over me.

At some deep and primitive level, her head and her heart knew someone had been watching over her all night long and she'd been able to just let go.

She was naked. Funny, she'd never slept naked before. Why on earth did people wear clothes to bed? How delicious to feel the smooth Egyptian cotton sheets under her, the weight of the covers on her bare skin, Bud's hard arms around her.

Bud's penis, hot and hard and fully erect, nestled in the small of her back.

"You're awake," his low, deep voice said, so close to her ear she could feel the puffs of air. She shivered.

"Mmm."

"Did you sleep well?" He licked the rim of her ear and goose bumps blossomed along her arms, and butterflies danced in her stomach.

Claire nodded, unable to form words.

Bud pulled back the covers and she could see his hands. One hand was slowly caressing her breasts, the other trailing across her stomach, right below where the butterflies were doing somersaults, moving his hand in ever-larger circles.

It was the hand with the snake tattoo. His hand moved lower, stroking her pubic hair, stroking lower still, his fingers sifting through the increasingly slick folds until his fingers disappeared and only the back of his hand was visible. It was the most erotic thing she'd ever seen—a snake over her mound, seemingly ready to enter her. The snake danced and writhed along Bud's powerful forearm muscles as his fingers moved in her, coaxing wetness out of her.

"You're wet, honey. You been dreaming about me?" Bud's tongue licked along the back of her ear while his thumb slid along to what she now knew to be her clitoris. Knew it because there, right *there* where he was touching her, heat blossomed and shimmered.

It hadn't done anything for her at all when, with the help of a mirror and an anatomy textbook, she'd tried to locate her clitoris herself. Oh, there'd been a little extrusion of flesh there, all right, just like the book had said and Claire had drawn a sigh of relief that at least all her body parts were in working order. But when she rubbed it, she'd felt nothing beyond a little pleasure. *Very* little. The equivalent of, say, downing a Coke in the summer when you're thirsty.

Not anything like now, with Bud's fingers, wet from *her*, slipping and sliding in slow, controlled movements in and out of her vagina, then swirling up to circle her clitoris, sparking off bursts of sensation so powerful they danced and shimmered along the edge of pain.

"It's tomorrow." The deep voice sinking into her, so close she could feel his lips moving against her ear. "You remember what I said we'd be doing all day today?"

I'm going to fuck you all day tomorrow.

No one had ever said fuck to her, in her entire life. It had been a word relegated to books and movies. Funnily enough, she wasn't offended at all when Bud said it to her. It wasn't an expletive, it was a description, an apt word for an earthy act.

I'm going to fuck you all day.

"Oh, yeah," she sighed.

He tensed against her back, fitting himself more closely to her, lifting her leg over his hip. She was completely open to his hand, sliding slickly in and out.

Bud's lips moved against her ear, raising goose bumps. "When I said all day, I meant it. We'll stop to eat and I'll put up those shelves I saw in your storeroom earlier." He kissed her neck and she could feel his lips curve in a smile against her throat. "Maybe I'll catch the game this afternoon. Recover a little. But for the rest of the day you'll be on your back, or on top or in whatever position you want to be, as long as I'm inside you."

Claire was burning up. His words, the snake-hand moving in her, the feel of his fingers delving deeply inside her, where no one else had ever reached—they all combined to move liquid heat through her veins. She gasped when he moved his thigh under hers to open her more widely and slipped a second finger in.

"I'll let you wear clothes," he growled roughly as he spread his fingers, opening her up. The tip of his penis fit to her opening and he slid his fingers out to make room for it. He started pushing in. "But no underwear."

Pressing in. So hot. So hard.

"You hear me, honey? I don't want you wearing any underwear at all."

"Okay," she gasped. He was halfway in, stopping, letting her adjust to him, to the hot thick size of him.

"Wear something loose, something I can take off fast. I want to be able to put my hands on you, my cock in you, in one second flat."

She didn't answer, couldn't. There was no breath in her lungs for words. His penis burned, hurting just a little but the pleasure was greater than the pain.

"Claire?" He prodded with his penis, still just halfway in. "Am I hurting you?" He wasn't moving, waiting for her response. She wanted him to move. She *needed* him to move.

Claire reached behind her to grasp his thigh, hairy and hard, and let him feel the bite of her nails. The muscles were too hard for her to sink her nails into his flesh but she knew she'd made her point as he chuckled.

"You're torturing me," she breathed. "So start moving. *Now.*"

Another low rough chuckle and he did as she asked. Started moving. *Now.*

Slowly. It was terrible. It was bliss.

He finally stopped when there was no more of her, though she suspected there might still be more of *him.*

"God." The word came out low and rough. Claire could feel him hot at her back, trembling. "So tight."

"Mmm."

Yes, she was. She was clasped very tightly around his penis, though that was more because of his size than because of her smallness. He was enormous, stretching her. Yet when he started pulling out again, slowly, she missed him. Her vagina felt empty, as if it were made to be filled by him. She barely had time to register the emptiness, though, when she felt his muscles tense and he started moving back in. Still slowly, so she could feel every inch of his passage inside her.

Oh, Lord. She'd had no idea of the intensity of lovemaking.

No. Not lovemaking. Sex.

Lovemaking was for lovers. For all she knew, they were having a one-night stand. Well, one-weekend stand, since he seemed to have big plans for the day.

Live for the moment. Don't think of tomorrow. Her creed.

The snake-hand kept a forefinger on her clitoris as he started moving more quickly and heavily in her. The other hand was holding her breast. His grasp was hard and unyielding. The effect was to hold her still for him, like a female animal immobilized for servicing. She couldn't have moved if she wanted to and to her surprise, it excited her.

Him, too. The strokes grew heavy and fast, making the bed creak. The heat was amazing, incandescent. Her hand was still on his thigh and she could feel the muscles in his legs as he worked her. Sounds came from deep in his chest. Not words. Animal noises.

Everything about it was animal. The scent of his musk, the smells generated from their joined sexes rising sharp in the air, overpowering the delicate fragrance of the scented candles and flowers, as was right. What they were doing was much more real than her feminine world of pretty, fragile things. What they were doing was elemental. The bed creaked harder as his thrusts grew in intensity, hard hands holding her tightly. She couldn't move, could hardly breathe, his left hand curling around her rib cage and squeezing tightly.

The sounds grew louder. His wordless noises, the bed, now thudding against the wall, the slick sounds of his penis moving in her. Every sense was overloaded and when Bud put his mouth against her neck and bit her, lightly, it was too much. With a cry, she exploded, contracting sharply around him.

"Jesus!"

It was as if she'd taken him completely by surprise. His shout was so loud she could feel the reverberations in his chest against her back. He bucked strongly, once, twice, then swelled even larger inside her, grinding heavily against her as he climaxed, too, in a frenzy of noise and movement. Grunting and groaning and jerking.

When he finally stopped, there was silence in the small room except for his heavy breathing, slowly slowing.

A long silence, then a rough exhalation of breath.

"Whoa, that was quick," he rumbled. "I swear, I usually last longer than this. I can go for hours, I promise, but with you...I don't know what it is about you, hon...I have a hair trigger."

Claire would have been indignant if she'd have more strength and were feeling less languid and sated.

Suzanne had warned her about this. Modern men are weak and find excuses for everything, she'd said. They'll blame you for their shortcomings. No matter what, it's always your fault. Suzanne was so disappointed in men she'd basically stopped dating altogether.

Claire sighed. "So I suppose it's my fault?" She wriggled a little and felt Bud still hard inside her. Not iron hard like before, but still filling her completely. What was he complaining about?

He sighed back. "Nah, it's mine. Absolutely. Your only fault is being too desirable." Bud pressed with his snake hand to hold her still as he slowly pulled out. "Sometime today we'll fuck for a long time. I just don't know when it'll be. I get inside you and..." His short hair rasped against the pillow as he shook his head behind her. He kissed her neck. "Pow, I come like a teenager in the back seat of Dad's car."

He sounded cheerful enough, though. And looked cheerful when Claire finally turned over. He kissed her lips, briefly, lifted his mouth to look down on her, gaze circling her face. He started to bend down again then stopped.

"Nope. Nuh-uh. " Bud put a finger to the dimple in her chin. "You've gotta work on getting ugly, honey. Grow a wart or two or lose some teeth. Do *something*. Otherwise, we'll never get out of this bed. We'll just stay in bed and fuck until we starve to death and they find our bodies. That's not good."

No, it wouldn't be good to starve to death. Not when she'd just discovered how much fun sex could be.

Bud rolled over and sat up, back to her. He stretched long muscles, then stood and turned. "I'll shower first," he announced, mouth lifted in a half smile, eyes pure hot gold. "And cook us breakfast while you take your shower. Then I'll put up those shelves for you. Then we'll fuck some more."

Claire wanted to make some snappy comment but he took her breath away, standing there by her bed, bathed in the pale light of a winter morning. He seemed more enormous than ever, now that she knew intimately the feel of his body, the deep strength contained in those muscles. His penis jutted out from his body at an angle instead of lying flat against his stomach like last night, but it wasn't any smaller or softer after his climax that she could see. It was covered in a condom, which explained the crackling sound she'd heard as she was emerging from sleep.

He walked into the bathroom and a few seconds later she could hear the shower running, while he whistled cheerfully.

Norwegian Wood. Badly out of tune.

Claire took stock of the morning. Her first morning as a woman. She had big picture windows without curtains because according to Suzanne, 'window treatments', as she called them, were passé. Curtains were out, small slatted blinds were in. The house was isolated so it didn't make much difference. Claire's bedroom windows looked out over a small back yard, completely white with snow, contrasting with the dark bare branches of a crab-apple tree and the shrubs.

It must have snowed all night. The snow reached halfway up her pruned rose bushes. A preternatural quiet reigned outside, all sounds dampened by the snow. It was like being marooned on a cold desert island.

Fine.

Wonderful, in fact.

In a way, they *were* marooned. Nobody on earth knew she was here, except for Bud. And Suzanne, of course. But Suzanne was out of town, as was Dad. Her father had been in Paris for the past two weeks negotiating with the Russians for a collection of Fabergè eggs from the Hermitage in St.

Petersburg to be added to an upcoming show of Russian jewels at the Parks Foundation. He wasn't due back for another week.

Dad had no idea she'd moved out of the house. Claire hated deceiving him, but knew she had to move out from his suffocating embrace. He'd find out when he came home next weekend that it was a done deal. He would forgive her because he loved her. He might even understand, with time.

So no one on earth knew she was here in her little house with her fabulously sexy lumberjack. They were all alone.

There was a clatter from the kitchen. Claire hoped Bud could cook because she only knew how to boil tea and eggs. Even if he didn't know how to cook, though, he knew how to do other things. Very well, indeed.

Claire stared at the ceiling with its pretty pale blue stencils and smiled.

It was so *good* to be alive.

Chapter Seven

∽

Bud smelled her before he saw her.

He was busy cooking a big breakfast. She had a fully equipped kitchen, of almost professional quality, so she must be a good cook.

Well, so was he. His competitive nature rose to the fore. He was going to give her the breakfast of her life. He was also going to give her the fuck of her life, at some point during the day. Something he hadn't managed up until now.

She'd been a virgin, and she'd never had sex before. So she couldn't know that it wasn't normal for the man to start coming after only a few minutes. Or at least it sure wasn't normal for him.

Bud had never in his life had stamina problems. Sex had always been easy. Fun. Uncomplicated.

Fucking was like jogging. Hard, rhythmic exercise that gave him mental alpha waves and made him sweat. He'd actually once solved a case while fucking. In his head he'd reached The Zone, while pumping in and out of…

God, he couldn't remember her name…bottle blonde, worked for…he closed his eyes, trying to remember…an insurance agency. That was it. Very athletic. They'd fucked for hours and, at the end, she'd been grateful and he'd realized that the husband of the murder victim in a current case was lying. A quick phone call had verified that his hunch was right and Bud had received a commendation. If he had jogged for a couple of hours he'd have come to the same conclusion.

Jogging, fucking.

Same thing.

Until now. Until Claire.

No way could he solve a crime while fucking Claire. His mind shorted while his body spiraled out of control. He could barely remember his name, let alone do some serious thinking, while he was in her. He became pure animal.

Like now, smelling her over the scent of bacon and eggs and toast and coffee from the imported Italian espresso machine.

She probably had girl breakfasts, half a pot of low fat yogurt and tea, but he didn't. He liked his food and he'd cooked oversized portions. He had every intention of fucking a lot today and he needed calories for that.

Claire moved into the kitchen wearing cherry red sweats. With nothing underneath, like he'd told her? He looked carefully. She certainly didn't have a bra on, because he could see her little nipples, still hard from her orgasm, poking the front of the top. If she wasn't wearing a bra, then she probably wasn't wearing panties, either...

His cock reared up at the thought. *Stop that*, he told his cock.

They needed to eat. He also really wanted to fix her shelves. He was good with his hands and somehow wanted — needed — to do something for her.

"Hey." Claire smiled shyly, amazing when you thought he'd been inside her half an hour ago. Bud had to remind himself she was new to this sex business.

"Hey yourself." He cracked eggs and heard the microwave ping. "Breakfast is ready."

"Wow. Whatever it is, it smells good." Claire pulled out a chair and sat down.

"Not as good as you do."

She smiled, one of those mysterious womanly smiles. Where had she got it? Last night she'd been a virgin, innocent and unsure of herself. Now she was smiling like the Mona

Lisa. He sure as hell hadn't given her a smile like that. She'd got it all on her own. *Women.* He'd never understand them.

"My smell is Chanel." She tilted her head, long hair flowing in great shiny waves over her shoulders. She leaned over and sniffed him delicately. "What's yours?"

Bud put plates on the table, a skillet of bacon and sausages on a trivet, Danish butter and whole wheat toast on a plate. She had an amazing variety of designer jams and jellies and he put a selection on the table.

Steam rose from a stack of buckwheat pancakes while he pulled the syrup from the microwave. He lifted the edges of the omelet and decided it was time to flip it over. He had a pretty mean hand with omelets. He was cooking basically for himself but thought he'd show off a little. The patented Morrison twist of the wrist and the omelet flipped and settled. Perfect. A shake of the pan, heat up to maximum, then he deftly slid it onto a plate.

Man, he was good.

"Well, I showered using one of those funny soaps shaped like a flower you have in your shower stall and used your shampoo. You don't seem to have anything in your bathroom that doesn't reek like a friggin' flower garden, so I smell like I've been rolling in petals. You should have something that smells like gym socks just to keep the yin yang balance together. Though I don't guess I smell as good as..." His voice trailed off.

Bud stopped and watched Claire in astonishment. She wasn't picking at her food, lip curled, like most women did. As if it were radioactive. She was serenely putting enough food on her plate to feed a family of ten.

Four pancakes, two link sausages and half the omelet. She heavily buttered a slice of toast, piled on blueberry jam and started chomping away with every sign of intense pleasure. Soon the omelet was gone. A couple of minutes after that and she was helping herself to more link sausage. Bud watched, amazed, as she packed it away like a stevedore.

Claire looked pointedly at his empty plate. "Better grab something for yourself before I finish it all."

She wasn't kidding. Bud filled his plate, wondering if he'd have to cook more.

Claire swallowed and attacked the pancakes again. "You're a great cook. My compliments."

Bud shrugged. "I like to eat well and can't afford fancy restaurants all the time, so I've learned to make do in the kitchen. Judging by your kitchen though, you must be a good cook, too."

"Nope," Claire said cheerfully, as she polished off the last bite of pancake. "Can barely boil water. It's way up there on my to do list, though. This is my first house and I want to be able to do everything."

Bud stared. "You can't cook?" He looked around at the kitchen. "Good grief, woman. You've got every kitchen utensil known to man and enough food supplies to last out World War III."

Claire smiled and sighed. "Suzanne."

"Suzanne…what?"

"Barron. Suzanne Barron, one of my best friends. She decorated this house for me. When I told her I wanted to learn how to cook, she said she'd make sure I had everything I need to learn how."

"Including omelet pans in five sizes, an electronic nutmeg grinder and a bread-making machine. And everything in between. So you're all set."

"You could teach me to cook," Claire replied between bites. She ate daintily but steadily and quickly. "I'm a fast learner and it would be fun…" She broke off, a slice of sausage speared on her fork, an appalled look on her face. "Sorry," she mumbled. "I didn't mean to imply…" She bit her lip and stared into her plate.

There it was.

She didn't mean to imply that he'd be around long enough to teach her to cook. She didn't mean to imply that they might become a couple.

But she had.

His cue to pick up and leave. Bud was always antsy the morning after, watching like a hawk for suggestive comments about where 'the relationship' was going from here. Fending off invitations to a concert next week, dinner with friends or — God forbid — a visit to the family.

Any other time, with any other woman, he'd be making noncommittal comments and half an hour later he'd be out the door.

He fucked. He fucked well, by all accounts, or at least he hadn't had any complaints on that score so far. But that was it. He didn't *do* relationships.

Now, he settled more deeply into the dainty little kitchen chair and decided she needed to buy sturdier chairs. And she needed to stock up on some beer. She only had a couple of bottles in the fridge, the fancy imported kind, and some prissy white wine. That was the extent of her alcohol supply.

"Yeah, I'll teach you to cook," he said easily. "It's not rocket science. It's all a question of touch and timing." He winked when she looked up, happy to see her smiling again, that tense look gone. "Like some other activities I could mention."

Claire giggled and he smiled at the sound as he got up. A few minutes later, huevos rancheros were cooking on the stove and this time he meant to have a bite of it himself. You had to watch your step around pretty little Claire Schuyler, otherwise you'd end up starving.

"You've changed your clothes." Claire looked at him, at his gray sweat suit, a small frown between the dark wings of her eyebrows. "How'd you do that?"

"Yeah, I changed." They'd been in the kitchen almost three quarters of an hour and she'd just now noticed. Zero powers of observation. She was a reader and most readers, he'd noticed, lived inside their heads. Claire Schuyler would never make a cop. Cops were attentive to the outside world, always. They noticed everything, always, off duty and on. Their lives depended on it. "I had an overnight case in the trunk of my car. I thought maybe I'd head out to the coast for the weekend." He looked her up and down warmly, lingering over the good bits. "Never made it, though. Got waylaid by a pretty brunette. But I have spare clothes, sweats, my toothbrush, shaver, everything I need." He winked. "Also got a whole box of condoms and I plan on using every single one with you."

Claire reddened, as he imagined she would. But then she surprised him by putting down her fork and looking at him soberly. Long enough and intently enough to make him start to squirm.

"What?"

Silence then a sigh. "You, um, look very healthy, Bud."

Healthy? "Yeah, of course I'm healthy," he answered, puzzled. "Absolutely. I take good care of myself. Healthy as a horse. Always have been."

"And you were careful to use condoms with me. Are you always careful?"

"God yeah. Always. No exceptions, ever." It was an article of faith with him, one of his few hard and fast rules. No fucking without rubbers. He knew only too well what was out there. And most of the women he fucked had been around the block a few times. If he had to clock out before his time, better a bullet than disease. "No problems on that account, hon. Believe me, you're safe as safe can be with me."

"Good." She sighed and bit her lip, working something out in her head. She seemed to come to some kind of resolution finally, and she nodded, as if to herself.

"What's going on in that pretty head of yours?"

"Well, the thing is—" Claire pursed her lips, watching him carefully. "The thing is that I was…um…not well. For a while. I'm fine now. *Fine*. But I…while I was…not well…I was put on the pill. And since of course I can't have any diseases, if you wanted to—ummff!"

The rest of what she wanted to say was lost in his mouth. A red mist rose in his head. Fast as lightning, he picked her up, stripped her, pulled off his sweatshirt, pushed his sweat pants down—he deliberately hadn't put on underwear, either—and embedded his cock in her. Just shoved it in because he'd die if he didn't have his cock in her *now*.

He didn't think at all, he acted on pure instinct. The instant the words were out of her mouth, the instant he realized he could fuck her bareback, *feel* that tight little cunt around his cock without latex, he was a goner.

"Oh, God, you're not ready," he whispered. Trembling, he put his forehead to hers, eyes closed. He could barely think, hardly speak, he was so taken up with the feel of her around him. With the burning hot, intense emotions roiling inside him. "Sorry."

It was a lie. He wasn't sorry at all.

He'd never fucked without a condom. Ever. Would have liked to—what man wanted to use a rubber?—but he'd never ever really been tempted. So being in Claire was a double delight. *Feeling* her with his cock—and now that he had, he wondered how he'd ever go back to rubbers—and knowing it was her, Claire.

She was tight and dry. He knew better than this but couldn't stop. He was shaking, sweating. Helpless. Sliding out of control. Scared of what was happening to him.

"Sorry sorry sorry," he repeated like a whispered mantra. "I should pull out."

What an asshole he was. He had no intention whatsoever of pulling out, though he had no idea what to do now. They couldn't fuck because she was dry. He'd hurt her if he started moving. He was probably hurting her now. Her feet didn't reach the floor and she was sitting on him with her entire body weight holding her down and no leverage to get off. She couldn't move and he couldn't, either. He could only sit tensely with her impaled on his cock, holding her tightly, trembling.

He was frozen, unable to go forward and unable to pull out.

"Sorry," he choked out again.

"Shh." Claire rubbed the back of his head, somehow feeling his distress. "It's okay, Bud," she whispered. She leaned forward and kissed him, breasts brushing against his chest as she lifted a little to find his mouth, lips gentle against his. And the feel of her soft warm mouth against his set him off. Just like that.

Jesus.

A kiss and he came.

Not even one stroke, just the feel of her mouth and he exploded. His arms clamped against her, holding her tightly, hips arching up, grinding hard against her as he came and came and came, his cock red hot and inflamed, shaking so hard he thought he would fly apart.

He clung to Claire desperately, as if she were the only thing in the world that could keep him together, his cock stabbing brutally up into her in short violent strokes as he pumped every drop of liquid in his body into her. The first time in his life he'd ever come inside a woman, not a rubber, and *JesusfuckingChrist* it was so intense for a moment there he thought he'd pass out.

He realized he'd shouted only when he heard the echo of the noise in the quiet room. He was still grinding into her and realized that he was holding her down on his cock with almost brutal force, a degree of violence he'd never used on a woman, ever.

And this was *Claire*. Delicate, fragile Claire. Claire, who was new to sex.

Claire.

There was no stopping; it was like he was on a freight train to hell, plunging out over the canyon though the bridge was down, crashing and burning. Coming in spurts so fierce he was surprised he didn't break something inside her, punch right through her.

Even when he calmed down a little, when he'd pumped every drop of come into her, he was still hard as a rock, still shaking, so excited he could hardly speak. He couldn't look at her, couldn't talk to her. What could he say? He was behaving like an animal. He was always in control with women, but now he'd lost the reins and was fumbling.

The only good thing was that she was wet now. Not because of *her* excitement, because of his...but still. He could move in her. He'd pumped so much of his seed into her, their groins were wet, the liquid seeping out from where they were joined. They were still kissing and he deepened the kiss with a groan, holding her head still for his mouth. God, her mouth was as exciting as her cunt, tongue, lips soft, wet...

She was into it, thank you God, slanting her head to move her mouth against his, her tongue meeting his, arms around his neck.

Maybe it wasn't too late for her to get a little something out of it.

Bud had almost zero control but he was willing to try. Too late for foreplay, he thought. That comes *before* you stick your cock in the woman. Maybe he should kiss her breasts, but that meant leaving her mouth.

No. No way.

He wrapped his right arm around her, hand sliding up and down that narrow satiny back, through the silk waterfall of her hair.

His left hand caressed her breast, full and soft, lightly circling the nipple and oh, yes, that was definitely a moan, right into his mouth. Yes.

Bud fisted his hand in the thick spill of Claire's hair and tugged her head backwards, tilting forward following her, still kissing her deeply. She trusted him to support her and he held her rock steady. His other hand left her breast, drifted down over her soft little belly, forefinger circling the cute little outie. She moaned again.

Amazingly, another climax was bubbling up again. His nerve endings were on fire and his skin felt hot and too tight. This was uncharted territory here. He could continue fucking after coming, and often did, but the edge of excitement was lost and he was always in control.

No control now, none. He was going to lose it again, soon, and had to make her come first.

Bud reached down to where he was embedded in her, to where she was stretched tightly around him. He could tell by touch the difference between his pubic hair and hers. Hers was soft and silky. They were both drenching wet, the first time this had ever happened to him. He'd never felt his come on a woman before and it made him feel hot, primitive, raw.

Bud touched her, index and middle fingers on either side of his cock, following her around him until he reached her clitoris. He rubbed her there, shuddering when she gasped in his mouth. He had to be quick because a hot wire was flashing down his spine and his balls were tightening. He leaned forward, opening her up to him at a sharp angle, so that his short heavy strokes ground directly against her clitoris. Pumping hard and fast, clutching her tightly, tongue deep in her mouth…

Yes!

Oh God, yes, Claire started climaxing, tight little contractions, cries that were lost in his mouth.

Lost. He was lost, too, pumping and grinding in her forever until with one last thrust which raised them both off the chair he started spurting. Grinding and aching and shaking and lost.

Bud abandoned her mouth to bury his face in her hair, groping for control. He felt as if something in him had cracked wide open, leaving him raw and exposed. Helpless. Defenseless. He came in long red hot jets, filling her.

It wound finally down, a climax so intense it had almost been painful. Nothing — *nothing* — like the sex he'd ever had before. Something else entirely. To his horror, tears leaked out of his eyes.

No, not tears. They couldn't be tears.

He hadn't cried since he was eight years old and his stepfather had beaten tears right out of him. Screaming in time with the swings of the fucker's hard leather belt that men don't cry.

Bud had buried his murdered mother without crying.

So they couldn't be tears.

Still, he wiped his face against the cloudy fragrant mass of Claire's hair, waiting for his heartbeat to slow. Waiting to get a slippery grip on *something*, so he could face her.

He had to say something. Something to put this right. He hardly recognized himself. He had a lot of experience at sex. He'd fucked thousands of times before with more partners than he cared to tally up.

It was always the same sequence. A little foreplay, stick it in, start moving. Make sure she comes, more than once if possible. Try to remember her name afterwards, thank her before falling asleep. Get out by morning. It always worked out more or less okay. His partners usually left pretty happy. Sex cleared his head, made him feel better. Made the woman feel better, too, he hoped.

He was never out of control, particularly not after coming. Not like now, one big jittery nerve ending, feelings too big to contain. Now he felt as if his entire world had slipped right out of focus and nothing was familiar, nothing felt the same.

He had no idea whatsoever to say to Claire. He tightened his grip on her, hoping he wasn't leaving bruises, searching in his depths for something to say.

He wasn't smooth, but he had a few lines up his sleeve. Something to make the woman feel special. If there was a woman in the world who deserved a romantic line or two, it was Claire, who'd given herself so generously to him. Who had given him the gift of being her first lover. Who was sweet and gentle.

In return, he'd fucked her like a prisoner on furlough fucks a whore.

She deserved something romantic, something gentle. Soft words. Delicate ones.

But when he opened his mouth, his voice was hoarse and the words raw. The truth came tumbling out, uncontrollable and as real as his heartbeat, tripping wildly in his chest. "I love fucking you without a rubber."

Her face was buried on his shoulder. To his surprise, instead of becoming angry at his crudeness, he could feel her lips curving in a smile against the skin of his neck.

She sighed and nodded, dark gleaming hair rippling over his shoulders.

"I could tell," she whispered.

Chapter Eight

෪

Bud was in heaven.

Or at least that's what it sounded like. An angelic voice singing something about green fields and lost souls. There was even a Goddamned harp.

It was beautiful soothing music, just what he needed for his inflamed nerves.

With great reluctance, he'd finally released his death grip on Claire and lifted her off him. Even after coming twice he'd still been hard, cock red and inflamed, but he knew he had to call it quits for the moment. She would be too sore to continue and he…he needed to get his feet under him, get his bearings, get a grip.

So he'd carried her into the main bathroom and left her there with a kiss, washed up in the service bathroom off the kitchen and gone straight to the store room to start measuring and drilling, hammering and fitting. He loved working with his hands and right now he needed something simple and straightforward to do, something he could understand, something familiar and normal, not…not like the scary enormous…*things* roiling around in his chest he had no name for and didn't know how to handle.

Maybe Claire understood he needed a little time on his own. He'd been working for half an hour alone, and he'd calmed down some, feeling he could face her now.

He'd spent the time putting it all in perspective. Claire was an unusually beautiful woman, incredibly desirable in every way there was. What man wouldn't get a little…overexcited fucking her?

It had been sex, just sex. Okay, really really hot and intense sex, but nothing more. That was it. Nothing to get scared about, nothing he hadn't had a thousand times before. So when he heard the bathroom door open and his heart rate sped up, it was only the thought of getting more mind-blowing sex, which any red-blooded American male would want, right? Though there weren't any red-blooded American males he'd allow to come within ten feet of *her*, that's for sure.

Whoa.

Since when was he jealous or possessive? He was never jealous, ever. Oh sure, he steered clear of the married ones and the ones with fiancés, on principle, because he believed in not stirring up unnecessary trouble and anyway there were plenty of unattached ones around. But what the women he bedded did on their own time was no concern of his.

So why did the thought of another man fucking Claire feel like someone ripping his heart out of his chest with red hot pincers?

He heard sounds in the living room, and then the music from heaven started up. A voice so pure it was hardly human. An eerily beautiful voice, a voice to fill you with longing and hope and sadness all at once. A voice so haunting it was almost unreal, liquid beauty to soothe the soul.

With a fucking *harp*, no less.

Bud looked down at the hammer in his hand and snorted. He didn't recognize his own head, his own thoughts. Something was messing with his head and he knew what it was. *Who*. A gorgeous brunette.

"Hi. Sorry I took so long." The gorgeous brunette in question stuck her head in, smiling and smelling like a meadow in spring, a couple of books in her hands. "Wow." Wide deep blue eyes took in the four walls. "You've been busy. I was going to try my hand at putting the shelves up myself today, but I don't think I could have put up more than one or two. Maybe. And they wouldn't have been straight, they'd have been all over the wall. The pockmarked wall. You've almost got the whole job done and you didn't gouge any holes at all. My hero." She stood on tiptoe and kissed his cheek. "Thanks so much, Bud. I really appreciate it."

Jesus, his cheek burned. His heart was hammering. He had to clear his throat before speaking. "You're—ah— welcome." The room was suddenly too small. He felt awkward, hands too big and clumsy.

Trilling notes like crystal shimmered in the air, the harp almost indistinguishable from the voice. Some song about a shepherd losing his love to the wind. The words and the notes seemed to sink straight into his stomach and vibrate there. Which was crazy because Bud wasn't a shepherd and didn't have a love to lose to the wind. And his stomach *never* vibrated. Not even after too many beers.

Notes lingered in the air, voice and the harp together lamenting lost love in shimmering gliding clouds of music.

"Nice music." Bud found himself waiting between songs to start drilling again. It seemed somehow…wrong to make noise while the song lasted. Like pissing in church. Which was crazy, of course, it was just a recording.

"Yes." Claire smiled. "She's a dear friend of mine and of Suzanne's. Her name's Allegra. Allegra Ennis. Suzanne and Allegra are my best friends and I love them both. We try to get together as often as we can. We're like this little trio. Didn't you see the photograph on the mantelpiece? We were at a charity ball at the Parks…Parks Foundation." Claire fumbled as a book fell to the floor. She rose with it in her hand, flushed and flustered. Bud took note of that to think about later. Right now he was interested in Claire's descriptions of her friends. "I, ahm…used to work there. As a librarian."

"Yeah, I saw the photograph. Couldn't miss it. Three gorgeous chicks."

Claire laughed. "Well, it was a formal do and we were all dressed up. Suzanne and Allegra were working. Suzanne designed these amazing floral arrangements. Calla lilies inserted into green shoots of bamboo that had been trained to grow in a spiral and a long planter with baby roses in peat running down the main table at the gala dinner. And of course Allegra sang. She was brilliant. I'm the only one of the three who doesn't have any creative abilities at all. But they love me anyway."

He'd seen the photograph. Curious, Bud had studied the large wood-framed enlargement of a snapshot, thinking that outside magazines and the movies, he'd rarely seen three more beautiful women together. Three women with their arms around each other's waists, heads together, smiling. All three elegantly dressed in evening wear. In the background, he could see a huge crystal chandelier above a grand piano. Tuxedoed waiters holding trays. The snapshot showed Claire framed by a cool, luscious blonde on one side and an ethereal-looking redhead with a far-away smile on the other. Claire was the lovely dark-haired imp between them.

"Which one is Allegra? The blonde or the redhead?" Bud hardly needed to ask. He was a cop and good at reading faces. The blonde was cool and elegant and remote. Clearly the decorator. The redhead's face went with the soaring angelic voice he'd heard. So he'd answered his own question. But it was so pleasant in this little storeroom talking to Claire without hormones fogging the air. They'd fuck again soon—he could feel it building up—but right now he was content to just talk with her. 'Chat' maybe a chick'd call it.

Whatever.

There was a nice feel in the air, listening to her talk about her friends in the cozy little room, where he'd spent a satisfying and productive half hour doing something useful that didn't involve his cock.

Claire drove him wild, sexually. For some reason he still didn't understand, she'd gotten under his skin, and sex with her was about as intense as he'd ever had it. But apart from the sex, Bud was beginning to realize he *liked* Claire. Liked her innocent enthusiasm for life, her friendly nature, the good spirits bubbling under the surface when he wasn't grinding almost violently in her...

His cock stirred and he reined his hormones in. No. Now wasn't the time. He wanted to hear what she had to say. He wanted to know more about her. Hearing her talk about her friends was very revealing. For the first time in his life, he found he'd rather talk to a woman than fuck her. For now, anyway. He was definitely taking a rain check on the sex.

Amazing.

Actually, not so amazing when you considered what Claire had to offer besides a fabulous face and sexy body. Besides long legs and a soft mouth. She was good-natured and cheerful and probably better educated than him. Certainly more well-read, judging by the walls of books in the living room. Though that was probably professional, since she was a librarian.

Luckily, he wasn't intimidated. All the books in the world can't give you street smarts. Only the street can do that. Bud had street smarts in spades.

"The redhead is Allegra," Claire answered his question. "The blonde is Suzanne. Allegra's Irish. Her father was a famous musicologist from Dublin who emigrated here to teach at Reed when she was seven and she speaks with this charming slight Irish lilt. Has the second sight, or so she says." Claire bit her lip. "It deserted her at the wrong time, though. She didn't see it coming."

Bud frowned. "See what coming?"

"Tragedy. Nobody saw it coming, really. We were all so happy for Allegra. She was doing so well. Her career was really taking off—she was booked two years in advance for tours. Her three CDs were selling steadily. You're listening to one now. "Seasons". It's my favorite."

He could hear why it would be her favorite. The soaring notes rose in the air, hung there in crystalline perfection, fragile, delicate, eerily beautiful. Like music piped in from another world. Or heaven. "Was? You're talking in the past tense. What happened? She stop singing?"

"Yes." Claire's eyes were suddenly shiny, face tense. "I guess you could say she's stopped singing. Was forced to. When she was just starting out, she landed one of the best managers in the business. She was so excited. He was a really big name in the music world—a famous producer who'd produced a string of hits in the 80s. He was retired but said he'd come out of retirement for her. Allegra didn't find out until later—much too late—that he was a has-been and had lost all his contacts because of alcoholism and outbursts of rage. He was known for his wild temper tantrums. He trashed one hotel room too many, got drunk once too often, insulted one corporate bigwig too many. Allegra had no idea when she signed up with him. She was on the verge of becoming very famous when he started wrecking her career. And then she had...an accident."

"Accident?" Bud measured and lifted. "She okay now?"

Claire bit her lip, pain in her eyes. "No, actually, she's not. And it wasn't really an accident. She was assaulted. Beaten so badly it damaged the optic nerve. It...it left her blind."

Bud stilled. He put the hammer down slowly and turned to Claire. Something on his face made her eyes widen.

"Bud?"

"Who assaulted her? Did they find the guy?" His voice was tight.

"Find the...?" Claire swallowed. "Oh, the man who did it. Yes. Her manager. He beat her up. I still can't fathom how anyone could hurt Allegra. Allegra is—I don't know how to describe her. She's such a wonderful person, warm and funny. Well, she *was* warm and funny. Now she's scared and...and lost. She's so unworldly. A real artist. She needed someone tough on her side to manage her career and she thought she'd found him. He was pushing her to go to bed with him but she didn't want that. And then he—he started…changing."

"I just bet he did," Bud said grimly, focused in on what she was saying. He didn't know anything about being a librarian or a musician but he sure as hell knew all about this. Men changing and becoming violent were his business. He'd seen it happen over and over and over again. The woman can't be controlled any more and the man loses it. Bud knew only too well how the story was going to end but he wanted to hear it anyway. "Go on," he prodded.

"Well, she said he became demanding, impossible to please. Nothing she did was good enough. He had temper tantrums and nothing she did could calm him down, you know?"

Bud nodded. He knew.

"He wanted her to go in impossible directions, musically. I mean—can you imagine someone with a voice like hers, singing rap? That's what he wanted. Then hip hop and salsa. He tried them all. He wanted her to do commercial stuff that just didn't suit her. She tried. She tried really hard but it never worked. And the more it didn't work and the harder she tried, the angrier he got. And the CDs weren't selling well any more and there were a few cancelled concerts because ticket sales were low. And he got madder and madder."

Oh yeah. Bud knew that trip. Knew how a weak son of a bitch could lash out against those around him, refusing to take the blame for his own failures.

"She talked things over with us—with Suzanne and me. I'm not much of a businesswoman but Suzanne sure is. Suzanne's a lot tougher than she looks and she told Allegra to cut loose from her manager. He was dragging her down. So Allegra decided to break the contract. There was a clause that allowed her to do that." Claire smiled faintly and shook her head admiringly. "Suzanne had made sure that clause was there. Anyway, Allegra took her father along when she went to tell her manager that she was rescinding the contract."

Claire stopped. Bud waited, then shook her shoulder gently. "And?"

Claire took in a deep, shaky breath. "And...and I don't know. Allegra doesn't talk about what happened. She can't remember. But at midnight that night, Suzanne and I got phone calls from the hospital. They'd found our names in Allegra's purse. A nurse called us."

Oh God. Bud closed his eyes, remembering the times his mom had been put in the hospital by his step-dad's fists. He knew the tone the nurse would have – brisk, no-nonsense, with sympathy and pity underneath the brusqueness.

"Allegra's father was dead. Hit his head on a glass table, or so her manager said. Allegra doesn't remember anything about it. All she knows is she woke up a week later with her jaw wired shut, a massive cerebral hematoma and she was blind."

Bud's jaws clenched. Oldest story in the world, but it got to him every time. "What's the fu – what's the guy's name?"

Again, Claire looked at him curiously, but she answered his question. "Corey. Corey Sanderson. As I said, he was a big name in the 80s. I think that might have helped. His defense attorney negotiated a deal. Said the death of Allegra's father was an accident and that her client had temper control issues. Allegra couldn't remember a thing and she couldn't testify anyway. She was in the hospital and couldn't talk with her jaw wired. She's barely back on her feet now. She was still in the hospital when the trial was held."

"What did he get?"

"You mean the sentence?"

Bud nodded, throat thick. Yeah, the sentence. His stepfather barely did time for murdering his mother.

"Seven years, I think. For manslaughter, assault and battery. Plus he has to undergo compulsory psychiatric treatment. He's in a psychiatric clinic now."

Corey Sanderson. Bud took note of the fucker's name. He was going to track the case down, study the evidence. Sounded like shoddy police work to him. Sounded like a man got away with murder. Bud was damned well going to investigate the file, though his gut told him what had gone down. This Sanderson sonovabitch had lawyered up fast and well. He'd had the bucks to hire the best mouthpiece, the Ennis woman had been too sick to testify to murder and the shithead had gotten off way too light. Manslaughter and grievous assault should be good for at least 15 to 20 in a federal prison, not 7 in some cushy clinic. Not to mention the fact that it should have been homicide, if not murder one. It might even have been premeditated. His meal ticket was rebelling and had a father. Get rid of the dad and teach her a lesson. But double jeopardy meant the asshole who'd killed a man—and beaten and blinded a woman while he was at it—would never stand trial for murder again.

Bud thought of the photograph he'd seen. Allegra Ennis was a slight woman, delicately built, with a lovely heart-shaped face. The idea of a man taking his fists to her…his own fists closed and he forced himself to open them again.

This was why—this was *exactly* why—he'd joined the navy and why he'd later become a cop. To protect the weak. He was too late to protect his mom, but by *God* he'd had the pleasure of putting away his share of scumbags. Particularly tough guys who liked to take it out on women and kids.

Claire was scanning his face anxiously. He knew he was giving off almost palpable waves of frustration and hot anger and she couldn't know it wasn't directed at her. Didn't know him well enough. For all she knew, *he* was a violent man, capable of beating a woman.

She was alone with him and he could snap her neck like snapping a green bean. He'd always been a good street fighter and the navy had taken that and refined it. Had taught him how to be a killing machine. He'd taken to military training like a duck to water and he was equally good with a rock, his fists, a knife or a gun. As a cop, he'd learned other tricks. He'd breezed through the Police Academy, excelling at everything except Law Enforcement Theory. Oh, yeah. There were all sorts of ways he could hurt her and she wouldn't stand a chance.

They'd fucked, sure, but that didn't stop a man from attacking a woman. On the contrary, sex just heated things up, if that's the direction they were headed in. For all Claire knew, the first time they disagreed he could turn on her, beat her up. Kill her, even.

Bud had killed before—in the line of duty, of course. Two enemy soldiers while he was in the navy, during the first Gulf War. And, as a cop, he'd taken down a scum-sucking motherfucker who'd kidnapped a sick little girl from the hospital. The Parks heiress. Bud had gotten a bullet through the chest and a commendation for that one.

None of that meant anything as far as Claire was concerned. She had absolutely nothing to fear from him. He'd tear out his own throat before hurting Claire or any woman, but how could she know that?

Now was the time. The time to tell her he was a cop. That he had a vested interest in the story of Allegra's beating and the murder of her father. He wasn't mad at her; he was mad at the system. She could trust him, absolutely. He couldn't raise a hand to her or to any other woman, unless it was in the line of duty, and to protect someone weaker.

He opened his mouth to tell her all of that, tell her who he was, and was surprised at what came out. "Why are you holding those books?"

Claire relaxed, moving her shoulders gently in time with the music floating into the room, a Celtic dance tune. "These?" The smile was back as she held the books up.

Why the *hell* hadn't he told her? It was right there, a big gaping hole in the conversation, waiting for him to fill it. They were spending an intense weekend together, had already had screaming hot sex and he was looking forward to more of the same before tomorrow morning, when he'd go back to the cop shop and she'd go back to...wherever it was she worked. It was a perfect time to share confidences. Talk about each other's lives.

He knew why he wasn't talking. This was a weekend stolen out of time. He didn't want anything disturbing it. Didn't want the petty details of life to interfere.

"Yeah, those."

Claire hefted the two books, big ones, a hardback and a paperback, with dull dust jackets. They looked a thousand years old. "Well, I thought since you were doing something manly and competent in here, I could do something womanly in return. And no..." she evaded him deftly, slapping at the hands reaching for her. "I didn't mean that. I'm going to read you some poetry while you work."

Poetry? She was going to read him poetry? Dear sweet God.

Bud plastered a smile on his face. "Oh. Um, poetry. That's...ah...nice, honey."

Claire threw her head back and laughed. "Oh, Bud. You should see the expression on your face." She hitched herself up on the top of the washing machine, then sat cross-legged, and smiled secretively. She looked like a wickedly beautiful elf as she opened the first book. *Very thick* book, Bud noted uneasily. Very thick, dark, dull, dusty tome. "You'll like this." She turned pages furiously, looking for something, a small frown between dark eyebrows. "Go ahead and continue," she said without looking up. "Consider me background noise, like Allegra."

The brackets needed tightening so, with a sigh, Bud picked up a Philips screwdriver from his toolbox. Good thing he always traveled with a spare toolbox in the trunk of his car. Suzanne might have fitted Claire out with everything she needed, but tools sure didn't figure into it. Claire had a cute little brass hammer that might be useful for tapping knees to figure out if someone was dead or not, but not much good for anything else. A little graduated set of screwdrivers with pretty colored handles that would snap at the first heavy-duty use. And that was it.

""Don Juan"," Claire announced. She had a slender finger pointing at the page but she was watching him. "Byron."

"Great." Bud tried to drum up some enthusiasm in his voice. "Grecian urns."

"No," Claire said serenely. "That's Keats. Byron is sex and sin, you'll like him. Now hush and listen. Poetry is good for you. I'll skip the prologue where Byron insults the most important and stuffy poets of his time and go right to where as a sixteen-year-old, Don Juan seduces his father's best friend's wife."

Claire started reading and despite his prejudice against Literature with a capital L, Bud listened. She interrupted every once in a while to explain a few references. She read well, with passion and drama, and Bud was interested despite himself. Oh yeah, that Don Juan was a real...Don Juan. A mean and smart motherfucker with an eye for the ladies. Bud lost track of the number of women the man bedded.

Claire's voice rose and fell with the emotions of the poem. That light soft voice, clear as a bell, seemed to fill the room. She was a wonderful reader and soon Bud was into the rhythm of the thing. She read through several *cantos* while he worked, almost unconsciously to the rhythm of the cadences of the poem. Bud was lifting the next to the last shelf when she stopped.

The time had passed quickly, he realized with a start. He'd tightened almost all the brackets while Claire read. Damned if he didn't miss her voice, miss the story. "That was fun," he said in surprise.

With a secretive smile, Claire put away the big dusty dun-colored book and opened another. An ancient well-thumbed paperback entitled Modern Satirical Poetry. "You'll like this one even better. Just wait." She hummed softly as she leafed through the pages until she found the one she was looking for. Sighing with pleasure, she announced, "Ogden Nash."

Bud had heard the name but couldn't quite place him. It was someone he should know, which meant boring. Bud prepared to be bored and was surprised right out of his skin.

The first poem—"Candy is Dandy but Liquor is Quicker"—startled a belly-laugh out of him and made him narrowly miss hammering his own thumb. Claire read poem after poem while he snickered and tried to keep his face and the shelves straight, her voice rolling over him reading out the funniest, most skewed-thinking poetry he'd ever heard. When Claire read the last one, "Further Reflections on Parsley", the entirety of which was 'Parsley is gharsley', he gave up and threw his head back. Tools slid to the floor and he followed, tears leaking out of his eyes, holding his sides, laughing so hard his stomach hurt. He couldn't remember the last time he'd laughed so long and so hard.

Pleased, Claire kept riffling through the pages. "Another one," she said, a gleam in the deep blue eyes.

Bud held up his hand, the other holding his sore stomach. "Stop," he pleaded, out of breath. "Can't take any more."

When the laughter subsided and he was able to think straight, he looked up at Claire, perched daintily on the washing machine, looking smug and enormously pleased with herself.

She'd changed and now wore hot pink sweats. The color brought out the healthy peach undertones of her ivory skin and accentuated the deep summer-sky blue of her eyes. She was so beautiful, so desirable it took his breath away. Lightning-hot lust speared through him, almost electric in its intensity. The hairs on his forearms stood up. A clamor set up in his head, bells ringing, horns sounding, cymbals crashing.

Bud stopped laughing, just like that. Unfolded himself from the floor and stepped to the washing machine, towering over her.

"Bud?" Claire breathed, looking up at him. He didn't answer. He couldn't speak, could hardly think past the noise in his head.

"Lift your arms," he said thickly.

"Okay." Slender arms rose immediately toward the ceiling, the thick sleeves of the sweatshirt falling down from her delicate wrists. Claire was nothing if not obedient. It was one of the many things he loved about her.

Loved?

Don't even go there, he told himself. Go with the moment. And at the moment, he wanted her naked more than he wanted his next breath. She was watching him steadily, eyes as clear and blue as the sky of a late summer evening. Clear and calm, totally unafraid.

Good, he didn't want her scared of him, in any way. It was a miracle she was even speaking to him, after the almost violent fuck at breakfast. It had gotten way out of control. But now he knew he could enter her bareback, so he had no excuse to go wild, though his pulse spiked as he slowly drew the sweatshirt up, sliding it over her arms. He pulled those funny sticks out of her hair and relished the wild spill of dark shiny hair falling over his hands. He lifted a heavy lock and fingered it. The scent of her shampoo rose sharply and he stopped himself just in time from taking it to his nose and sniffing deeply at it, like a dog. He was so excited his cock hurt and he realized with hindsight that it had been hard for a while, it's just that he'd been laughing so much he hadn't really noticed.

He threw her pink top over his shoulder, wrapped an arm around her to lift her and to pull the sweatpants off, too, stroking down the long length of her legs and then—oh yes!— there she was. Naked. Ready, too, if the look in her eyes was anything to go by.

111

Only one way to find out. He touched her, fingers carefully rimming the smooth little cunt, sliding through the folds. She was wet. Not as wet as he'd like, but wet enough. With an inward sigh, Bud realized that there wasn't going to be much foreplay this time, either.

Maybe next time.

Bud whipped off his own top and looked down. She had to be cold sitting there, naked, on top of the washing machine. He didn't want her to be cold, didn't want her to be uncomfortable in any way. He lifted her up with one arm and placed his sweat top under her and stepped between her legs. Claire opened her legs to accommodate him and then, to his surprise, placed her hands over his groin. She was looking down to where he was lodged between her thighs, so close his cloth-covered hard-on brushed her sex.

"May I?'" she breathed, reaching out to touch his cock through the material.

She took the strangled noise in his throat for a yes and touched him with a forefinger, running up and down his hard-on. She was totally concentrated on what she was doing, a faint smile on her lips as she saw and felt what she was doing to him. If he got any harder he could have used his cock to hammer in the nails. His hips were surging forward in time with her hand. She lifted it away and he nearly shouted—*Hey! You come right back here!*

But she was only inserting her hands into the waistband of his sweats to tug them down. In a second there he was— hard as stone and raring to go. Cock pointed straight at where it wanted to go. She tugged slightly harder and his sweats fell to his ankles. He was barefoot. Another second and he'd stepped out of the sweats and shunted them to one side with his foot. There was a whole lot to be said in favor of sweats with no underwear. They'd gotten naked in less than five seconds.

Claire's legs were so open he could easily see the internal folds of her sweet little cunt. Dark pink and glistening. Bud's breathing speeded up and he was that close to losing it. Again.

With an amount of self-control that should have won him a Nobel Prize, he fit himself to her and stopped. Some kind of self-restraint was necessary here. This time it had to be a proper fuck, not just jerking off inside her in an insane frenzy.

Shoving it in and doing her hard wasn't going to cut it. Not this time. Claire needed to know that sex was about more than what she'd had up to now. There had to be something he could do to slow it down, make it lovemaking and not fucking. Find some rhythm, some method of controlling his movements. Like what?

Bud gritted his back teeth. He wanted to ram into her so hard he had to grind his molars in an effort to keep still.

He pressed his cock to her, felt himself slip in, felt himself slip out of control…breathing hard, he pulled back. He had to do this right.

Well, she'd quoted poetry at him and managed to turn him on and keep him working to the beat. Maybe that could work.

He dragged his gaze up from where his cock was barely in her to meet her eyes. What little blood was left in his head allowed his brain to marvel at the expression on her face. Soft, slightly flushed. Even in the midst of passion, a slight smile curved her lips. The smile he'd yet to see completely wiped off her face. He would kill himself before he saw that smile disappear. He met her gaze, nearly hypnotized by the vivid blue of her eyes, clear and deep.

He pushed forward a little and the head of his cock slid all the way in. He pushed in a little further.

Jesus!

Further.

Bud took a deep breath and started talking, while he still could. He pulled back a little, savoring the feel of her.

"I was a hellion in high school. Basically a juvenile delinquent." Barely in her, he experimentally rotated his cock, stretching her a little, tormenting himself. A vein was beating in her throat and he bent to lick and nip along it, rewarded by a wet little pull from her cunt. *Yes!* "Except for drugs, there wasn't anything I didn't do, including gluing all the sophomore lockers shut and dumping a can of green paint over the statue on the front lawn of the school. Some governor." Claire's smile widened slightly. He could see her heartbeat over her left breast and resisted the urge to bite her there, too. He didn't do it because he knew it would be hard to stop. "I drank a six pack every night, smoked a pack a day, cut school and drag raced. Earned my living cheating at poker, messing with the rich kids' heads. It was a miracle I escaped juvie hall. The one good thing I had was this English teacher, Mr. Roth. Tough as nails. Tougher than me." Bud slid a little further in, rotating his hips instead of thrusting. Claire was so wet, they were making little sucking sounds.

Claire gazed up at him. "That's...*oh!*" He'd started a little rocking motion which she liked, judging by the slitted eyes and open, wet mouth. "That's...interesting," she gasped, eyes unfocused.

He laughed.

"Really," she protested. But her eyes were half closed and her head tilted, as if it took too much energy to keep her head straight on her neck.

"It gets better." Bud smiled down at her, loving everything about this. The sight of her flushed face, the feel of the slim muscles of her back against the palms of his hands, the creamy softness where he penetrated her. "Mr. Roth made me memorize things. Long lists of things. Boring things. The more tedious the better. American Presidents, Kings and Queens of England, state capitals, poetry. Didn't matter what. If it was boring and hard to do, that's what he went for." The lists and poems were still embedded in his head, written on the neurons of his brain and would be until the day he died.

"He said he'd report me to the police himself if I didn't memorize his lists and he meant it. So I spent a whole summer mumbling and memorizing and hating him. Kept me out of trouble for an entire three months."

Slowly, Bud slid all the way into her and leaned forward until his forehead rested against hers, exhaling shakily. She was clasped so tightly around him. Every sense he had shrieked pleasure. Soft skin under his hands, waves of fragrant hair over his arms and shoulders, long slender thighs gripping his hips, high round breasts flattened against his chest so tightly he could feel the hard little nipples.

She was definitely aroused, thank God. He could feel her breath against his face, breathing fast, thickly lashed lids half-hiding eyes brilliant as stars. He rotated his cock again, experimentally. She was very wet. It was okay.

"I still remember some poems," he whispered. He'd called them 'pomes' way back then.

"Do you?" she whispered back. "Let me hear them."

"Okay," he croaked.

Bud's cock was hitting the back of her pussy. She was creamy but so tight he was afraid of hurting her. Talking gave him a shaky hold on control. Here goes, he thought.

"Once-up-on – " In and out and in.

"-a mid- night-drea-ry," Four thrusts, tunneling in time with the meter.

"While-I-pon-dered-weak-and-wea-ry." The rhythm of the words gave him a handle on things, kept his movements regular and smooth.

"O-ver-ma-ny-a-quaint-and-cu-ri-ous-vo-lume-of-for-got-ten-lore." Oh yeah, it was going better, a stroke a word.

Claire's eyelids lifted and her smile grew. He gazed straight into her eyes, the words pulled out from a twenty-year-old lobe in his brain. Hips keeping time with the meter of the poem, gaze locked with hers, he went straight through

Poe's "The Raven". He was thrusting a little faster by the time he got to *'dark-ness there and no-thing more.'*

Bud shifted his hands, pulling her closer, fitting her more tightly to him and stopped, deep inside her.

"That was a good one," Claire sighed. "A fabulous one to—" she stopped and bit her lip.

"To…?"

"To…ahm…you know."

"To fuck to?" Bud asked, voice harsh.

"Mm-hmm."

"Say it." He prodded with his cock, grinding, lifting her a little with the force of it.

"Say…it?"

"Yeah."

He held himself still inside her, watching her eyes. She was close to coming, he could feel it. Shaking thighs, strained breathing. Pupils so large there was only a narrow deep blue nimbus around them. Her arms were wound around his neck, face so close to his their noses touched, so close he could see every detail of arousal on her face. She was flushed down to her breasts, breathing quickly in soft little inhalations of need.

"Say it. Go on. Lightning won't come down from the sky to strike you dead. Say it was a good poem to fuck to."

Claire opened her mouth then closed it. "I—I…can't."

"Sure you can. It's English, as Anglo-Saxon as it comes." He pulled back and pushed in, hard, one fast strong stroke and she jolted. She was trembling all over. He nudged upwards with his cock. Most women had a little spot, right there…"Say it. *Say it!*"

"Bud, I can't."

"Sure you can." Pressing harder.

Bud had no idea why he was pushing her so hard. Maybe because he needed to feel that she was as out of her depth as

116

he was. Saying fuck was probably as far from normal as it got for little Marian the Librarian. Well, good. He was way outside his comfort zone, himself.

Bud reached down to stroke her clitoris, watching her heartbeat over her left breast. The tissues were stretched around him, but she was wet. He rubbed and watched her flush more deeply. "Go on."

"I, ah—"

He grabbed her ass more tightly and leaned forward. He was as deep as it was possible to go. "Say it," he growled.

"A...a good poem," Claire gasped, "to fu—to fu—to fuck to. Oh, *God!*"

The words pushed her right over the edge. Her legs tightened around his hips, she arched against him and he could feel her coming, her strongest orgasm yet, wet little cunt pulsing sharply around him. She was shaking, arms and legs gripping him in time with the contractions. Her arms tightened around his neck, one hand clasping the back of his head. Her face was pressed to his, cheek to cheek, and she was gasping right into his ear. Jesus, he could feel the gusts. Bud had to grit his teeth not to come, holding himself stiff and still inside her while she went wild.

She calmed finally, still holding him tightly around the neck. She rested her flushed cheek on his shoulder and he kissed her ear. "I know other ones," he murmured and felt her shiver.

"Other ones? Oh...other poems." Claire closed her eyes and smiled. "I don't know if I can survive any more poetry."

"Sure you can." Bud licked her ear and she shivered again. He felt a last contraction coming from her cunt and smiled. Oh, yeah. He slid his hands under her ass and held her still as he started thrusting again, gently at first. It was easier now that she'd come. She was deliciously soft and creamy, tissues parting easily for him. So they should. It was *his* cunt. Made for him. Just for him.

"Listen to this one," Bud growled in her ear, starting to move in time to the cadence. *"The-out-look was-n't bril-liant-for-the-Mud-ville-nine-that-day,-the   score-stood-four-to-two-with-but-one-in-ning-more-to-play."*

Claire jolted, breath exhaling over his shoulder. ""Casey at the Bat"? You're going to...fuck me to "Casey at the Bat"?" Her stomach muscles contracted against him as she threw back her head and laughed in delight.

"Hush." Bud held her tighter. He was on the edge himself—maybe next time he'd have more control, though he was beginning to doubt he'd ever have it with her. Reciting kept his mind just enough off-center to keep a grip on himself. Next time he'd have to recite "Hiawatha". All 500 lines.

"Listen." He had a good little rhythm going now, sliding in her deep and slick. By God the poem was working.

"There-was-ease-in-Ca-sey's-man-ner-as-he-stepped-in-to-his-place; there-was-pride-in-Ca-sey's bear-ing-and-a-smile-on-Ca-sey's-face —"

He pumped in her to the rhythm of Mudville's finest, pinning their hopes on Casey. By the time the umpire called 'strike two', Bud was panting and shaking. Only reciting the words from memory kept him on this side of the razor's edge, kept a little blood in his head. Claire was clinging to him, soft and flushed, soft thighs wide open. He held her more tightly, pumped harder, faster. He was reciting purely by rote, his senses dead to the outside world, all his attention concentrated on his cock, moving in and out of Claire's softness...

"And-some-where-men-are-laugh-ing-and-some-where-chil-dren-shout —" Claire bit his neck, lightly, the mare nipping her stallion. It was too much and he shouted himself, the sound muffled in her hair as he exploded into her in fierce hot jets, pumping wild and hot. The semen came directly from his liquefied spinal cord because when it was over, he had to lean his knees heavily against the washing machine and lock them. He could barely stand. He'd never been sick a day in his life but all of a sudden he had a flash of what it must be like to be

weak and ill. His muscles felt rubbery and insubstantial. He could barely stand and his grip on Claire was all that kept him from sinking to the floor. His heart hammered and he had spots in front of his eyes.

Jesus, was it possible to fuck yourself to death?

"Well." Claire sighed heavily and nestled her head between his shoulder and neck. He could hear the smile in her voice. "I guess Ernest Thayer was wrong. Mighty Casey certainly did *not* strike out."

It startled a laugh out of him, a sound so rare he almost didn't recognize the noise coming from his own throat. He hardly ever laughed. Life just wasn't that funny and he sure as hell didn't see much that could make him laugh in his job. He rarely even smiled. And here he'd laughed a couple of times already today. Genuine laughter, coming directly from deep inside himself. Amazing.

It was all amazing. This beautiful woman in his arms, the outrageously intense sex, his wild reaction.

And now this.

He thought he'd known everything there was to know about fucking. Thought he'd seen it all and done it all, every position there was, every orifice there was, every which way.

But it was definitely the first time he'd ever fucked in iambic pentameter.

Chapter Nine

೮౧

That evening, Claire stood under the hot shower for a long time, warming sore muscles. Remembering how those muscles had become sore made her smile. Bud had jumped her bones again in the afternoon, after cooking her a gourmet meal for lunch, feeding her choice bits of exquisite veal piccata from his own fork. Claire had been fed before, of course, when she had been too weak to hold a fork by herself.

But never like that. Never by a handsome hunk of walking talking sex looking at her with glittering golden eyes, telling her to open up.

And she had.

She'd opened everything up. Mouth, thighs, sex…heart.

They'd lingered over lunch and then Bud had easily and expertly operated her wicked-looking imported Italian coffee maker. Two perfect espressos boiled out, the scent of the fragrant brew filling her house. The man knew how to do everything perfectly. Drive in the snow, cook, make espresso coffee, put up shelves.

Fuck.

Bud was rubbing off on her.

Claire smiled and lifted her face into the water streaming down. Never in her life had she said the word or even thought it. Yet it was such a deliciously apt description, the perfect word for a perfect act. And anyway, it was so true. He *did* know how to fuck perfectly.

After a while, they'd moved to the living room where Bud had propped amazingly large bare feet on her Chinese carved chest that doubled as a coffee table and switched on the TV.

It was a football game, one Bud took seriously because he said he had ten bucks riding on the outcome. She'd never watched a football game before and had no idea of the rules. It was loud and colorful and shockingly violent. Vast, agitated cheering crowds in riotously garish clothes. Cute girls in abbreviated outfits waving pom-poms energetically. Enormous men with huge shoulders and relatively spindly legs running madly all over an immense field following what Bud called the 'playbook'. It was all mysterious and alien to her, like watching the rites of some remote Amazon tribe.

After one particularly large man tucked the ball under his arm and barreled through a crowd of other frighteningly large men, she'd turned to Bud, puzzled. "I thought they weren't supposed to touch the ball. And isn't the ball round?"

He'd laughed, still watching the TV. "That's soccer, honey. This is football."

"Oh. Okay." Claire had put her crossed bare feet up right next to his and sat back within the circle of the large arm he'd thrown across the back of her couch. She found the contrast of their feet far more interesting than what was on the screen past them. Even Bud's feet were perfect. Long, lean, sinewy, with a dusting of gold hairs on the toes. "Who are we rooting for?"

"Seattle Seahawks," he'd said, frowning at the screen, remote in hand. He hadn't relinquished the remote once since they'd sat down. So it was true, then. Y chromosome humans had a genetic compulsion to hold the remote control. She'd read about it but never seen it in action before. "Not that my support has helped them any."

He snorted at something happening on the screen that involved cheerful and colorful violence. Claire found herself wincing more than once. Surely that had to *hurt*?

"Clowns," Bud snorted when one large man barreled into another large man and knocked him down. "Come on, Nate, you wuss. Kick ass for once."

It was all so...so *normal*. A man and a woman. A cold winter Sunday afternoon spent in front of the TV after lunch, watching a football game.

Until today, it had never even occurred to her that all of this could be part of her life. How incredibly delicious it was, this feeling of doing something a million other women were doing, right this minute. Watching TV with their mates. Boyfriends. Significant others. Lover du jour. Whatever the term was nowadays.

Only the other women weren't watching TV with someone as handsome and desirable as Bud. Claire smugly watched Bud frowning over some play on the screen, looking sexy and disgruntled and cute, if cute was a term that could be applied to a man as big and tough-looking as he was. Something happened on-screen that involved a lot of the big men tumbling over themselves, piling twenty deep on top of some poor sucker on the bottom. Bud slapped his knee in disgust. Claire laughed out loud in delight at his expression, and he looked over at her.

And just like that, it happened again.

Bud's gaze narrowed and he thumbed the remote, never looking away from her. The TV sound dimmed while she met his intent gaze.

Her breath choked in her throat. That golden predatory look was back as he focused in on her, hands reaching for her. In seconds, they were both naked and he was thrusting heavily in her while her thighs clasped his hips. This time, Bud didn't stop until the game was over. She was lying limply beneath him, a little breathless because, though she loved the feel of him on top of her, he was incredibly heavy. She was debating which she wanted more—feeling him on top of her or breathing—when the television erupted with noise, loud even though the volume had been turned down. Half the stadium was on its feet, roaring. Klaxons blared as the players filed off the field.

Claire tried to pull in enough air to speak. Lord, the man weighed a ton. He was lying fully on her, face turned into her neck.

"Who won?" she asked breathlessly.

"Who the fuck cares?" he murmured, and kissed her neck.

Claire would never again sit on her pretty yellow sofa that Suzanne had ordered especially for her from Italy without thinking of that hour and a half spent with Bud deep inside her.

Dinner had followed, a lavish three-course meal. She'd savored every delicious bite as the sky outside her window turned gray then black. It had snowed intermittently throughout the day, just enough to keep them in a little white cocoon. Claire had deliberately kept herself from thinking about tomorrow. Monday mornings were bad for everybody, but for her it would spell the end of the most fantastic interlude of her life.

Claire stepped out of the shower, dried her hair and moisturized everywhere, lingering over bits of her Bud had shown particular attention to, then slipped on her nightgown. Her pretty, frilly pale yellow silk nightgown that she hoped would drive Bud insane.

He was already in her bed, waiting for her. Her heart beat heavily at the thought, all that sexy maleness, waiting just for her. Right now, Claire was feeling every cell in her body, every hair on her head, every beat of her heart. Every single sense she had was wide open. She was perfectly aware of the fact that she had never had a day like this in her whole life and might not ever have one like this again. And it wasn't over, by a long shot.

She hesitated outside the bedroom door. Her door was lacquered dove gray, a color she and Suzanne had chosen together. When she'd talked with Suzanne about decorating the house, she'd imagined long solitary evenings in her pretty little house, listening to music and reading. Maybe nuking a frozen pizza full of cholesterol and bad carbohydrates now and again for danger and excitement. She'd been toying with the idea of getting a cat, just to have something else living in the house.

It had never, ever occurred to her that behind her elegant dove gray door there might be a mouth-watering hunk of man waiting for her, the door prize to end all door prizes. It probably wouldn't have occurred to Suzanne, either. Suzanne hadn't been sick, but she was incredibly picky and fussy when it came to the other sex; there hadn't been too many men waiting in Suzanne's bed. Certainly no one like Bud. And Allegra—beautiful as she was—had no men in her life. Allegra was off men entirely after Corey.

So here she was, Claire Parks. Ex-virgin. Having lots of sex both for herself and her girlfriends, to keep the averages up.

Claire laid her hand flat against the door, excitement so thick in her chest it was hard to breathe. Trembling slightly, she turned the doorknob, entered. And blinked.

There were no lights on in the room, but there was no need of them. Bud had discovered every candle in the house, had lit them and had placed them on her dresser, in a perfumed shrine to sex. She had a predilection for vanilla-scented candles and the fragrance wrapped itself around her, seeped into her bones, licked along her veins, warm and golden. The flickering flames cast a glimmering bronze light over the warm scented room. Further light came from a pale yellow full moon visible through her bedroom window, reflected off the snow.

It was enough to see Bud by, enough for her mouth to water. He was sitting up against the bedstead, massively broad shoulders gleaming in the half-light. Naked, fully and completely aroused. His face was in shadow; only those golden eyes gleaming in the darkness were visible.

"Stop right there." Bud's voice was a low growl.

Obediently, Claire stopped. Her toes dug into the pile of the carpeting, curling with excitement. She recognized that tone, that gleam. It meant very thrilling things were about to happen, very soon.

"Pretty nightgown," he said roughly. "Now, take it off."

"Off? Me?" She pouted a little. She'd had plans for this nightgown, and they'd involved Bud touching her. Taking her nightgown off herself wasn't part of the fantasy. "You don't want to do it yourself?"

"No." His voice was low and deep. "Off. Now."

Funny how his vocabulary went way down when he got excited. One syllable words usually came just before he lost control.

Claire fingered the heavy silk of her gown and lifted the hem. Slowly. Just a little. Bud had spent the day driving her insane and she felt honor-bound to return the favor.

His penis lifted a little away from his stomach and lengthened.

She felt so connected to Bud she could almost feel his erection herself. She had no idea how he could still be excited after the excesses of today, but he was. Boy, was he. Her romance novels hadn't in any way prepared her for the full force of a man's desire.

So he wanted her to take off her nightgown? She'd thought he might want to do that himself. Considering the speed with which he'd stripped her several times today, he'd be good at it, too. He was very good at getting her naked. Perfect, in fact. But if he wanted a change of pace... Claire pulled the slippery silk of the nightgown up past her ankles, calves.

She could hear Bud's breathing. It was visible, too. His chest was expanding with each breath, so hard his arms opened. She could see his heartbeat in the erect penis.

She was doing this to him! Oh, God, this was so exciting.

125

Higher. She tugged the nightgown higher and watched his penis swell with every move she made. Oh, boy, she *rocked*.

"Off." Bud's voice sounded choked. "Stop fooling around. I want that damned thing off you *now*."

"Oh?" Claire bunched the soft folds, letting the ruffled hem brush her knees. She swished the material back and forth, like a little girl showing off her new party dress. "Now? Like right now?"

She wasn't quite ready to relinquish that deliciously heady sense of power over him. She'd been able to gauge how high the hem had risen by his rib cage, his penis and increasingly white knuckles.

"*Right* now." Large jaw muscles jumped. "Fast."

Okay.

Wonderful as it was tormenting Bud, being naked right now was too great a temptation.

With a sigh and an internal promise to herself to do a proper strip tease some other time, Claire pulled the gown up and off, letting it flutter and fall to the floor in a pale yellow silken heap. She was rewarded by the pure fire in Bud's eyes.

Show time.

Claire moved forward and was halted by a large hand held up, broad callused palm out. "Stop," he said, his voice hoarse.

Stop?

"Don't come any closer."

Claire stopped a foot away from the bed, puzzled. "Why not?"

Bud looked like a pagan God on her bed, sleek skin a burnished gold. The light from the candles showed off the heavy sculpted shape of his muscles, the hard valleys and ridges in deep relief. Even his penis seemed somehow otherworldly, so large and rock-hard, casting a cylindrical shadow across his washboard stomach.

"This is how it is," he said harshly. "A second after I touch you, I'm going to be inside you and I won't stop for foreplay. I promised myself you'd get some foreplay tonight. But then you walked in and…" He let out his breath in a heavy gust. "No. Not going to happen, not now. So you'll just have to do it yourself."

He wasn't making sense. "Do what myself?"

"Foreplay." Bud fisted his hands in the sheets, as if to anchor himself. "You're going to have to do it all yourself, honey. Get yourself wet and excited because I'm too far gone to do it for you. So help me out, here. Lick your index finger."

Still puzzled, Claire did what he said. She licked her finger, rewarded by his eyes narrowing. He was so intensely focused on her, she was sure a grenade could have gone off in the room and he wouldn't have noticed. She held her wet index finger up. It glistened in the candlelight and he nodded.

"Now touch your nipple."

Ah. A new game.

Claire's lips curved in a smile. She ran her index finger down her neck then slowly around the outer curve of her breast, watching Bud's eyes circle in his head as he followed her finger…

Mmm.

The circles became smaller, then she was rimming her aureole and, finally, brushing her nipple. It pulsed at her touch, turning small and hard. Touching herself with her wet fingertip wasn't anything like as exciting as when Bud did it or when—God!—he took her breast in his mouth and sucked hard. Just the memory of it made her nipple super sensitive as she brushed her fingertip over it. Bud cupped her breast when he suckled her, as if offering her breast to himself as an exquisite treat. He sometimes bit her lightly, just enough excite her, not enough to hurt.

The memory aroused her. Her breath speeded up and Bud's eyes narrowed. He was watching her so intently she knew he could see every step of her arousal. Was he feeling as connected to her as she was to him? Were his nipples hardening, too? They were hidden in the thick mat of dark blond hair on his chest so she couldn't tell.

Excitement, arousal, passion. Such mysterious workings of the human body. Like illness, they could be hidden from view, yet work their powerful magic like a rushing underground stream.

Claire licked her finger again and touched her other nipple. It would have been nice to do that slow circling thing with her finger again, watching Bud's eyes roll in his head like a pony's, but she was getting into it and her nipple was already hard. Touching herself was starting to be frustrating, not exciting. She needed more stimulation, like when Bud bit her. She pinched her nipple, then let go immediately, surprised. It hurt. It hit her, all of a sudden, how very careful Bud had been with her, though he'd often been so excited he could barely speak. Powerful as Bud was, he hadn't hurt her, not once, not even inadvertently.

Both nipples were hard now, and wet from her finger.

"Lower," he whispered.

She *was* going to have to do it all by herself.

"Okay," she whispered back. She brought her finger slowly up to her mouth, Bud's hot eyes following every move. She licked her finger, slowly, wetting it thoroughly, then outlined her lips with her finger. Slowly, smiling a little as a groan escaped from deep in Bud's chest. Then she licked her lips. Slowly. Remembering how he'd licked her lips on the couch while making love to her.

She flashed on the sensory memory, hot liquid moving through her veins as she remembered—could almost *feel*—him moving in her, hot and hard, thrusting so fast at the end it was a miracle she hadn't caught fire there from the friction. She'd climaxed twice. Both times, he'd continued the hard thrusts, doing something with his hands and his penis so that the climax had continued for long minutes.

What a complete surprise. She'd masturbated a couple of times and the few orgasms she'd managed to give herself had been hard, tight little ones, over in literally a second. Bud had kept her going forever, rubbing up against some secret spot only he knew about. The second time she'd cried with the intensity.

"What are you thinking about?" He was watching her so closely, he must have been able to tell she was exciting herself with her thoughts as well as her hand.

"I was thinking about us on the couch, during the football game." She was feeling so sexy even her *voice* changed. It was low and husky, liquid sex. Who knew her voice could do that? "When you were in me, and fu—fucked me all through my orgasms."

"Jesus." Bud's eyes closed tightly for a second, then he opened them again to glare at her. Hot golden indignation. "I'm working really hard here to keep a grip. What are you trying to do to me?"

Drive him crazy, that's what she was trying to do to him.

She took a step forward. Lips, check. Nipples, check. Hmm. That left one biggie of an erogenous zone.

Smiling, Claire placed her finger between her breasts and drew a line straight down her middle. She circled her belly button, slowly, enjoying Bud's rapt gaze. Down again, until she reached her pubic hair. She widened her stance and cupped herself.

"Are you wet?" Bud rasped. The veins were standing out in his neck and arms. His knuckles were as white as the sheets.

Claire touched herself with her middle finger. She was a little slippery. "Some," she replied. "Not as wet as when *you* touch me." She slid her middle finger all the way in.

There. Take that. He wanted her to take care of her own foreplay, but she couldn't do as good a job at it as he could. He was perfect in that, too.

Bud closed his eyes in pain, then opened them to glare at her. "Come on, let's speed things up, here. Get wet *fast*."

Claire widened her stance. She was able to insert two fingers now. She slid them around inside herself, starting to get a little worked up. Her fingers couldn't work magic like Bud's, though she was starting to get a little buzz. She slid her fingers in and out, touching the clitoris briefly, then sliding back in again.

"You ready yet?" Bud asked harshly.

Claire felt so languid. It was really nice touching herself while he watched with golden fire in his eyes. It took a second for his question to penetrate. "Ready for what?" she murmured, breath suspended. Maybe she'd found that spot. The one Bud found unerringly, without fail. Her fingers brushed a point and the hairs on the nape of her neck rose.

"Ready for *this*."

Bud's big hands reached out and he lifted her effortlessly over him. In a second, she was laying flat on her back and he was kneeing her legs apart as he mounted her. Another second, and Bud was sliding into her, hot and hard and deep.

He stopped deep inside her, holding himself still. He was holding his torso up on his forearms and he was trembling. His head hung low as he breathed heavily. It was as if he were afraid to move.

He finally opened his eyes, gaze as yellow and fierce as an eagle's. "Are you comfortable?"

"Comfortable?" Claire wriggled a little. He didn't have his entire weight on her, so she was able to breathe. "Yes. Pretty much. Why?"

"No wrinkles in the sheet under your back? Your hair's not pulling you?" When he'd lifted her over him, he'd swept her hair up before laying her on her back, so that it rippled in waves around her head.

"I'm comfortable," Claire assured him. She smiled up at him. He wasn't smiling back. His face was set, almost grim. The skin over his cheekbones was flushed and pulled tight. His jaw muscles worked as he stared at her out of slitted eyes. It looked like anger but it wasn't. With any other man, Claire would have been a little afraid, his expression was so fierce and dangerous-looking. She wasn't frightened. This was *Bud*. He would never hurt her. "Why are you asking?"

Bud shifted his hips, pushing forward, moving even more deeply into her. "I want you to be comfortable," he whispered, "because this is the position you're going to be in for a long, long while." His gaze held hers. "I'm going to fuck you all night."

Chapter Ten
December 14th

ත

The next morning, Claire stretched and winced. She was sore all over, particularly between her legs. Sticky, too.

At some point during the endless, heated night, Bud had stretched her legs wide apart and back in on themselves, holding them open with his hands on her knees as he pounded into her. She'd been completely open to him and he had used that fact mercilessly. She'd lost count of the number of orgasms she had. Twice during the night she tried to call a halt. "I can't take any more," she gasped. His answer was to growl, "Sure you can," and thrust even harder.

He'd been right. She'd ended up clinging to him, shaking and pleading for more.

It had been fierce and wild and, at times, almost scary. He pushed her way beyond anything she recognized as herself. She'd gone up in fire and smoke to be reborn a new woman. This sexy wild woman who took risks, who pushed the envelope. Who dared, and won.

Claire Parks, Wonder Woman.

When she woke up she was instantly aware of herself, of her body, of his. She was completely in the moment, completely in her body. Her sore, well used body. Her happy body. No mind tricks pretending she was somewhere else. She didn't have to. She was right here in bed with Bud. Warm, and not alone.

She was sleeping with her head on Bud's chest, the hairs tickling her nose. Though she'd only slept a few hours she was completely and totally rested. Revved, even.

And completely, totally happy.

The future was a bright and shiny path ahead of her. Her new job during the day, Bud at night. Weekends together.

Her father would be a problem, that was true. Bud wasn't like anyone her father would have dreamed of for her, but he was what *she* dreamed of. Or would have, if she had known men like Bud existed. Bud was her mate, made just for her. Her father would just have to recognize that fact. Daddy would come around. And if not—fuck him.

It took a second for Claire to recognize her own thoughts. She was immediately ashamed of herself. Her father loved her. If he was suffocatingly protective of her, it was because he'd lived so long with her illness, had been so scared for her and thought of her as an eternally needy and sick child. Her father would have trouble imagining her with any lover, let alone a tattooed lumberjack lover. Maybe he would have preferred someone who worked at the Parks Foundation, cultivated, terminally boring but properly respectful, though there were precious few men there who'd want a woman.

Accepting Bud as her lover would be hard for her father at first. Still, though he was a Parks, the fourth-generation heir to a family fortune, he was no snob. He never stopped talking about the police officer who'd rescued her from Rory Gavett. He recognized quality in people, notwithstanding their origins. Eventually he'd grow to love Bud as much as she did.

Love?

Oh, yes. Claire loved Bud. There was no doubt in her mind, in her heart. From the outside it might look as if she were a child. Younger than her years, certainly. And she'd been a virgin, with no experience of men and sex. That didn't mean she didn't know her own heart. Couldn't recognize the strong, manly virtues of Bud.

She lifted her face to smile at him, expecting a warm greeting and a hot kiss. Instead she met cool, sober eyes. He was lying with both arms behind his head, fully awake, serious, watching her carefully. She blinked at the expression on his face. Not warm, not sexy, not welcoming.

"Claire," he said, his voice somber, "we have to talk."

Oh, God.

Claire's heart took a violent swoop in her chest, landing with a thud. Bud had the expression—the *very same* expression—her oncologist had had when he'd told her the bone marrow transplant hadn't taken. That there was nothing more they could do for her. That she had only a few more months to live. That she was doomed.

OhGodohGod. Why hadn't she realized? It was only a one-night stand. Two night stand. She'd let her heart, her feelings get away from her. There probably had been signs this was only a weekend affair—a hot fuck, why not call it by its real name?—but she hadn't had the experience to read them. She'd thought this was so much more…and it *was* so much more.

For her. Clearly not for him.

What was she to do?

Claire switched immediately into Gratitude Mode, the only way she'd survived all these years. Whenever horrible things were happening to her, she always scrambled to find something to be grateful for. Had to. Any other mindset would have dragged her down and under.

There was a lot to be grateful for. She owed Bud the best possible introduction to sex a woman could hope for. She'd probably packed more good sex into the past two days than Suzanne and Allegra together had had in the past two years. It had been fabulous and she was grateful. If the thought of saying goodbye to Bud was so painful she was suffocating, well…she'd been in pain before. And survived.

She ruthlessly repressed the tears. Tears were for later, when she was alone. She always shed her tears alone. She knew how to do this.

"Okay," she said calmly. Her face was smooth, bland. Bud couldn't see her racing heart and sick, churning stomach. She could play this game. She always had. "Let's talk."

He watched her eyes for a moment then nodded, as if coming to some secret conclusion.

"I love you, Claire," he said quietly.

Her jaw dropped.

Noises rang in her head, the muffled clangings of shock. It took her a second to realize that the far off noise wasn't jangled neurons in her brain, but the front doorbell ringing incessantly, interspersed with a fist pounding on the front door. She turned her head toward the living room, frowning. "Who could that be?" she mused. "Nobody knows I live here…"

She turned back and watched Bud disappear completely from sight. Her sexy teasing lover with the hot golden eyes had vanished into thin air, and another man had taken his place—a being as cold and inhuman as a cyborg. A frightening, feral stranger with a blank expression and flat yellow eyes. Warriors on a battlefield would look like that.

He pushed down on her shoulder with one big hand. "Stay here," he whispered. "Don't move."

In one swift, silent movement, he rolled out of bed and pulled on his sweat pants. He reached into the carryall with his toiletry items and spare clothes and, to her shock, his hand came away with a gun. A big black gun that he carried as if it were an extension of his hand. He did something to the side of the gun. It snicked and she realized from reading a million thrillers he'd turned the safety off.

This man—this immensely large and powerful man with the frighteningly cold and dangerous eyes—was now armed and moving swiftly toward the front door.

She stared after him, open-mouthed, frozen with shock. She could see him at the door, standing to one side, gun held up beside his ear. The bell rang again, a fist pounded and she heard a faint, tremulous voice calling. "Claire! Claire, open up! I know you're in there!"

Dear sweet God, her father! He'd come back from Paris early.

Claire scrambled out of bed, pulling on her nightgown. She ran into the living room, screaming. "Bud! Bud, don't shoot! It's my…!"

She was too late. He'd peeked through the peephole, dropping his gun hand so it was aligned with his leg. He pulled the door open and her father half-fell in. Bud steadied him with his free hand.

"Mr. Parks!" Bud growled, astonished.

"Lieutenant Morrison!" her father gasped.

"Daddy!" Claire cried.

Bud turned to her, frowning. "*Daddy?*"

She stared back at him. "*Lieutenant?*"

Chapter Eleven
December 14th
Parks Mansion

❧

So she really *was* a Princess, after all, Bud thought glumly that evening, over dinner in the Parks mansion.

Oh, not a real Princess, with a crown and a country, but close enough. The Parks family was the next best thing to royalty. At least in Oregon. There was a Parks Foundation, a Parks Museum of Modern Art, an Elisa Parks Memorial Wing of Pediatric Medicine at the St. Jude hospital and a Parks Medieval Music Festival in the summer.

Parks money kept the PPDHQ computer system state of the art — because after Bud had rescued Claire, Old Man Parks had made it clear to the Parks Foundation that what the police wanted, they got. It was a standing joke on the 13th floor that Bud was the Golden Boy who could goose the Parks Foundation to lay a lot of golden eggs.

So that heartbreaking, terrified bald little bag of bones he'd picked up from the filthy floor of Rory Gavett's van was *his* Claire? No wonder he hadn't recognized her at The Warehouse.

Though she'd been — what? fifteen? — at the time, she must have weighed less than 70 pounds, had lost all her hair, and had been blindfolded, gagged and bound. He remembered clearly cutting through the duct tape around her mouth, wrists and ankles and lifting her out. It had been hard for him to move because the pain of the bullet he'd taken was starting to push through the shock and he was losing a lot of blood. But the little girl — he'd have put her at seven or eight, not fifteen—weighed next to nothing and he'd carried her easily.

He remembered big blue eyes, wide with shock, and her trembling so fearsomely he'd been afraid she'd break her fragile bones. No, there was no way he could have recognized the slender-yet-sexy woman Claire had become.

No wonder she hadn't recognized him, either. The last time she'd seen him she'd been clinging terrified to his shoulders, face buried in his neck. He'd been in uniform then, a young patrolman who'd happened to catch the APB for a blue '87 Chevy van, with a kidnapped little girl inside. People always remember the uniform, not the man inside, anyway.

Plus he'd been covered head to toe in mud and blood. He'd called it in and held her until the cavalry arrived, in the form of two units who'd been patrolling nearby and the EMTs. Bud had managed to stay conscious until he could hand the little girl over to the medics, then he'd collapsed from blood loss, only gaining consciousness three days later. By that time, Claire was far away. Old Man Parks had had Claire flown to a clinic in Switzerland which offered superb medical care and 24 hour a day armed guards.

Who could have guessed that he'd been fucking Claire Parks these past two days? It boggled the mind. He had no business whatsoever with a Parks.

The Parks mansion could easily be a palace.

Coming up the driveway he'd had a sinking feeling in his gut. This was way *way* out of his league. The place was enormous, a four-story gray stone mansion fit for the king of a medium-sized kingdom. The trailer he grew up in would have fit neatly in a corner of the immense foyer, only it would have looked wildly out of place on the black and white marble flooring.

The silverware alone on the 20 foot long mahogany dining table was worth more than his monthly salary and he'd bet anything that the paintings on the wall were worth more than what he could earn in a lifetime.

It was a very lucky thing he knew which fork to use. There were four of them, plus three spoons, four knives and four crystal glasses with gold rims.

He knew what each fork was for.

The navy was one giant man-processing outfit. At one end it sucked in rough lower class guys like himself, who'd never sat down to a formal meal and more often than not had grown up eating out of cans, and spat them out the other end as killing machines who knew how to use forks.

So he knew how to use all the silverware, and even in what order, though outside the officer's mess and the annual dinner with the Police Commissioner, he'd never had occasion to use that knowledge. Still, he wasn't going to disgrace himself. He wasn't going to drink red wine out of the water glass, he wasn't going to use the meat knife to spread butter and he wasn't going to drink the water in the finger bowls. That didn't mean he wasn't almost violently uncomfortable.

Why the fuck was he here?

Claire and her father had both insisted, that's why. He knew Claire's father had always been almost embarrassingly grateful. When he was in the hospital recovering from the lucky shot that fucker Gavett had got off, old Horace Parks had sent over a check for an indecent amount of money, which Bud had sent right back.

"More roast beef, Lieutenant?" Rosa, the cook, beamed at him from over a serving platter with a surface area about as big as his desktop. She was another case.

When Bud had walked warily through the front door, prepared for anything, he'd encountered a round ball running smack into him, gray head bumping his sternum. Soft round arms hugged him as she cried out, "You saved her! You saved her, *la mia bambina!*" in a thick foreign accent. Italian, it turned out. Two seconds later, she broke down and bawled all over him.

It had been intensely embarrassing. Claire and her father hadn't intervened to rescue him, either. They just stood by, indulgently watching as Rosa cried all over his brand new dress shirt as he awkwardly tried to pat her back.

Since he'd sat down, Rosa had done nothing but ply him with food. Rosa had heaped his plate, no *plates* — they'd gone through five of them — full of food, all of it delicious, and he'd polished each one off. He'd eaten everything, because Rosa's lower lip quivered whenever he refused seconds — or thirds. Bud was starting to feel like a beached whale.

"Tyler, my boy," Horace Parks said, smiling, "you must try the gratin potatoes. It's Rosa's specialty." He should talk. Old Parks himself had picked at his food. He was a very old man, frail and thin, the kind that looked like a bird and ate like one. He beamed at Bud. "You have to keep your strength up."

If Bud had been able to blush, he would have. Surely Old Man Parks had to have some idea of how he'd used up all his calories over the weekend?

Rosa smiled adoringly at him and served another slice of perfect roast beef on his plate. The fourth. She then spooned enough potatoes on the plate to choke a horse. Bud felt uneasy, like a sacrificial bull being fattened for the kill. Why was he being served so much food?

"That's it, Tyler, my boy." Old Man Parks beamed. "We don't want to disappoint Rosa now, do we? She's been cooking all day for you."

"Yes, *Lieutenant Tyler*," Claire chimed in, faint irony in her tone. "Do have some more meat. Make Rosa happy."

Ever since she'd discovered his real name and profession, Claire had been slightly sarcastic. Yes, he was officially Tyler Morrison, but he'd been called Bud all his life. And he hadn't gotten around to telling her he was a police officer, it was true, but part of that was because they'd spent most of their time having sex. And anyway, she was one to talk.

Bud swiveled his head and narrowed his eyes. "I surely will, Ms. *Schuyler*." At least Claire had the good grace to blush a little. He'd just hidden a few facts, while she'd out and out lied to him. Claire Schuyler, indeed.

The old guy coughed. "So, Lieutenant," he said, "who do you think the new Police Commissioner will be when Longman retires?"

Jesus, now the old guy wanted to talk politics. This was a friggin' mine field, considering how powerful Parks was, and what clout he wielded.

Talking politics with one of the most powerful men in Portland was right up there with root canal work in his opinion. Bud was a field man, not a front office desk jockey. He could easily slip and crash, here.

"Well..." Bud played for time by sipping a glass of truly excellent red wine. He'd grown up in a household of alcoholics who drank the kind of wine that came with a screw top. Still, he'd learned to appreciate the good stuff and this was the best he'd ever had. He savored the wine, having learned the hard way to take life's little pleasures whenever he could. "Robert Mansfield seems to have the trust of the present Commissioner. And he knows a lot of guys on the city council and in the state legislature. That could be good for us, come budget time."

Robert Mansfield was a total shithead, a bottom dweller who sucked the cock of anyone higher up in the pecking order, and stepped on the face of anyone lower down. He was made-for-TV handsome, though. Tall, broad, with a shock of thick white hair. And as dumb as they come — basically a good-looking rock with lips. Still, he seemed to be the guy the powers-that-be loved. Bud hated the politics of this shit.

The only guy who was made for the job was the one who'd never get it: Carlos Jimenez Sanchez. Competent, honest, tough as nails and totally unafraid to step on big toes to get the job done. He was completely dedicated to the men and women under him. He knew the names of even the lowliest candy-assed rookie and would step on a land mine before he betrayed them. He had excellent community relations. On top of it all, he was an ex-marine. But Carlos had pissed off some very powerful people, was short and wiry and came off like a rabid terrier on TV. He would never get anywhere near the 16th floor.

"Robert Mansfield, eh?" Parks played with the stem of his wine glass in a way Bud was terrified to do. Bud had big hands and was scared he'd break the delicate crystal. Parks had grown up with this stuff, had probably drunk his baby milk out of Waterford glasses. After a long moment of contemplation, the old guy sighed. "Yes, Bob seems to have the ear of the current Commissioner and of a number of the members sitting on the city council. It's just that the man is such a complete ass."

Bud was sipping his wine and nearly choked.

"Now how about Carlos Sanchez?" the old man mused, watching him carefully. "He'd make a great Commissioner, don't you think?"

Bud blinked and realized that something important was going on here. Horace Parks had real power. He could make or break careers. He'd made Bud's, as a matter of fact, though Bud would have made Lieutenant eventually, no matter what. He was damned good at his job.

"Carlos would be perfect for the job," Bud said carefully. "He'd have it now if he hadn't—" Bud paused, wondering how to put it delicately.

"If he hadn't broken the jaw of that TV reporter?" Parks asked. "The one who broadcast the news that the police were closing in on the Tigard serial rapist, letting him get away? That was unfortunate, yes. Completely understandable, of course, but maybe he should have…er…pulled his punches."

"Pulling his punches isn't Carlos's forte." Bud had to be clear on this. If he could put in a good word for Carlos, by God he would do it. The man deserved it. But he couldn't lie about Carlos's nature. Carlos was a warrior and he put fighting the enemy before everything else. He'd be efficient and ruthless, just what the situation demanded. Bud knew some very bad people were contemplating making Portland their base. They'd think twice with someone like Carlos keeping a vigilant eye on the situation. But fighting crime the real way, the hard way—step by step, scumbag by scumbag—isn't pretty and doesn't always look good on TV. "He'd be a very effective Commissioner if he could be given free rein and didn't have people second-guessing him all the time. Carlos is dedicated to the community and he has good relations with minorities but he's no politician."

"I understand what you're saying." The old man was nodding, watching Bud carefully. "Still, he'd be a good Police Commissioner." There was a faint question in his statement.

"He'd be a fabulous Police Commissioner," Bud said firmly. "Strong and dedicated. The Russian Mafiya's eyeing us, thinking of turning us into the next Vladivostok. Money and people are pouring in. All the signs are there. They'll think twice with Carlos at the helm. Nothing slips under his radar."

Parks nodded.

"Besides, Robert Mansfield is such a dirty old man," Claire said unexpectedly, and they both turned in surprise to her. "He pinched my bottom at a fund raiser and when I confronted him, he pretended it was the waiter. A poor Pakistani kid. He tried to get him fired. The creep pinched me so hard I was black and blue for a week."

Bud heard a rushing sound in his ears. It took him a second to find his voice. And when he did, it was thick with rage. "Jesus fucking Christ. He hurt you? Robert Mansfield *hurt* you?" Robert Mansfield was a walking dead man. He half rose, ready to rush out right now and beat Mansfield to a pulp. "That fucking son of a b—"

"I think we'll retire to the library, my dear." Horace Park's quavery voice broke in. He was old but he was savvy. All that money and all that breeding gave him antenna telling him Bud was about ready to lose it, maybe make a scene. And he was. It took him a whole minute to get his breathing under control, unclench his fists.

You do not use swear words and you do not lose control in the finest house in Portland. Bud would have been ashamed of himself, but the thought of that fucker Mansfield hurting Claire pulsed through him, making his control slip, making it hard to sit still through the static of rage in his head.

"No cigars, Daddy," Claire said sternly. She pointed a slender finger at him and shook it. "And no brandy. You can have a sherry. *One*."

The old man sighed deeply and piteously. "Yes, my dear." He turned to Bud, opening long, narrow, soft mottled hands in a *See what I have to cope with?* gesture. "There you have it, Lieutenant. I have no freedom any more. My daughter, my own flesh and blood, is slowly taking all the pleasures of life away from me." A heavy sigh as he stared at the Persian carpet on the floor, seemingly lost in contemplation of life's injustices.

What he was doing was giving Bud a minute to get a grip on himself. Animal rages probably weren't a frequent occurrence in the Parks dining room.

Claire walked around the table—the damned thing was so long it took forever to get to the other side—and held her hand out to her father. She lifted the old man up and put her arm around his waist. They stood there for a moment, heads together, smiling. Then Claire reached up to kiss a papery wrinkled cheek.

They made a pretty picture in the candlelight—the beautiful young daughter and elderly distinguished father—in the elegant dining room, everything whispering refinement, sophistication and civilization. Right there, Bud could see the resemblance between them. Not in features and coloring so much as a certain style. A lightness, a grace.

What the *fuck* was he doing here? He had no place here at all, amid the priceless antiques, original artwork on the walls and atmosphere of ageless elegance.

He knew exactly why the old guy wanted to drag him away to the library. He could almost write his speech for him.

I am extremely grateful to you, Lieutenant, for saving my daughter's life. Anything you want, anything at all, all you have to do is ask. But, of course, surely you can see that any relationship between yourself and my daughter is impossible…

Yada yada yada.

The hell of it was, the old guy was right. He and Claire were an impossible couple.

"Don't keep *Tyler* too long, Daddy. I want to make an early night of it." Behind her father's back, Claire winked and smiled warmly at him and just like that Bud knew.

He'd known already, of course. The instant attraction, the intense sex, hotter and wilder than anything he'd had before. Just being in her presence gave him a funny feeling in his chest so unfamiliar it had taken him two full days to realize it was happiness. He knew he was in love with Claire Parks. That hadn't stopped him from steeling himself to let her go.

But she smiled at him and wham, there it was—the truth.

No. No fucking way would he give her up.

He'd fight for Claire with every breath he took. Claire was *his*.

He'd never been in love before, had never felt any woman to be particularly special. There was absolutely no precedent for what was going on inside himself, for what he felt for Claire. But with every cell in his body, he knew Claire was meant for him. He'd do anything in his power, fight Satan himself, to keep her with him.

Horace Parks was Claire's father, and therefore deserving of respect. But if he elected to stand between him and Claire, all bets were off. The Parks had generations of breeding and money behind them but Bud was used to fighting and fighting hard for everything he'd ever had in his life. Guts and determination trumped money any day. He'd never lost yet.

He followed Horace Parks, grimly determined to prevail.

The library was everything you'd expect a library in a mansion to be. Dark wooden shelves filled with leather-bound books disappearing into the shadowy reaches of a ceiling at least twenty feet high. Carpets and banker's lamps and lots of old silver. Oil paintings of disapproving guys with sour expressions, whiskers and mutton chops. The smell of leather and paper and money, the old kind. The kind that had been around for generations.

Once the big studded door had closed with a whump like a bank vault door behind them, the old guy perked up. He scuttled over to a big wet bar, poured two giant glasses of a gold-colored liquid and walked over to him.

"Sit down, sit down, Lieutenant," Parks said, pressing a glass in his hand. Cut crystal, heavy and solid-feeling.

Bud sniffed the pungent apple-scented fumes rising up. "This isn't sherry."

Parks sat down in an armchair next to his and sighed. "No, indeed, it isn't," he said, shuddering. "Sweet, weak, nasty drink with no punch to it. No, this is Calvados. *Père Magloire*, best in the world." He sniffed appreciatively and took a deep sip. "I acquired a taste for Calvados when I spent a year in Paris after the war, in a fruitless attempt to master the basics of international law. I did, however, acquire a deep knowledge of French brandies and an appreciation of French women." He reached into a heavily carved wooden box on a round table between the two armchairs. Instantly, the smell of fine tobacco mingled with the fumes of the brandy. They made for a potent mix.

"Here you go, my boy, Havana's finest. I'll open the windows when we leave, otherwise Claire will have my head." He clipped the cigars with a silver clipper, handed one to Bud and lit them both up from an ancient, battered gold lighter. Bud exhaled, sending the smoke up into lazy spirals, and sipped, savoring the fine smooth apple-scented brandy.

He held the cigar up. Darkly rich and pungent and contraband. "This is illegal, you know," he said mildly.

"Yes." Parks smiled and puffed. "But I have friends on the police force."

They sat awhile in silence. Bud didn't have breeding but he knew tactics and strategy. This was the lull just before a battle, when both sides took stock of the situation and the weapons they had to fight it. They sat and puffed and sipped until Bud judged the time was right. Time to unsheathe the swords.

Bud kept his voice quiet, but firm. "I think a few things need to be said, Mr. Parks. About Claire and me."

"Horace, my boy. Call me Horace." He gestured with the cigar. "Go right ahead. I'm listening."

"Okay." Bud looked over at the old guy. He was watching Bud attentively, expression completely neutral.

Round One.

"I grew up in a trailer park," Bud began. "The term trailer trash was invented to describe families just like mine, so I probably have lousy genes. My father died before I was born. I think. That's what my mom said, anyway. They weren't married and I have no idea who he was. She probably didn't either. Morrison is my mom's name. She was an alcoholic and so was my step-dad. I wasn't what you'd call a real studious kid. I got into a lot of trouble and never finished high school. Then my mom died and I joined the navy as soon as I was legally able to do so — got my GED with them. When I left the navy, I joined the police force, been there ever since. Will be until I die or retire, whichever comes first. I make about

$65,000 a year and I'll probably never make much more than that. I have some savings, not much, and I own my apartment but that's about it. I'll never be a rich man and I'll never be anything but a cop. I don't have anything to offer Claire that she doesn't already have a million times over. But I love her with all my heart and, if she'll have me, I intend to marry her. The only thing I can promise is that I'll be faithful to her and I'll try to be the best husband I know how to be."

Their eyes met, Bud's clear and cool. Parks stared, unblinking. His eyes were a pale blue, the watery eyes of an old man, but the gaze was direct. He didn't say anything for a while, puffing on his cigar. Probably trying to find the words to tell Bud that he was crazy.

"Well, Lieutenant, that was short and sweet." Parks studied the glowing tip of his cigar. "Of course, you left out a few particulars. Such as the fact that your stepfather was violent and your mother ended up regularly in the hospital. As did you, for defending her against a man twice your size. You forgot to mention the two medals for bravery in battle while you were in the navy. You also forgot to mention your citations and commendations as a police officer, the fact that you got yourself a degree in criminology while working and that you're the finest shot on the force. Longman tells me you're the best officer he's ever had under his command. And, of course, there is that pesky little detail that you saved my daughter's life.

"You're not rich because you're not greedy. You could easily have kept that check I sent you in the hospital. The amount was three times your annual salary. I checked. At the time you had five hundred dollars in the bank and a heavy mortgage. I checked that, too." He smiled blandly at the look of surprise on Bud's face and shrugged. "I grew up with Walter Bordas, the president of your bank, and I asked him a few questions about you. And yes, I know it was illegal, but we rich guys play by our own rules."

Bud tensed. "If you're saying I was stupid for not taking your check, you're probably right," he growled. "But I couldn't take money for just doing my job. It wasn't right." If Old Man Parks was trying to prove Bud would never be rich, he was doing a good job of it.

"No, indeed, your sense of honor wouldn't let you, and I find that commendable. Did you think I was criticizing you? I get the impression you think I somehow disapprove of working men, when nothing could be further from the truth. I myself am very wealthy but I didn't do anything to earn it. Nor did my father, nor his father before him. I have a great deal of admiration for someone like yourself who started out with nothing and who has made a success of his life. The state of your bank account means less than nothing to me. And as far as Claire is concerned, well, it would be hard to find a less materialistic girl — sorry, *woman* — than Claire. She's never been interested in money and has very simple tastes. No, my worries are completely different in nature."

So…the attack would come from an unexpected quarter. Bud braced himself.

Parks sighed and was quiet for a moment, staring into his glass.

"I was 55 and Elisa, my wife, was 45 when we discovered she was pregnant." He swirled the amber liquid slowly, then took a long draft. "I won't lie and say that we were pleased when we got the news. We led a very pleasant and satisfying life, which involved an active social life and a great deal of travel, none of which is compatible with a small child. We probably would have chosen to terminate the pregnancy, but Elisa was too far along. She thought she was in early menopause and didn't go to a doctor until she was in her fifth month. I imagine, in the normal course of events, we would have taken the path most people of our class take. Our kind rarely let children cramp our lifestyles and we take appropriate measures. Hire a full-time nanny, make sure the child has plenty of material possessions and decent manners.

149

Send the child away to an expensive prep school when he or she is old enough. It's what our own parents did. And then...then Claire was born and she simply stole our hearts.

"From the moment she was put in my arms, I fell in love with her. She was a delight from day one. Charming and beautiful and smart. Elisa and I found that we much preferred evenings at home with our little daughter to evenings out with our usual social set." He sighed, the sound quavery, the exhalation of air of a very old man. "Looking back on it, maybe that was our first mistake. Claire grew up in a little enchanted world of elderly doting parents, an affectionate nanny and Rosa, who loves her like a daughter. She was a fragile little girl and got sick often. The pediatrician told us that children of elderly parents were often frail, so we were very careful of her. One year she missed a lot of school and we hired tutors for her. It was easier that way and she ended up doing most of her schooling here at home. She rarely played with other children—we were frightened that she'd catch something. That's not the way kids are supposed to grow up, I can see that now. The upshot is that Claire has no notion of the outside world, how ugly and violent it can be. She's been surrounded by loving adults all her life. I imagine that would have changed with adolescence, but when she was thirteen...she..."

Parks' voice changed, grew hoarse. He swallowed heavily. "She fell ill. Fulminating leukemia. We were devastated." He looked down into his drink, at the little waves of Calvados raised by his trembling hand. "It killed Elisa. She had a heart attack a few days after the doctors told us there was very little hope for Claire. One day we were so happy, a fortunate little island of three. I was a loving husband and a doting father. The next, I'd lost my wife and risked losing my child. My whole family wiped out in the space of a few days."

He brought the glass to his forehead, rolling it. When he looked up, the pale eyes were bloodshot. He looked every one of his eighty years and more. "For someone who'd been so sheltered, Claire surprised us all. She fought like a tigress for her life. That first year she was taken to the hospital by ambulance five times. Each time they told me there was no hope—and yet she pulled out of it. She understood everything about the illness, read everything she could get her hands on. I couldn't believe it when I saw my thirteen-year-old child poring over *The Merck Manual*, understanding every word. She insisted on subjecting herself to every experimental treatment she could find on the internet. Most of the treatments were extremely painful, but she never cried, never complained. Not once. Not ever. She was much, much stronger than I was. She often ended up comforting *me*."

The trembling was worse now, and he had to put his glass down on the table next to his armchair. "Around her fifteenth birthday, she had a bone marrow transplant as a last chance at life. It didn't take. There was nothing more they could do. The doctors started talking to me about living wills and when to pull the plug..." He stopped to take a shuddering breath. "She was put on a respirator. I sat through the nights with her. I was exhausted by that time, too. The doctors told me I was essentially on a death watch. One night..." He stopped, breathing hard, fighting for control. "One night, Claire spent the night in pain, barely able to breathe. I thought I'd go crazy, listening to her desperate sucking sounds, listening to her moan through clenched teeth, because she didn't want painkillers. Over medicating pain is a polite way of finishing off very sick patients and she knew that. At one point..." He stopped and wheezed. Bud could see a vein beating in the old man's wrinkled temple. "At one point during that endless night," he whispered, "listening to Claire gasping, watching her tremble with pain, I prayed to God to take her. I actually hoped and prayed...my little girl would just...hurry up... and...*die*."

He broke down then, and Bud looked away, the same way you'd avert your gaze from a bad car accident.

Bud memorized book titles and studied family portraits, thinking of how he'd feel sitting by a dying Claire's bedside.

He waited until the choking sounds quieted down and turned back. "Nobody likes to see someone they love suffer." It was the only comfort he could offer.

"No." Parks pulled out a handkerchief as big as a sheet and wiped his nose. His voice was hoarse and watery. "I'm so ashamed of myself. I think, in my dread and exhaustion, I was hoping she would...pass away so the ordeal would finally just be *over*. Luckily, Claire is much stronger than I am. She survived that night, and the next. And the next. She insisted on another bone marrow transplant with an experimental protocol. To everyone's surprise, that one took. And then— and then, she was kidnapped." He looked across to Bud, tears in the rheumy old eyes. "That only lasted a few hours, thanks to you. You caught him right away, and took a bullet for it."

Bud waved that away. Horace Parks was trying to tell him something important. His rescue of Claire was old news.

Parks was silent a moment, gathering his thoughts. "After the Gavett...episode, I sent Claire off to Switzerland, where she essentially lived for the next five years in a compound. She read, learned French and German and read some more. She caught up on her schoolwork, surpassed her peers and took a correspondence degree in library science. When she came home, I insisted she live here and work at the Parks Foundation, where she was very unhappy. That's something I should have noticed, but I simply didn't want to see it. Like I didn't want to see that she wanted a place of her own. She's an adult and she's been disease-free for five years now but I'm still treating her like a sick child. When I left for Paris for two weeks, it was like she made a jail break. She quit her job at the Foundation, found herself a new job and a new house. And then I discovered she'd found herself a lover, too."

Bud froze. "Uh, about that, Mr. Parks, uh, Horace..."

Parks waved that away. "Oh, I don't mind that, my boy. I'm not a prude. Claire's a beautiful young woman. She should have started her love life long ago. I imagine she was a virgin, wasn't she?"

For the very first time in his life, Bud could feel himself turning red.

Then Parks surprised the hell out of him. He echoed Claire. "I'm glad it was *you*, Lieutenant. She was very lucky." He got up to pour himself another drink. The guy could sure hold his alcohol. There'd been several glasses of *Chateauneuf du Pape* over dinner. He sat back with a sigh and drank half the Calvados, watching Bud the whole time. There was silence in the large shadowy room. Bud didn't mind silence and he didn't mind the intense scrutiny to which he was being subjected. The old guy had something on his mind and he'd say it when he was good and ready.

"There's a reason I'm telling you all of this. I'm a very old man, Lieutenant," he said finally, his voice quiet. "All in all, I've had a very good life and I feel in my bones it's winding down. No…" He held a soft white hand up as Bud opened his mouth to protest. "No platitudes, please. We all must die sooner or later. That's not what I'm worried about." With effort, he scooted his armchair closer to Bud. "No, there's something else eating me alive. I'm worried sick about dying and leaving Claire on her own, with no one to protect her. She's a highly intelligent young woman. She reads more books in a year than you and I will in a lifetime. But she's — she's innocent in a way that's hard for a normal person to understand. She has spent her entire lifetime enclosed in a little bubble. First the one created by my wife and myself and then one created by her illness. She has no notion — no idea of the nastiness of the world. She's never encountered evil and cruelty. She has no way of recognizing them. I fear--I fear *so much* that, like her friend Allegra, she could fall into the hands of someone who could hurt her and hurt her badly if I'm not there to look out for her."

The hair on the nape of Bud's neck rose. In a sudden, electric moment, it occurred to Bud for the very first time what a risk Claire had taken in sleeping with a guy she'd just met at a dance club known for its rough trade. He'd been so blindsided by his attraction, the sexual heat, the unnerving experience of falling in love for the first time, that he hadn't even thought about the danger she could have put herself in.

She'd chosen *him*, sure. Great. But what if she hadn't? What if she'd chosen wrong? As a cop he'd seen too many women end up battered and raped by some guy they'd met in a bar. If not worse.

Just last week, he'd inspected the dismembered remains of a young woman whose friends had last seen her leaving a trendy bar with someone described as a 'nice, clean-cut guy'. The nice, clean-cut fucker had used a knife. The ME said it took her a long time to die.

Jesus.

Parks put his glass aside and leaned forward, placing a hand on Bud's forearm. There were tears in his eyes. The hand shook.

"Lieutenant. Tyler. Listen to me." Parks's voice was trembling and hoarse but the grip of his hand was strong now, the grip of desperation. "I can't sleep at night for the thought of what could happen to Claire after I die. You say you love her. Can I entrust my daughter to you? Will you look after her, protect her when I'm no longer here? If I know I've given her into your hands, I can rest easy." Pale blue eyes bored into his. *"Will you give me your word of honor you'll take care of my daughter?"*

Everything the old guy felt—the love and desperation and burgeoning hope that he could lay down his burden at last—it was all right there in his tear-filled eyes, in the tight, trembling grip of his hand.

Horace Parks at that moment was stripped of all his money and breeding and privilege. He was reduced to essentials. A frail old man with not long to live, trying desperately to protect a loved and vulnerable daughter, from beyond the grave, if necessary.

Bud took a moment to find his voice because suddenly his throat was too tight.

"Yeah." He cleared his throat. "I promise you, Horace. You have my word of honor. I'll love Claire and look after her for the rest of her days. Nothing will ever happen to her that I can prevent. I'll protect her with my life. Count on it." He placed his hand over the old guy's and squeezed gently. They both stared at the symbolism of their hands together. Bud's hand was large, tanned and strong. The hand of a powerful man in his prime. Horace Parks's hand was old, soft, mottled. The hand of a man who could no longer protect his loved one.

Together, they forged a bond.

They both understood that Horace Parks had just handed over care of Claire to Bud.

From that moment on, Claire was his.

* * * * *

"Let's go, honey," Bud said softly. He shook Claire's shoulder gently. She'd fallen asleep in the enormous living room while waiting for them. Well, she hadn't had much sleep these past two nights. He'd promised the old man he'd take care of Claire and he would. Taking care of her didn't mean fucking her all night, two nights in a row. She must be exhausted. Maybe she was over the disease but she'd been very sick and she needed her rest.

He was going to take real good care of her from now on, starting right now.

Claire started and opened her eyes. She looked up at him and smiled, pushing back her hair with one hand. "Hi. Wow. I guess I fell asleep." She straightened and looked around. "Where's Daddy?"

"He stayed in the library. I left him snoring," Bud lied. The truth was that old man Parks didn't want Claire to see he'd been crying.

"Oh, okay." She shook her head. "Jet lag. He probably didn't rest in the afternoon."

"He'll be okay." Bud held her coat. "Come on, honey, let's get you home. It's late. You must be tired."

Claire looked up swiftly. "Not *too* tired," she said and smiled, blushing.

Fuck.

No, no, not fuck. Don't even think the word, Bud told himself and his suddenly alert cock. Not tonight. He winced at the thought of how hard he'd used her the night before. He'd just pounded into her for hours. He'd held her legs up and apart so he could have better access and had gone wild inside her.

Now look at her. Bud traced the soft skin under her eyes. It was slightly bruised. "You need your rest, honey." He buttoned up her coat, frowning, glancing out the window. It was sleeting. "Is this coat warm enough? It must be way below zero. And you should have something covering your head."

Claire was watching him, puzzled. "I don't like hats," she said.

"*Ecco*, Lieutenant." Rosa bustled up. She handed him a handsome oversized red woolen scarf.

Bud nodded. "Thanks, Rosa." Billowing it out, he folded it into a triangle then placed it over Claire's head and shoulders, babuschka-style. At least it would keep her warm on the way to the car. "There you go, honey. I don't want you catching cold."

"*Sì.*" Rosa folded her hands, looking at him and Claire, eyes switching back and forth. She nodded once, approving. "*Sì.*"

Bud put on his own coat, and took Claire's arm. "Goodbye, Rosa. Thanks for the great dinner." He opened the door, bracing against the blast of cold sleety wind. Lucky thing he'd parked the car at the end of the driveway close to the mansion. He didn't want Claire out in this weather a second more than necessary. He hurried her over, arm around her back.

He started the car, glad to feel the heat starting almost immediately.

"So," Claire said, brushing off some of the slivers of ice from her coat. "What did you and Daddy talk about? You were gone a long time."

"This and that. Oh, and I asked for your hand in marriage."

Claire's hands stilled. "What? Oh, my God. You did *what*? What—what did he say?"

Bud smiled at her, his beautiful Claire. He leaned over to kiss her mouth, sweetly slack with surprise. A soft kiss, over almost before it began.

"What did your Dad say?" Bud shifted gears and started driving. "He said sure."

Chapter Twelve
December 20th
Armand's

ജ

"So..." Suzanne Barron said, with a snigger and a quick glance to make sure Bud was still talking on his cell phone in the restaurant's elegant atrium. He'd excused himself from the dinner table to take the call. Obviously job-related. "You're engaged. That was quick. I leave you alone for one weekend in your new house and I turn around and next thing I know you're sporting a diamond ring." She peered closely at the monster rock on Claire's hand and shook her head in admiration. "And not just any diamond ring. Princess cut, flawless, no inclusions. At least two carats." Suzanne was a woman who knew her jewels. "That's one serious engagement ring."

"Yes, it *was* quick." Claire flexed her left hand with the enormous brilliant diamond on the ring finger and was nearly blinded by the reflections thrown off. The diamond was huge and made it difficult to wear gloves or to wash dishes. She'd already snagged dozens of stockings on it. It sat on her hand, a huge lump of diamond, a little like the hard lump of anxiety she sometimes had in her stomach.

When Bud found out that there was such a thing as a princess-cut diamond, he'd insisted that nothing less would be good enough for her. She'd have been happy with a Coke tab and here he'd paid a considerable portion of his annual salary for a huge gaudy ring she neither needed nor wanted.

"I'll bet that sucker cost $10,000," Suzanne mused.

"Ten thousand, five hundred," Claire said glumly. She'd been appalled when Bud had insisted on spending so much money.

"Not to mention the walking hunk of sex that goes with it," Todd Armstrong added, with another admiring glance at Bud over his shoulder. "Lucky, lucky you." He swung his head back, the golden fall of shoulder-length hair belling out. Candlelight was reflected in the long gold crucifix in his right ear dangling from a chain. Todd, Suzanne's friend and sometimes partner in interior decorating, was famous for his earrings and predatory dating habits. "Hon...if this—" he tapped her diamond engagement ring, "doesn't work out, I don't suppose he swings both ways?"

Claire laughed and Suzanne smiled.

"No," Claire answered. "He is very definitely straight. I don't imagine he could be enticed to the other side."

"Pity," Todd sighed. "I thought as much, but there's no harm in asking. He is so yummy. All those muscles and that quiet air of power, like he could arrest you at any moment and do delicious things to you involving handcuffs. Yesss!" He shivered, eyes closed. "Oh, well. A guy can always dream." He glanced over his shoulder again longingly, earring swinging. "Still...wow. That man is seriously sexy."

"Yes," Claire sighed, too. "He is."

Bud's broad back was to them, then he turned in profile, speaking soberly into his phone. Bud—*Lieutenant Tyler Morrison*—cleaned up very nicely. He looked like someone you'd bring home to mother but also like someone you wouldn't want to meet in a dark alley. Or someone you'd want on your side if you did meet something nasty in a dark alley.

He was in an elegant dark suit, well-cut, that fit his broad frame perfectly. Claire knew perfectly well that he'd suited up, so to speak, to make a good impression on her friends and he had. He'd been courteous, interesting, well-informed.

They sure hadn't got around to talking politics or world affairs over their hot sexy weekend, and she was surprised to learn how interesting he was, how fascinating his tough take on life was. He spoke very little of the specifics of his job, but he was clearly a man of authority and power.

In his Lieutenant incarnation, he was immensely attractive and—Todd was right—extremely sexy.

Not that she was benefiting from any of that sexiness.

Bud was definitely not gay, but he might as well be, for all the sex Claire had had since their engagement. Bud had somehow got it into his exceedingly thick skull that sex was something that tired her out, or used her up or…something. From not being able to keep his hands off her, he morphed into a fiancé who treated her with kid gloves.

They slept together every night at her house, but they'd only made love once in the past six nights. Polite, respectful love, suitable for broadcasting on the Disney Channel, lasting just long enough for her to have what he probably considered the requisite two climaxes. Then he'd immediately pulled out and cuddled her. Still hard as a rock.

Claire might have considered that he'd reached his limit, that their wild weekend of fucking—there was no other word for it—was an anomaly if it weren't for the fact that he had an erection most of the time he was around her, and when they went to bed, it lasted all night. Or at least he went to bed fully erect at night and woke up in the same state. Not that it had done *her* any good.

Maybe she should ask if she could borrow it? Just for a while?

From being her wild sex-on-a-stick lumberjack, a really really good fuck, better than any romance novel hero, he'd become her loving fiancé-nanny. He surrounded her—smothered her—in tender loving care. She didn't need that. She'd had that all her life. What she needed was for a man to look at her with golden heat in his eyes, to reach for her unexpectedly, as if he couldn't control himself any more, to tremble when he touched her.

The rough sex over the weekend had excited her, electrified her, made her feel hot, alive and wildly sexy. In comparison, the boring, controlled lovemaking the other night made her feel like a matron in her fiftieth year of marriage to an accountant.

"Sweetie." Suzanne covered Claire's hand with her own. She leaned forward, curling a lock of blonde hair behind her ear with her other hand. "This has been so sudden. Is it a good idea to get engaged so quickly? You know you haven't had…a lot of experience with men." Suzanne was being polite, as only she could be. She knew perfectly well Claire had had *no* experience with men. "Maybe you and Bud should wait a little? See how things turn out? Do you love him?"

"Yes." It came out clearly because it was a question Claire could answer clearly. She was in love with Bud. She loved Tyler, too, only he exasperated her.

"That's good." Suzanne smiled at her, nodding. It was one of the many things Claire adored about her. Suzanne treated Claire like an adult. Claire said she was in love with Bud and that was that. Suzanne took her at her word.

"Well, how could she not be in love with that fox?" Todd asked indignantly. "Just look at those shoulders. And he always carries a gun and knows how to use it. I mean how exciting can you get? Mmm. I wonder if he's carrying now?"

"Yes," Claire answered. Another surprise. One of many. Apparently Bud—no, Tyler—was always armed or could put his hand on a gun in seconds. All the time she'd been having hot sex with her lumberjack, he'd kept his gun near him. It was the most alien concept she could imagine—being involved with an armed man. And not just a normal armed man, no. A crack shot, apparently.

"Guns are penis substitutes," Todd said solemnly. "That's what my shrinks say, anyway. Though something tells me that guy doesn't really need a substitute, that he has the real thing right there in his pants. Just look at the size of those hands and feet. I'll bet he has a really really *big*..." He sat up straight and slapped himself on the hand. "Behave, Todd. So—" brightly, "when are you two getting married? I have a fabulous wedding gift in mind for you."

"Oh," Claire replied, a little alarmed at the thought of an actual wedding, when she was still adjusting to the thought of being engaged, "not for a long t—"

"As soon as we can manage it," a deep voice replied. Bud slipped back in his seat and covered her hand with his. He brought her hand to his mouth and kissed it. Holding her hand, he nodded to Suzanne and Todd. "I apologize for leaving you. I had to take the call."

"A dead body?" Todd asked.

"Nothing as exciting as that, Todd," Bud answered. "If it were, I'd have to go. Luckily, Portland seems to be murder-free this evening. No, it was just an administrative matter that needed clearing up. All officers are on call after ten p.m."

Suzanne leaned forward into the candlelight. She was a stunningly beautiful woman, and Claire had never seen a man who hadn't done a double take upon meeting her. Bless him, though, Bud didn't even appear to notice. He treated her with careful impersonal courtesy, as if she were an elderly maiden aunt with a double chin and warts.

"Don't talk to me about red tape." Suzanne rolled her eyes. "I nearly drowned in it when restoring the factory. This city needs to loosen up."

"Tell me about it. You should see the red tape a murder investigation produces."

"All those DNA tests and autopsies and cute little chain of evidence bags," Todd chimed in, shrugging when Suzanne raised an eyebrow. "What? I watch C.S.I. every week. Very exciting."

Bud smiled. "That's actually 'Forensics', Todd. All detectives do is put together the pieces so that it makes a logical picture that can hold up in court. Pretty boring, actually."

There was a slight lull in the conversation as the waiter brought dessert for her, Suzanne and Todd and a whiskey for Bud. The waiter presented Bud with a gold-embossed leather folder with the check inside. Bud had made it clear that this was his treat. It was a very expensive restaurant, another thing Bud had insisted on. Claire wasn't too happy with the way Bud was lavishing money on her, as if he felt he had to keep up with something. She didn't need money lavished on her and neither did Todd or Suzanne. Todd and Suzanne had sophisticated tastes, it was true, but the three of them and Allegra often met at Lo Chow's, a dingy hole in the wall where you could eat to-die-for dim sum out of tin plates for less than five dollars.

Though it was much too expensive, the evening had gone well so far. For all his tough-guy macho nature, Bud wasn't a homophobe. He got on with Todd and they even discovered a shared passion for fly-fishing. Todd was incredibly knowledgeable, and he and Bud had amicably discussed hand-made lures over the blanquette de veau.

Todd, an angler. This was new to Claire, and, judging from the raised eyebrows, new to Suzanne too.

"Suzanne lives in an old shoe factory her grandparents left her, Bud. She's done a beautiful job restoring it. It's absolutely gorgeous." Claire was so proud of Suzanne.

"Yeah?" Bud slipped a credit card in the brown leather folder. "Where's that, Suzanne?"

"Pearl," she replied. "Rose Street."

"Pearl. Rose Street." Bud, convivial dinner companion, disappeared. Lieutenant Tyler Morrison narrowed his eyes and frowned disapprovingly. "That's a real rough part of town. Not at all the kind of place for a single lady to live in."

"I suppose you're right." Suzanne shrugged ruefully. "Such a pity. The area was a perfectly nice one forty years ago, or so they tell me. I couldn't have hoped to find that much space anywhere else. And anyway—the building is mine. It's been in the family for three generations and I couldn't bear to sell it. I might not be alone for long, though. Part of the building is designed to be a rental unit and I've already got a prospective tenant lined up. A businessman. We have an appointment the day after tomorrow."

Claire yawned, too quick for her to stifle it, as she usually did. Bud overreacted to any sign of tiredness. Sure enough, he stood immediately and cupped Claire's elbow, lifting her. "Time to go, ladies. Gentleman. It's been a very enjoyable evening. The first of many, I hope."

"Bud, I'm fine," Claire protested. It was such a pity to cut the evening short because of a yawn. "We've got plenty of time—"

Bud wasn't even listening. He pointed a long finger at Suzanne. "Make sure you check the guy out—this prospective tenant—before you sign the lease and make sure you get decent building security," he ordered. "I could advise you on that, if you want."

"Thanks, Bud. And thanks so much for the lovely meal." Suzanne stood and Todd followed.

"Yes, thank you very much," Todd echoed.

Bud nodded and speared Todd with a hard gaze. "You'll see Suzanne gets safely home."

It wasn't a suggestion.

"Yessir, Lieutenant, sir." Todd's dimple twinkled. "Should I salute?"

"No, I'm not that kind of Lieutenant. Make sure you see her go in the door. Claire, honey, let's go. You're looking tired. They're working you to death at that ad agency. You've worked overtime three times this week. They're pushing you way too hard."

Claire barely had time to say goodbye to Suzanne and Todd before Bud clasped her upper arm and started walking toward the exit.

They'd had this argument before. Claire liked her job at the ad agency. It was so different from the boring and staid work done at the Parks Foundation. The people working at the ad agency were wild and fun and a little crazy, like Lucy. Bud had it in for Lucy for abandoning her that night at The Warehouse, though Claire had long since forgiven her. Lucy was fun and irresponsible and that was that. Bud acted as if he'd like to arrest her.

She'd been working hard at Semantika but it wasn't the work that was tiring her out. No, the reason Claire was tired was that she spent most nights awake, staring at the ceiling, waiting for Bud to jump her bones. Waiting in vain.

There had to be something she could do to jog Bud out of his over-protectiveness and back into sex mode. They drove in silence through the dark streets, Bud easily navigating his car through the rainy sleety night. He was a magnificent driver, something Claire admired. She hated driving and wasn't good at it. Bud was good at a lot of things, sex included.

If she was going to get any more sex out of him, however, it looked like she'd have to scheme for it. Maybe a change of setting would work.

"Bud, I've never seen where you live. I'd really like to see that. Could we sleep over at your house, just for a change?"

"You want to sleep over at my place?" His hands tightened on the wheel. "What the f— whatever for? I'm not too sure you'd like my house. It's pretty basic." He stole a wary glance at her. "I don't spend much time there and haven't done it up at all. It's not as nice as your place."

"Well, no, how could it be? Mine was designed by Suzanne. She's one of the most talented decorators in the country. I'm not expecting Italian sofas, Shaker furniture and hand-crafted lamps. How basic are we talking here? Do you have indoor plumbing? Heating? Electricity?"

His hard mouth curved. "Yeah," he admitted. "I've got all of that. I suppose you'd be comfortable enough."

"Well, then. I promise not to pick at the mold in the refrigerator or bury your smelly socks in the back yard. I just want to see where you live. Here we are, engaged—" She shook her head because she still couldn't believe it, "and I don't have any idea where you live."

"Sure you do," Bud protested. "1432 Fuller. About eight blocks from your house. And I don't have a back yard. It's an apartment on the fourth floor."

"See? I didn't even know that. Come on, Bud," she pleaded. "I'll bring my own sheets and towels. I'll even cook for you."

"*No*," he growled. They'd done that once and it hadn't worked out. Claire had a steep culinary learning curve ahead of her. "I'll do the cooking. And I have sheets and towels. Okay, okay." He sounded resigned as he pulled up in front of her house. "I'm leaving tomorrow for Chico—have to take a deposition. I'll be back late the following day. When I come back we'll sleep at my place, if that's what you really want. Just don't expect too fancy a place."

Claire hadn't had any idea that he had to leave town. That he even had the kind of job that required him to go out of town. He never discussed work with her, never told her how his day had gone. What he did instead was fuss over her.

It was clear what he and Daddy had been talking about in the library. Her. Poor Claire. Poor sick Claire. Eternally ill, eternally a child.

Well she was *fine* now. *Fine*. All grown up. And now that she'd been introduced to good sex, she wanted more, lots more.

They already had a little routine now, like old married folks. Claire showered in the main bathroom and Bud took the service bathroom off the laundry room. How on earth could he cross the laundry room and not remember what they'd done there? To the beat of poetry. It would be forever seared in her mind.

There had to be something that would jog Bud out of his sex-is-bad-for-Claire's-health mindset. Maybe the pale yellow silk nightgown? The one that had driven him so crazy she'd had to take it off herself?

Claire dried and powdered and moisturized and perfumed herself to within an inch of her life, determined that tonight she'd see some action. Bud was waiting in bed. He always took less time than her. Moving quietly, she stepped into the room. This time, there weren't any candles but there were a few familiar features. Bud was naked and aroused.

He usually slept naked, which would have been very handy had they been having more sex, and his erect penis was clearly visible under the sheet. Bud was a human furnace and, until she got in bed, he didn't pull the eiderdown up.

He watched her enter the room, tracking her movements, eyes hot, glowing, golden, features sharp and predatory. Ah, yes.

"I really like that nightgown," he whispered.

"I know," she whispered back. "I put it on specially for you. And I'm hoping this time you'll take it off me yourself."

Hot, hot golden eyes. "Oh, yeah. Come right on over and—" he sobered suddenly, the heat in his eyes fading, dimming to concern. "I don't know, honey. You were so tired. Maybe we should just—"

"Shut up, Bud." Claire whipped the nightgown up off her head and walked naked to the bed.

Bud shut up and reached for her, big hands trembling. He pulled her down on top of him and kissed her, hot and deep, one hand holding her head still for his mouth, the other anchoring her hips to his. She opened her legs and slid her vagina up and down the base of his hot, hard penis. The big hand holding her hips caressed her buttocks then moved down, down and touched her, right where she wanted to be touched. He inserted a long finger and stroked.

Oh, she'd missed this *so much.*

The heat and the power, the misty steamy fog rising in her head so she was pure feeling, pure body. Bud's tongue stroking hers, in time with his finger exploring her vagina. Wet mouth, wet sheath, hard nipples rubbing against the hair of his chest. She gripped him as hard as she could with her arms and legs, loving the feel of his powerful muscles against her. She was a second from exploding when Bud kicked the eiderdown off the bed. An errant feather wafted in the air. Bud was turning with her in his arms when the feather drifted across her face.

She sneezed and Bud froze.

He stopped kissing her, stopped touching her and turned to lay her gently on her back. "Sorry, honey," he whispered, drawing the sheet up over her. He reached for the eiderdown on the floor and carefully tucked it around her, as if she were three years old. He kissed her carefully on the forehead and leaned over to turn the bedside lamp out. "I shouldn't have started that when you need your rest. Good night, love."

Claire was paralyzed. She was an inch from orgasm and didn't know what to do about it. She was too shy to ask Bud to continue, too shy to reach down and touch herself. And any orgasm she gave herself would pale in comparison to what he could to do her — for her.

Tears leaked out of her eyes, but she didn't dare swipe at them. Bud would immediately rise up and ask her frantically what was wrong. What was wrong was that he had left her hanging, trembling, on the thin edge of completion. Claire lay awake grinding her teeth, staring up into the dark ceiling, until her body slowly cooled down. Frustration, anger and sadness tangled in her chest.

She loved Bud.

But she wanted to kill Tyler.

Chapter Thirteen
December 23rd
1432 Fuller
Early morning

છ

Claire shifted and sighed in his arms and Bud broke out in a sweat. Her knee was nudging his cock. His tremendously erect, ready-to-burst-out-of-its skin cock. Waking her up for a hard and furious fuck was out of the question, though. Even if it wasn't out of the question, he'd be too violent. He was so worked up, there was no way he could control his strokes once he got into her. So he sweated and suffered.

She'd been fast asleep when he arrived home two hours ago, exhausted and horny as hell. Curled up on his couch with a cold cup of tea on the coffee table, looking about twelve years old. The thought of Claire waiting for him in his apartment had kept his foot on the accelerator all the way up from Chico, breaking speed laws all the way.

The deposition of a Slovenian gunrunner with ties to Semis Ruden, the world's largest supplier of arms to guerrilla armies, operating out of a mafiya-run semi-state in the Ukraine called Trans-Dneiper, had taken longer than expected. Though the idea of a waiting Claire was enticing, Bud was too much of a pro to hurry the proceedings. They were questioning the informant through an interpreter whose English was shaky at best and it was very slow going.

He was tired because he'd spent the entire night in a hotel jerking off. This engagement business was exhausting. Bud rarely had to beat the meat. There was always a willing woman somewhere within reach; all he had to do was look.

The Slovenian interpreter, for example. She'd cast admiring glances his way a number of times, screwing up the English even more. Bud didn't want the Slovenian interpreter, he didn't want the duty officer at the Chico PD, he didn't want the waitress in the all-night diner where he'd grabbed a bite to eat, he didn't want the hotel receptionist.

He wanted Claire.

Sleeping with Claire and not fucking her was taking its toll. Night after night, he lay in bed with her, hard and horny, wishing Claire didn't look tired and didn't have slight bruises under her eyes. But shit, it was hard, sleeping in the same bed as Claire every night without touching her. He had a couple of medals from his time in the navy, but facing enemy fire hadn't required anything like the grit not fucking Claire did.

Whenever his hands itched to touch her and his cock felt like it was going to burst out of its skin, all he had to do was remember Claire's father in the library, trembling voice talking about sitting beside Claire, waiting for her to die, and he was able to restrain himself. Nothing was ever going to happen to Claire, he'd given his word of honor.

That particularly meant not fucking her brains out.

Walking into his apartment, he'd smelled her first. Claire's smell was imprinted on his brain; he'd recognize her blindfolded. Maybe tonight…then he walked into the living room to find her slumped in her pajamas on the couch, head on one folded arm. She'd looked pale and tired. He carried her to bed, put on his own pajamas—sleeping naked as he usually did was way too dangerous—and slipped in beside her.

She liked to sleep touching him. That was very nice, but it was also pure torture. Bud tried to hold her without touching her. Could cocks burst like balloons? If they could, his would.

The hell of it was, he couldn't just reach down and jerk off like he had last night. The movement would wake her and he'd probably spurt all over her. Embarrass the hell out of him, too.

She snuggled closer in her sleep, one soft slender arm across his chest. Would it be too much to take her hand, curl it around his cock and coax her to jerk him off? She'd only touched him once, in the laundry-room. Just the memory of them in that little room, smelling of wood varnish and detergent, a naked Claire on top of the washing machine, had his heart pounding. She'd touched him, lightly, gently. She'd even put her hands around the band of his sweatpants and slipped the bottoms off. That was the extent of it. Claire wasn't forward at all when it came to sex. He could wish that she could be more aggressive, but then he supposed she wouldn't be Claire, the woman he loved.

He'd had plenty of women who didn't make any bones about what they wanted. He'd had dinner partners who reached under the table to fondle him, more than a few who'd simply asked outright—*wanna fuck?*

Yes. Yes, he did.

He wanted to fuck Claire.

Her hair was spread all over his chest like a soft warm ebony blanket. She was breathing softly, gently. He could barely hear her. Everything about her was so light and delicate. It worried him. It had worried him that weekend, too. He'd been way too rough with her. At the time, though, his worry was that she'd been a virgin.

Still, virgins become unvirgins, really fast. He had no doubt that she would get up to speed with him soon. She hadn't said no, ever. She'd liked everything he'd done to her. Bud knew he had strong sexual appetites. He hadn't ever really thought much about having a permanent partner, but he knew that if he ever had one, she'd have to keep up. Before he knew about the illness, Bud was sure Claire would eventually keep up.

Now he wasn't so sure.

He loved Claire. He had every intention of being faithful to her for the rest of his life. But what would happen if they couldn't have as much sex as he wanted, needed? Would he be consigned to beating off in the men's room at work?

Jesus, his hard-on hurt.

Bud's hand was inching down to his groin—was it possible to jerk off without moving? Maybe instead of jerking off he could *squeeze* himself off—when the phone rang. It could only be one thing at one-thirty in the morning. A work emergency.

He was almost grateful for the distraction as he reached for the phone before it could ring twice.

"Morrison."

"Bud. John here. Huntington."

He didn't need the name. He'd have recognized that voice anywhere. Lieutenant Commander John Huntington, former SEAL. The Midnight Man. He hadn't seen him in twelve years, since they'd been on a training op together.

Turned out Suzanne's prospective tenant was Midnight, of all people, who'd surfaced unexpectedly in Portland. Suzanne had called to check with him because Midnight had put Bud's name down as a reference.

It had reassured Bud no end, knowing Midnight was with Suzanne in Pearl. Suzanne was a friend of Claire's and he felt responsible for her. A beautiful woman living alone on Rose was an invitation to trouble, but if her tenant was Midnight, well then, he could rest easy. Midnight was one of the most dangerous men on the planet. He wouldn't let anything happen to his landlady. Particularly if she was a beautiful woman.

Bud didn't waste time on small talk. "What's up, John? You in trouble?"

"Might say that," John said calmly. "I just killed a man."

That *was* trouble. Bad trouble. Bud sat up, rolling Claire off his chest and reaching for his pants while talking into the cordless.

"Sorry to wake you up at this hour, Bud, but I need you to call this in. I'm in Suzanne Barron's building on Rose Street. She had an intruder tonight. Armed. I took him down. You'd better get over here with your team. It's not pretty."

"Bud?" Claire said sleepily. She sat up, pushing hair out of her eyes and blinking. "You're back. I wanted to stay awake for you, but I must have fallen asleep." Damn, he'd hoped she wouldn't wake up. He put his hand over the receiver.

"Sorry I woke you up, hon. Go back to sleep."

"Is there a problem?" she asked, yawning.

"No," he lied. There *was* a problem and it involved her friend, but damned if he'd get her all worried until he knew exactly what the situation was. If Midnight was there with Suzanne, she was safe. It was pointless getting Claire all worked up. "Go back to sleep, honey. I have to go. I've been called out and I don't know when I'll be back. You have the keys if I'm not back by morning. Make sure you lock up."

Claire blinked owlishly, still half asleep. "'Kay," she mumbled and lay back down, falling asleep almost immediately.

Bud grabbed his clothes and the cordless handset and walked into the living room. "I'll be right over." Bud said quietly into the headset. "I'll call it in and go directly to Suzanne's house. The rest of the squad will be there in about a quarter of an hour."

"Door's open," John said. "Wide open. He trashed the security system. And you can use the sirens. He's not going anywhere. Hang on a second, Bud."

There was silence on the line. Bud used it to finish getting dressed.

John came back on the line. "I think we've got ourselves a hired hand here, Bud."

"Yeah? How so?" Bud held the handset between shoulder and ear while he put on his shoulder holster.

"He's got a Colt Woodsman with the serial number filed off. With a suppressor. You don't carry a weapon like that to make off with the silver tea service. And he's got body armor. That's not standard B & E fare, either. Hurry up, Bud."

A Colt Woodsman—standard assassin model—with a suppressor. Body armor. In Suzanne's house. This was not good.

"On my way, big guy." Bud said and walked out the door.

* * * * *

December 23rd
Portland Police Headquarters
Late morning

Nine hours later, Bud was in the cop shop, drinking engine sludge badly disguised as coffee and staring in frustration at the computer. It was top-of-the-line and was at that very moment hooked up with NCIC, in search mode for prints. Of two hired killers sent to murder Suzanne Barron.

NCIC processed over a billion requests a year. It worked fast on supercomputers but they couldn't be fast enough for him. Bud felt the urgency of a necessary answer. Suzanne's life was on the line.

Not only had there been an assassin in her house, there had been a second one. After the scene had been processed and the bag and tag techies had done their thing, they'd all trooped out to take it downtown to HQ. That was when the second shooter, who'd been waiting for just that moment on the second floor of a flophouse, had narrowly missed killing Suzanne. If it hadn't been for John's reflexes, Bud would have had to take Suzanne's shattered body to the morgue.

John had taken the second shooter down too, a perfect double tap to the head, then he'd disappeared with Suzanne. An already bad situation had all of a sudden gone south.

He had no idea where Midnight had taken Claire's friend. The cop in him deeply disapproved. Suzanne was clearly in the sights of a criminal for something she'd said or done or seen. She needed to be taken in for questioning.

The man in him understood completely. Their body language had told him John and Suzanne had become lovers. John would protect what was his. Someone was gunning for Suzanne, and John had simply taken her out of the equation, trusting Bud to get to the bottom of this business. If Midnight had taken Suzanne into hiding, no one was going to find them, ever.

The ball was now in Bud's court, and he sat thinking furiously.

This had all the hallmarks of a mob hit. Second shooters were there to take out the assassin and wipe out all connections to the man who'd paid for the job.

This whole thing was ass backwards. Bud's job usually involved finding a murderer. He knew the killer already. John Huntington. Only it had been legitimate defense, not murder. John wouldn't get any grief about rescuing Suzanne. Bud would see to that personally.

No, his job now was to find out *who* had been murdered. And then after that, why they'd been sent.

Ding!

Information coming through. Bud peered at the screen. The face that appeared, full frontal and profile, was familiar. It was the man who'd been sent to take Suzanne out. Body number one.

Bud was all of a sudden very grateful that Midnight had had the foresight to put a K-Bar through the first guy's throat instead of blowing his face away. They had a match. The police photographs showed a guy maybe a few years younger, with shorter hair, but definitely the scumbag he'd last seen dead in Suzanne's very pretty living room.

Roger Beckett, 36, last known address Salem State Correctional Facility.

Fuck. The guy had a rap sheet as long as his arm, starting from the age of 15. He was a drug addict, in and out of rehab, and recidivist criminal, in and out of jail. Not for petty crimes, either. Assault, armed robbery, drug dealing, rape.

Bud's heart lurched when he read that.

Rape.

Rapists never changed. Not ever.

Bud absolutely did not believe in therapy or behavior modification when it came to rapists or — God — child abusers. A very deep part of him, which he rarely let out, rarely even admitted to himself and certainly not to others, believed that sex offenders should be castrated. Just cut it off so they couldn't use it again, hurt someone vulnerable with it again, because that was the only thing that worked. These were men who were bent forever. Hard as it was for Bud to understand the sickness, he knew for a fact that a guy who was turned on by little girls or little boys was a sick fuck who could never get it up unless he had a helpless child in his clutches to torment. And rapists — they liked the violence, got off on the power of hurting women. Once a rapist always a rapist.

There was no doubt in his mind that if it weren't for John, Suzanne would have been brutally raped before being killed.

The second shooter's file was coming up when the desk sergeant walked in. "Lieutenant," she said. "There's someone to see you."

"Not now, Sergeant Lopez. I'm busy," he said absently. An attachment was coming in over the secure line. A big one. 40 megabytes; probably lots of .jpg files.

"I think you'll want to see this person," Carmela Lopez said dryly. She stepped aside to reveal a man of medium height, trim. Short, light brown hair, nondescript regular features. Cheap shiny black suit, white shirt, narrow black polyester tie.

He might as well have had F.B.I. tattooed on his forehead.

"Lieutenant Morrison, I'm Special Agent Sisman. New SAC of the Portland field office."

Bud had no time right now for interagency public relations. "I'm kind of busy right now, Special Agent," he said. "If this is about that memo we all got a couple of weeks ago to set up an interagency terrorist task force…"

"No," the F.B.I. agent replied. "My business is much more immediate than that." He nodded at the computer screen. "You put in a request for a fingerprint-based ID for an unsub. NCIC routes answers through us first. We have a red flag for any request for a specific set of fingerprints and that…" he pointed at the screen where the attachment had finally loaded, and was waiting, blinking, "…that's it."

Bud was confused. "What's it?"

Sisman walked over to the office computer and tapped the screen.

The data had finished loading when all of a sudden the screen went dark, then glowing pulsing letters appeared. INFORMATION RESTRICTED.

What the…? "Restricted? Who the hell to?" Bud growled.

"Me, for one," Agent Sisman replied. He met Bud's eyes in a hard stare. Sisman was about seven inches shorter and at least 60 pounds lighter than Bud but Bud had met his match in toughness. "You can access the information in that file if you tell me why you need it."

Bud thought that over for about three seconds, but there was no question what his answer would be. Suzanne's life was on the line. "Done. You first."

"Okay." Sisman walked over, sat down in the hard plastic chair and punched the keys of the keyboard. It was an interactive program, an operation organized in steps. Some kind of tight security system. A small beep sounded with each step. Bud couldn't follow the keystrokes and what presented on the screen were asterisks in fields. Code and passwords.

It took a few minutes, but finally the screen cleared and a face came up. Bud couldn't be certain it was the second shooter whose ravaged face he'd studied in the morgue. The top part of his head had been shot off. John had been careful to preserve the face of the contract killer in Suzanne's apartment, but he hadn't had the time to do that for the second shooter. He'd reacted instantaneously to the danger to Suzanne, getting off the best shot he could.

There are only two shots guaranteed to kill a human being on the spot. Frontally, a bullet to the bridge of the nose and, from the back, a bullet to the spot between the two tendons at the nape of the neck. Anything else—even severing an artery—allows the enemy enough time to get off a shot before dying.

The bullet to the bridge of the nose wipes out the frontal lobe of the brain and the bullet to the nape of the neck severs the spinal column. In both cases, the victim drops to the ground instantly. Dead.

John, in the space of a split second, had opted to wipe out the possibility of the shooter getting off a lucky shot and he'd been absolutely right. Bud could only admire the sharpshooter skills.

He might have been able to get off a shot like that once, but though he was far and away the best shot on the police force, he didn't know if he could manage a single-shot kill in the dark at 300 yards anymore.

Sharpshooting skills are perishable, like milk, though with a longer shelf life. He'd kept his own skills up, but his duties as a police officer had allowed the sharpest edge of that blade to dull a little. Clearly, the Midnight Man hadn't. Good for him. He'd saved Suzanne Barron's life twice.

The thing was that though Bud couldn't be absolutely certain they'd ID'd the second shooter, he could be 99% sure.

The dead meat on the slab in the morgue had dark blond hair, a gold cap on his left front incisor and a surgical scar above the collarbone, probably a thyroidectomy.

Bud read the biometric data on the screen in front of him.

Ryan McMillan, 47, 5'11", 187 pounds, dark blond hair, heavy dental work, thyroidectomy in prison in 1995. Bud read further and the hairs on his forearms rose.

Ryan McMillan was the top gun in the small circle of elite killers for hire in the continental United States. Suspected in the murders of Carmine 'Fish' Lo Pesce, Teamster head Vic Torrance and—Bud froze—the assassination of Senator Julius Lesley. The most famous unsolved crime in America after the disappearance of Jimmy Hoffa.

McMillan had a standard fee of $500,000 a hit.

Whoever wanted Suzanne dead was willing to pay at least $500,000 plus whatever Beckett asked. Over half a million dollars to kill an interior decorator. Bud was still reeling from the implications of that when he heard Special Agent Sisman's voice say dryly, "Your turn, now."

Bud turned to meet the agent's weary, ancient-looking eyes. Over the next twenty minutes, he gave a complete report of the past night's events to the feeb, up to his last look at the second shooter in the morgue.

There was a heavy silence for a full minute.

Special Agent Sisman stated the obvious. "We've got big, big trouble here."

* * * * *

December 23rd
Portland Police headquarters
6:00 p.m.

The cab left Claire at the entrance of the concrete and steel 16-story building. The Justice Center. There had been an article in *The Oregonian* a while back stating that parking within a few blocks of the Center was forbidden since 9/11. Dressed as she was, there was no way she could walk a few blocks in the freezing cold. She'd opted for a cab.

At work, she'd simply said she needed to get off early. She was ridiculously overqualified for her work as a secretary and had put in a lot of overtime. Her request had been granted immediately.

Claire bunched the soft folds of her thick coat in her fist. She was freezing cold, but she was sweating, too. She was about to do something very scary.

She kept her head down as she entered the lobby and rode up to the 13th floor. That was where the Homicide Squad was. She'd checked.

Her knees knocked and her heart beat against her rib cage as she rode slowly up.

This was scary.

Not doing it was scarier.

Start as you mean to go on.

Claire could remember her mother saying that, and it made sense. She and Bud had started a love affair that, in a ridiculously short amount of time, had morphed into an engagement, and he'd given off clear signs that he wanted to get married as soon as possible. Marriage for Claire meant a lifetime.

She couldn't bear a lifetime as they were now, with Bud tiptoeing around her, afraid to kiss her, touch her, make love to her. Much as she loved Bud, she knew she could never stand a lifetime of being treated like a little china doll that would break if handled too roughly. Claire wouldn't break, ever. She'd been through too much, withstood too much pain and despair to break. No matter how rough his lovemaking, he couldn't hurt her. The way he was behaving now was hurting her.

The only way she and Bud could possibly have a future was for Bud to treat her like a woman. A full-blooded strong woman who could take whatever he had to give. Including all the sex he and she could stand.

That was why she was going to do the most forward, most frightening thing she could imagine, to push herself off Bud's pedestal.

Claire was used to hiding her feelings. No one could possibly tell that she was trembling, almost sick with anxiety.

She knew perfectly well what kind of façade she was presenting to the world. To the 13th floor, actually, she thought, as the elevator doors opened. A well-dressed elegant young woman, self-confident in her looks and bearing.

She looked around the open-plan floor, bemused. Desks and ringing phones and harried police officers — men and women — all busy and competent-looking, and every single one of them armed.

So this was Bud's world. Rough and urgent and important.

He never, ever talked about his job. It was as if he wanted to keep her in a little bubble of pretty, refined fragile things. That was how she'd grown up, sure, but twelve years on the edge of death had turned her core to steel. She would love it if he told her about his day, even the terrible, cruel things he saw. After all, he was helping to make the world a better place.

Claire already knew the world was terrible and cruel.

There must have been a hundred people on this floor. The noise level was acute, what with people shouting into phones, shouting at each other, conversing across cubicles, phones ringing, computers dinging. The smells were sharp, too. Leather and paper and sweat and bad coffee.

She wavered, shaking inwardly. This might not be a good idea. And if Bud didn't have an office of his own, it was an impossible idea.

"Excuse me." The man she approached didn't even turn around in his chair. She cleared her throat, raised her voice. "Excuse me?"

He turned, surprised. Short, with a dark growth of beard and tufts of dark chest hair fluffing out from an open shirt. "Yeah?" He looked her up and down, probably considering that she looked a little out of place, with her dark red cashmere Valentino coat, soft black kid gloves and high heels. "You'll be wanting to go back downstairs, ma'am. There's an information desk on the…"

"Is this the homicide squad?" she interrupted.

"Department," the man answered. "Yeah."

Claire resisted the urge to lick dry lips. "Is—is Lieutenant Tyler Morrison here?"

"Bud? Yeah." The man pointed to the back of the room where there were two offices with frosted glass. And doors, Claire was relieved to see. "Left hand door. You got business, lady?" He looked her up and down again and snickered. "A murder to call in?"

"No," Claire replied pleasantly, thinking of how frustrated she was with Bud. "A murder to prevent."

She made her way across the crowded room. No one paid her any attention at all. It all looked chaotic, but wasn't, she realized. Everybody knew exactly what they were doing.

So did she.

Bucked up by that thought, she knocked on the left hand door, feeling her heart-beat rise as she heard a familiar voice growl, "Yeah? What is it?" She opened the door and walked in.

For the very first time, Claire saw Bud surprised. It took him a second to get his bearings. "Claire?" He stared blankly, then alarm crossed his face. "What the f—what are you doing here? Are you okay? Is anything wrong?" He braced his hands on the desk and started to rise.

"Stop right there, Bud." He sank back down, puzzled. She'd gotten the tone exactly right. Firm, commanding.

Claire reached behind her to lock the door and walked slowly into the room.

She looked at Bud. Really looked.

Recently, she'd been so angry with him and his sudden nanny-like attitude toward her that she forgot how sexy he was, how wildly attractive he was. Strong, tough, dangerous. Capable of enormous tenderness. One of the good guys in a world that didn't have too many of them.

This was a man worth fighting for. She was going to fight with every weapon at her disposal. Starting now.

Claire slowly unbuttoned her coat with a gloved hand, letting it hang open a moment, enjoying the sight of Bud's open mouth. She slowly brought her gloved hands up and slowly, oh so slowly, caressed her shoulders, opening the coat further. A shimmy, making her breasts quiver, and the coat dropped to the floor in the soft heavy slither only cashmere can manage.

She was naked underneath. All she had on was black gloves, black thigh-highs, high heels and lipstick. She looked like a high-class hooker. An aroused one, too. Her nipples were hard little buds, puckered up mainly from the cold but a little from excitement, too. Particularly now, watching Bud watching her.

Oh God, this was worth it. Worth every minute she'd agonized over the idea, worth every second of anxiety to see that red hot heat in Bud's eyes again.

"I thought of this, of you, all across town," she said softly, watching his eyes. She tugged at the gloves, finger by finger, taking off first the left one then the right one. "In the taxi, I imagined you touching me, all over. Whenever you touch me, I tingle. Did you know that? Thinking of you I got wet, right there in the taxi cab. When the driver took corners, I crossed my legs to add to the pressure and I almost came when he turned into Webster. And my breasts — they rubbed up against the lining of my coat as I thought of all the times you licked my nipples. But still—" she walked slowly toward him, " — nothing could possibly beat you touching me. Holding me." She skirted the desk, coming to a halt by his thigh. "Fucking me," she whispered. "That's the best thing of all."

He reached for her, urgently, with that hot golden look she loved, she craved, but Claire held his hands. She turned hers so their hands met, palm to palm, and she slid her fingers between his. Even the touch of his hands—so large and warm—the palms callused and hard, excited her. His hands were powerful yet they had never hurt her, ever. Exerting gentle pressure, she lowered their clasped hands to his thigh, sliding hers away. "Don't touch me, not yet," she said throatily. His hands twitched, as if tempted almost beyond bearing to touch her, then stilled. She wanted to be touched but she had to make her point first.

Claire looked at his lap, tilted her head to meet his hot golden gaze, then lowered her eyes again. She licked her lips, slowly. "You're happy to see me." His erection was hugely visible beneath the gray wool material.

"Fuck yes," he breathed and she rejoiced. He'd cleaned up his language for her over the past week, too, as if she were too delicate to stand strong language. She didn't need that. She loved the way he talked. She loved the way he watched her, she loved the way he touched her, she loved the way he fucked her.

She loved...him. Exactly the way he was. And at this precise moment in time, he was aroused as hell and she loved that, too.

She touched him there, running her hand up and down that smooth column beneath the wool. It was hot, the heat radiating through his underwear and pants. His penis twitched and grew harder and larger as she fondled him, opening her hand over him, sliding up and down.

"Claire." His voice was deep and rough. He caught her hand in his. He didn't push it away, just held it strongly. The effect was to press her even harder against his penis. "Do you know where we are?"

She smiled. "Of course I do. 1111 Southwest 2nd." Her lids drooped as her mouth curled upwards. "Police Headquarters."

"Yeah." A muscle jumped in his jaw. "Police headquarters. Where I work. We can't do this here, honey."

"You don't want to fuck now?" Claire pouted a little.

"No." The word was ground out between clenched teeth. "Fuck *here*? Are you crazy?"

He talked a good line, but she wasn't buying it. She looked up again at his face, delighted at what she found. Heat and lust. Jaw muscles jumping, flushed cheekbones, narrowed eyes zeroing in on her breasts.

Absolutely. That's exactly what he should be looking at, lusting after. Her breasts. And also…

Claire opened her legs, balancing lightly on the high heels, delighted to see Bud's head snap down. If he looked carefully, he could see the folds of her sex and maybe even see how wet she was. He looked exactly as if he were looking very carefully.

Just to make sure he didn't miss the point, Claire reached down to touch herself. She was slippery and swollen. Bud did that to her. She might have gotten a little excited in the cab ride at the thought of this, but being in the same room with Bud, yes, that was what did the trick. Claire swirled her finger around herself, then held her finger up. "See, Bud." Her voice must have dropped an octave. Marlene Dietrich in heels and thigh highs minus the top hat. "See what you do to me?"

Bud closed his eyes in pain. "Honey, this isn't the time or the place for this. It's a really…busy day and anyway, anyone can just walk in."

"No, they can't." Claire touched a nipple with her wet finger and listened with satisfaction to the sound he made deep in his chest. "I locked the door." She reached over suddenly to take his phone off the hook. "And no one's going to call you, either. So for a little while you're all mine."

"Not at *work*, I'm not." Bud was trying really hard to sound forceful but his eyes were hotter than any sun and his penis was almost vibrating.

Claire swung a leg over and straddled him.

"Claire!" She nearly laughed at his expression. He was battling two extreme emotions. Shock and lust. Claire opted for lust.

Luckily she was wearing high heels. Stiletto heels, killer heels. What Lucy called 'fuck me' shoes. They allowed her to rest her feet on the floor so she could find purchase. Bracing her feet, Claire moved until her naked sex rested directly over his penis. She slid back and forth over him, the rough texture of the woolen trousers and placket-covered metal zipper exciting her almost as much as the hot thick column beneath them. She was so wet she was staining his trousers.

Tough.

She braced her hands on his shoulders and leaned forward. She had on red crimson lipstick, the brazen wet kind, the kind that advertised the mouth as a sex organ. She couldn't kiss him—that would be going too far and leave marks—but she could lick him. Follow the shape of his ear with her tongue. Yes, she could, and she was delighted to feel that it made him shake and shudder. Beneath the folds of her sex, he swelled and jerked.

Bud had his hands on her hips. No doubt his original intention was to lift her away. He could do it. He was certainly strong enough. He'd carried her with ridiculous ease, lifted her over him in bed. He was as strong as an ox. Oh, yes, if he really wanted her off him, if he really wanted to put a stop to this, he could.

But he didn't.

The strong hands dug into her buttocks, following the movements of her hips as she rode him. Claire could start to feel that delicious feeling of losing herself, the sensation of slipping and sliding into a warm sensuous bath…

Before she lost all sense of time, she shifted slightly. One last lick at his ear, a nip of the lobe and she slithered off his lap to crouch on the floor before him.

"Claire," Bud breathed. He could no longer clutch her, so his hands gripped the arms of the chair so hard the knuckles were white. "Don't do this, not here, not now."

Claire would have stopped if she had any sense that Bud really didn't want this. He just *thought* he didn't, which wasn't the same thing at all.

Crouching at his feet, she placed her hands on his knees and spread them. She'd put on red nail polish and her pale red-tipped hands made a shockingly erotic contrast with the dark gray of his trousers. She unbuckled the belt and pulled the tab of the zipper slowly down. The sound was loud in the silent room. Not even the noises from the busy floor beyond the locked door penetrated. The slow ripping open of the zipper was the only sound in the world. The sound of things changing, the sound of sex on her terms.

"Claire…hon…" Bud said again. Then stopped, as if further words were beyond him. Another sign. During their hot weekend, Bud could barely speak while making love. Tyler, on the other hand, had talked non-stop during the single bout of polite sex they'd had. Lovely, stirring, tender words of love, but in full sentences and with a real vocabulary instead of the one-word grunts which were the only thing Bud had managed when overwhelmed with lust and excitement.

"Bud," Claire said on a sigh of wonder as she pushed down the front of his boxers and drew his penis out. He was as wet as she was, a miracle considering that she'd taken him from zero to a hundred miles an hour in a few minutes. She'd had all that time in the cab and even before, as she was working up the courage to confront him, to get excited. But in just a few minutes, the huge bulbous head of his penis was weeping clear liquid drops.

Claire leaned forward and delicately licked him clean, like a cat.

Bud shuddered, head back, eyes closed tight. He made sounds of pain from between clenched teeth.

Claire had never done this before. When reading about it, she'd actually been a little turned off. How could she have known what a huge turn on it was, instead? Her hands were splayed around his penis, thumbs pointing toward his testicles, framing his erection. It deserved framing. She sat back a little on her haunches, studying him. There really hadn't been the time or the opportunity to do it before, but now she studied him, studied the hardness and grace of him. She was so close she could smell him. It was his familiar scent, only concentrated and musky. His penis was pure power, thickly veined, darkly glistening. Fascinating.

She leaned forward again, shifting her hand to hold the base, sucking the head into her mouth. Bud groaned and placed his hands on her head. There was no question of taking the full length of him in her mouth. He was way too big and she'd choke, but the slow stroke of her hand along the base and a delicate swirl of her tongue along the slit of the head seemed to be more than enough for him.

"Baby," he gritted, fingers digging into her scalp, "we can't do this here…"

Claire lifted her mouth and her hand. "I know," she sighed.

Carefully, as if handling something infinitely precious and fragile, Claire pressed his penis against his abdomen, pulled the boxers up and—with difficulty—zipped him back up again.

Bud's eyes followed her hotly as she stood up. His hands had opened to let her rise and she took one of them. "Touch me," she whispered, bring his hand to her own sex. Widening her stance, she guided him.

"You can feel for yourself how wet I am, Bud." He was caressing her slowly, fitting a big finger inside her. Claire's legs trembled as she gasped for breath. Oh God, he knew exactly where to touch her, exactly how. Faster than she expected, faster than she wanted, a climax was building.

Not now. Not here.

While she still could, she stepped back, one step, two. Out of his reach. She watched his eyes, loving the hot golden heat in them.

"That was our foreplay, Bud." Walking away from him was like leaving a force field. She felt as if she were moving through molasses. She wanted to walk to him, not away. "We won't need any more tonight."

"Lieutenant!" A sharp knock sounded at the door, then someone rattled the knob.

Bud didn't move. Neither did she. Without looking away from him, Claire bent to pick up her coat. His gaze was hard, unblinking and fierce. Broad chest rising and falling rapidly. "I'm going home, now," she said quietly as she buttoned the coat back up, from sex kitten to young lady in six easy buttons. "When you come home, I'll be waiting for you, naked in bed. I won't want or need any foreplay. I want you to start fucking me immediately…"

"*Lieutenant!*" Another hard knock. "Get off the phone. We've got a case!"

Claire backed away, still holding his gaze. "…and I want you to fuck me all night," she finished in a whisper.

She reached behind her to unlock his office door and turned to see an officer with his fist raised. He blinked at her, round-eyed.

"Go right in, officer," Claire said coolly. "I've finished my business with the Lieutenant."

Chapter Fourteen
December 23rd
Abandoned house on the outskirts of Portland
Late evening

 හ

Bud blinked as the photographer's camera flashed one last time. The flare of the bulb brutally highlighted the cruel scene. The mutilated body, the blood spatters, the filthy garbage-strewn floor of an old abandoned house.

"Whoever the fuck this guy was," Dr. Allen Siteman, the ME, growled, "he pissed someone off, big time."

Whoever the fuck he was, he sure had.

Bud walked slowly around the body, careful to avoid blood and avoid stepping on anything or moving anything. The crime scene techies had spent the past two hours meticulously logging everything, bagging whatever could possibly be of use, so it could all be put together later in the lab to tell the story of what happened.

His turn now.

Bud knew he had a damned good crime scene team and he hadn't interfered in any of the proceedings so far. There was no hurry to a crime scene investigation. The investigators took whatever time was necessary. No one was going anywhere—least of all the victim. The team was well trained and they'd gathered up all the physical evidence possible and tagged it. The scene had been photographed in a clockwise pattern and from all four corners. The police artist in the meantime had been making freehand sketches. Latents had been taken from every conceivable surface.

The victim's prints were impossible to take, however, because both hands had been cut off at the wrist.

Bud and Siteman studied the very dead unsub.

Bud motioned to the pale rookie who'd found the body. Officer Sandy Potter. She'd been standing quietly to one side for hours while the techies did their thing, everyone politely ignoring the fact that she'd puked her dinner and probably lunch and breakfast into a tin pail. Potter walked over and assumed the at rest position, hands clasped behind her back. Clearly just out of the Academy and wanting to make a good impression. She had. Except for vomiting, which he'd done a few times himself, Bud found her competent and skilled.

"Let's run this through once more, officer."

Potter nodded, not showing any signs of impatience. She'd already told her story three times and had been standing, shivering, in the cold abandoned house for hours now. But she simply nodded and spoke clearly and slowly, so he could take notes. Bud was going to write a favorable report for her files.

"Two local kids found the body. The house has been abandoned for fifteen years and they say it's haunted. They swore it was the first time they'd ever been in the house. They'd lost a bet and had to spend the night in the house." She gave a pale smile. "I lost a bet like that myself when I was twelve."

Bud nodded. So had he. "You got the kids' names?"

"Yessir," Officer Potter replied, "and addresses. They were exploring when they found..." her eyes slid to the floor then back up again and she turned even paler, "...when they found the body. I happened to be on patrol with my partner and we called it in. My partner escorted the kids back to their parents."

"They'll have to be questioned."

"Yessir, they know that."

"Okay." Bud pulled on latex gloves and squatted next to Siteman, who'd been examining the body on his knees. "What do we have here, doc?"

On one level it was a dumb question. What they had was stretched out before him, a maimed and tortured body. The dead man was lying on his right side, bloody face pressed against the floor, hidden by a long spill of blood-soaked hair. There was so much blood it was hard to tell exactly what color his hair was except that it was a light color. Not brown. Not black.

The victim had taken a bullet to both kneecaps and an elbow. The bone of the kneecaps had burst outward from the force of the bullets, like ghastly, macabre mushrooms. The elbow was a pulpy mass of bone and flesh. The hands had been neatly, almost surgically removed. The radius and ulna gleamed whitely in the red flesh.

Siteman had been quietly talking into a miniature recorder. He pressed the 'off' button and sighed. "I'll have more after the post," he said. "For the moment what we have is a young white male, about 5'10", probably dead a little over two hours before we got here. I'll take his liver temperature to be sure."

"Tortured to death," Bud said quietly.

"Looks like it," Dr. Siteman agreed. "It was a very painful death. Judging from blood spillage, I'd say he took a bullet first to the right knee, then the left. By the time they got around to putting a bullet through his elbow, he was dying. There's very little bleeding from the elbow. It's going to be hard to identify him without prints. We might have to wait for someone to call in a missing person report. Permission to turn him over, Lieutenant."

Bud looked around. The crime scene squad photographer was very thorough as were the techs. They'd done their jobs. Now Dr. Siteman needed to test the liver temperature for an accurate reading. "Permission granted," he said.

Siteman reached out and slowly pulled at the left shoulder until the body flopped over into a supine position, the bloody hanks of hair falling away from the face—a familiar face—and revealing an earring nestling against blond hair. A crucifix on a long golden chain.

No!

Bud rose slowly, shock slowing his system. For a moment, the dead man's earring seemed to float up toward him and he took a step back in horror. He felt the blood drain from his head in an abrupt plummet and tottered for just a second on his feet. Time slowed, hung suspended, stopped. Noise disappeared and his head filled with the sound of rushing air. For the first time in his life, he felt faint.

"I'll see if I can schedule the post for first thing tomorrow morning. Lieutenant? Did you hear what I—" Siteman looked up swiftly and frowned. "Lieutenant?"

Bud heard him, but it was as if he were a million miles away.

"Bud?" Siteman's voice was sharper now. "What's the matter? You look like you've seen a ghost."

Not a ghost. A man he'd recently had dinner with. A friend.

Bud's mouth had gone completely, totally dry. He had to lick his lips to speak. He'd been in battle, had been under fire, but he'd never known fear like this before. Hadn't even known he could feel fear this intensely. It paralyzed him.

"Bud? You okay?"

Suddenly time rushed back in, a roaring river. He could hear the noises of the crime scene squad and feel the heavy hammering of his heart.

"We don't need anyone to call in a missing person report. I know who he is. The dead man's name is Todd Armstrong," he said hoarsely. His lips were numb, throat nearly closed with panic. "He has—had—an interior decorating business near Pioneer Square called 'Todd's Designs'." Bud tried to swallow but his mouth was too dry. "He was tortured to death because someone wanted information on the whereabouts of his occasional partner, another interior decorator named Suzanne Barron. She was the victim of a murder attempt last night. Mob-related, probably. They sent two shooters."

Bud looked around. His partner, Detective Lawrence Cook, was talking quietly to the photographer, but came swiftly over when Bud signaled to him. Bud scribbled on the duty sheet. He had to move fast.

"I'm signing off the crime scene to you, Cook. I need a car and the fastest driver we have here and I need them *now*." He strode toward the exit, barking instructions. "This is a SWAT call-up. Send the SWAT team to 1740 Lexington Road, tell them we have a possible hostage situation. I want a dynamic entry—flashbangs, breaching explosives, everything for close quarters battle." There were two possible SWAT entries into a hostage situation. Dynamic and stealth. He needed dynamic. Stealth took time to set up, and was geared to apprehending criminals and terrorists. Bud didn't give a shit about apprehending anyone, he wanted to stop anything that might—God!—be going on. Stop whatever what they were doing. Kill the fuckers where they stood. "Tell them we're facing men who are armed and extremely dangerous." He turned back for one last look at Todd Armstrong's tortured body. "They're responsible for this and they might be holding a young woman hostage or..." he choked, found it hard to take a breath, had to fight through the panic seizing his mind. "Or they might be torturing her."

He couldn't even say the words—*or she might already be dead.*

He met Cook's horrified gaze. "Call SWAT now," he said and ran.

* * * * *

195

December 23rd
1740 Lexington Road
11:30 p.m.

Bud was late. Well, she'd just have to get used to this. He had an important job that took up a lot of his time. Claire respected that and wasn't ever going to complain. Her thoughts were her own, though. Inside the privacy of her head, she could wish he were already here. She'd been waiting, naked, in bed for two hours now.

"Lieutenant, we have a case," the officer at headquarters had said.

A case.

What he meant, of course, was they had a murder.

Some poor soul had been killed and Bud was doing his very best to bring the killers to justice. Though Claire was sexually frustrated with Bud, that didn't affect her feelings for him. The more she knew him, the more she admired him, in every way.

For some crazy reason, Bud seemed to think that she was missing out on something with him because he wasn't rich. Claire had every intention of proving to him, day after day after day, that she didn't care at all about the money. The only thing she was missing out on was hot sex, but not for long. Bud might not have plenty of money but he had plenty of love and sex to share with her.

She turned over in bed, shivering at the thought of what they'd be doing when he finally did get home. Her excitement had lasted all afternoon and she had come home pleasantly buzzed, feeling soft and sexy, wet and primed. She'd wanted him to find her in bed so badly she'd actually eaten in bed. A sandwich and a glass of white wine. Naked. It had made her feel so deliciously decadent.

The romance novel couldn't hold her attention and she finally just put it down and switched off the light. There was nothing in the book half as exciting as Bud would be when he got home. He was the most exciting thing in the world.

It was snowing outside, little needles of sleety snow tapping at the window. Though she was naked, she was snug in her eiderdown. Bud would be heating her up soon enough, anyway. Claire didn't care when he came home, however late it was. She'd be awake. No way could she fall asleep, the way she was feeling.

Would he ring or just let himself in with the key? He'd had her key for a while, but he usually rang the bell if he came home after her. Maybe tonight he'd want to surprise her. Slip into bed with her in the dark.

Such a delicious thought. Claire smiled into the darkness.

And then her world exploded.

A bright explosive light flaring up out of nowhere like a sun gone nova blinded her. A blast so loud she was deafened. Claire sat up and screamed, though she couldn't hear herself. When she was able to focus again, she saw what looked like hundreds of insectoid aliens with big black carapaces surrounding her bed, thousands of laser lights criss-crossing the dark ceiling, the walls. She screamed again when she saw the insectoid aliens all held black, enormous-looking rifles aimed at her.

She scrunched up against the headboard, screaming, crying, terrified. The aliens were communicating in garbled sounds, rifles steady.

"*Clear!*" a deep male voice shouted from outside her window.

"*Clear!*" This time from her living room.

"*Clear!*" From an alien in her bedroom.

The light came on. As one, the aliens pointed their rifles at the floor and peeled their faces off.

It took Claire's terrified brain a moment to realize that they weren't aliens. They were men in gas masks and body armor. She couldn't breathe and clutched the blankets with bloodless fingers.

"Oh, God, honey, I was so fucking *scared.*" Someone was holding her, strong arms so tight she could barely suck in air. She would recognize that voice anywhere.

"*Bud!*" Claire clung, terrified, to his neck. She whimpered, trying to crawl into his skin. "Oh God, Bud, what's going on? What's happening?"

Bud was shaking. She'd felt him tremble with sexual excitement but had never felt this—deep tremors of fear shaking that strong body. He was holding her so hard it hurt— the first time he'd ever caused her pain. His face was buried in her neck, and she felt wetness against her skin.

He was crying. Bud was crying. She wouldn't have thought it possible. She was crying, too. Claire Parks, who never cried, not even in the fiercest pain. Not even when she'd received a death sentence.

She flashed suddenly on ten years ago, when she'd clung, terrified, to Bud.

He eased his hold, shrugged off his jacket and put it around her shoulders. The terror was easing off, and she realized she was naked, in a room full of armed men. They weren't looking at her. The men had all turned their backs to her and were facing outward.

Claire pulled back to look Bud in the face. "Bud," she whispered. "What's going on? Who are all these men? Why are they armed?"

He wasn't answering her. He lifted himself away from the bed and started giving orders to the men in the room. In a heartbeat, they left, slipping quietly out the door. One minute they were there, ringing her bed, a supernatural menace, and the next they were gone.

Bud rummaged in her closet and pulled out one of her suitcases. He opened it and started quickly throwing clothes from the closet in it. "Get dressed, honey," he said, barely looking at her. "Warm clothes, boots, gloves. Get a move on."

Get a move on?

Claire was frozen. She held the sheet up to her neck with a still-trembling hand. "Bud, tell me what's going on. Who were those men? What's happening?"

He still wasn't listening. He was shoving things into her suitcase with one hand, speaking rapidly into his cell phone with another, stopping every minute or so to go check the windows.

"I know. Shit, yes." His deep voice was ripe with frustration. "That doesn't mean they're not on their way. Clear everyone out but secure the perimeter. Is the decoy ready? Good. Does she have long hair? Then put a hat on. Get her going. We'll be exiting from the other side of the block. Get the safe house ready." He snapped the phone closed. "Come on, hon. They're waiting out back. Get dressed."

Her heart was still pounding, but she'd recovered enough to realize that he had led a bunch of armed men into her bedroom. And had terrified her.

Claire kept her voice steady, but it wasn't easy. "Why should I get dressed and where are we going?"

Bud snapped the suitcase closed. "To a safe house. A policewoman who looks like you is waiting in the front room. A decoy. Once she's left, we'll slip out. You'll need clothes and some reading material. I don't know how long you'll have to stay in the safe house." He'd made fun of her enormous To Be Read pile on the bedside table. With a swipe of his hand, he tumbled the entire pile of books into a duffel bag, closed it, and hefted it over his shoulder. He looked back, frowning. "Damn it, Claire, I told you to get dressed."

Circulation was returning, including some blood to her head. "Bud, I'm definitely not getting dressed until…"

He simply hauled her out of bed and shoved a sweater and pants into her hands. He was frowning, sweat on his forehead. She stood before him, dressed only in his oversized jacket that hung to her knees and covered her hands. "Goddamn it, Claire, I told you to get a move on. Don't make me repeat myself. We don't have any time." He threw one of her coats on the bed. Socks followed.

Bud had never spoken to her like this. There were shadows outside her windows, the crackle of a radio. The engine of a car started up. Bud looked at her, his face hard. Claire was frozen, clutching his jacket around her.

"Claire, if you don't get dressed right this minute, I'll drag you out of the house naked. Believe me, I'll do it if I have to."

She watched that implacable face and had no doubt he'd do exactly what he said. She slipped the clothes on, zipped up the ankle boots. Bud was looking out the window. He nodded, flipped the cell phone on. "Go," he murmured into it and Claire heard the rumble of a car engine taking off. Another quick glance out the window and he took her elbow. "Let's move."

Claire stiffened. She locked her knees. They were trembling anyway, so locking them made sense from a number of points of view. "I'm not going anywhere until you tell me why and where."

Bud had on an expression she'd never seen before. Hard and ruthless and utterly closed to her. "I'm saying this once, Claire. Someone's after Suzanne. Night before last, two killers came gunning for her. Her tenant took them down and disappeared with Suzanne. I just came from examining Todd Armstrong's body. He'd been tortured to death for information on Suzanne's whereabouts. Whoever wanted to take Suzanne down is gunning for her friends and anyone who knows anything about her knows about you. You're next on their hit list."

Claire's heart pounded. Suzanne in danger...another thought occurred to her. "*Allegra—*"

"Is safe. You told me she's in Boston, at the Eye Clinic. I called a friend at Boston PD in the car coming over here. Allegra's under armed guard. From now on you are, too. I'm taking you to a safe house until I figure out what's going on and who the guy behind all this is. You'll have armed guards 24/7. So will Suzanne's parents in Baja California. I notified the Mexican police. Now get moving."

A repeat of Switzerland. Claire's heart thudded and she sucked in air, feeling suddenly faint. "Bud, please *please* don't lock me up. Please. I couldn't stand it. I have a valid passport, and I could leave the country right now. I have a friend in Bermuda. Or I could go to an aunt in the south of France."

He wasn't listening to her. She got the impression he could barely see her. His eyes constantly flickered around the room, stopping at the door and the windows. He looked back at her, saw she wasn't moving. His hard face got harder when he saw her expression.

"Listen up, Claire. A very brave policewoman who looks a little like you just now left in a car, acting as a decoy. If this house is under surveillance they'll follow her. She's bought us some time, but I'm not going to have you waste that chance she's given us so you can have a little hissy fit or get in a pissing contest with me. I'm going out into the living room now. I'm giving you..." he checked his wristwatch, "...five minutes. You come out under your own steam with a packed bag or I'm handcuffing you and carrying you out. And don't think for a second I won't do it, because I will."

They stood for a few seconds, toe to toe. There was no arguing with Bud, no talking to him, no reasoning with him. This was Claire's worst nightmare.

"Decide now," he growled. He wasn't even looking at her. He was glancing out the window again. A big gun had appeared in his hand.

She nodded at the gun. "Otherwise you'll shoot me?"

"Don't be ridiculous."

"How long will this last?"

"As long as it takes. Now get going."

It was over, in more ways than one. "All right," she said quietly. She knew she had no choice. "I won't take more than a few minutes. Please leave me alone."

Bud turned and left the room immediately. She could hear his deep voice in the living room, issuing orders.

Claire added toiletry articles, underwear, warm woolens. Several nightgowns. More reading material. She locked her suitcase and put on her coat. She stood for a moment in her warm room, looking at the rumpled bed, thinking of the hopes she'd had. The dreams of a happy lifetime with Bud.

With steady hands, she took off her engagement ring and placed it carefully on the top of the dresser. She didn't need it.

She'd never wear it again.

Quietly, Claire rolled her suitcase out the door.

* * * * *

December 28th
Safe house, somewhere in Oregon
Late morning

Four days later, an exhausted and unshaven Bud pulled up in the driveway of one of the safe houses run by both the Portland PD and the FBI. This was a joint case and Claire had been living there, guarded by two FBI agents and two police officers. Bud had chosen the PD officers himself. Smart, tough and crack shots. And the FBI agents were no slouches. Claire had been kept safe. He'd made certain of that.

For four days, he'd been running on coffee and two or three hours' sleep a night on various cots and couches.

It was over. The long nightmare was finally over and a rough kind of justice—not one he'd have been able to hand out, as a sworn police officer, but justice all the same—had been done.

On Christmas Eve, John Huntington had called in from wherever it was he'd been keeping Suzanne. Suzanne had heard on the radio news of the death of Marissa Carson, her client. Leaving Marissa Carson's house two days earlier, she'd encountered Marissa's husband, Paul Carson, an underworld crime lord masquerading as a businessman, a man Bud had been after for years.

When Bud had heard that name, a jolt of electricity had run through him. Terror because it was clear he was involved in the danger to Suzanne and Claire, yet a fierce kind of joy at the thought of hanging something on him at last. Marissa had been found with her head bashed in, her husband swearing he'd been in Aruba at the time of his wife's murder.

Only he hadn't been. He'd been in Portland. The only person who could swear to that was Suzanne Barron. Suzanne could put him away forever in a place where his money and his mob connections couldn't help him.

No wonder Carson, powerful, rich and ruthless, had done everything in his power to find Suzanne and take her out, including torturing poor Todd Armstrong to death. The only thing standing between the electric chair and freedom was Suzanne Barron.

Suzanne had insisted on turning state's witness, though she was basically signing her own death sentence. If Carson didn't manage to actually have her killed before the trial, her testimony would put her into witness protection till the end of time. Suzanne's life essentially was over.

Then Carson was shot and killed last night. Felled by a sniper's bullet.

Freeing Suzanne and freeing Claire.

Bud knew that the Midnight Man loved Suzanne deeply and would do anything to protect her. He knew also that Midnight was one of the most talented snipers in the country.

He refused to put the two things together.

Paul Carson's death spared Suzanne a life in hiding and above all, spared Claire.

These past four days he'd been sitting through the endless FBI debriefings of Suzanne and busting his balls to put together an air-tight case against Carson. And then...someone...had taken the matter out of his hands and taken Carson's life.

Exhausted and disheveled, he was still jubilant. Suzanne was free. Midnight was free to love her. Claire was free and safe. It had been hell, but they'd come through it.

Life was fragile; hopes and dreams hung from a thin slender thread that could be cut at any time. Bud had almost lost Claire as soon as he'd found her. He had no intention of wasting any more time.

They were going to get married as soon as it was legally possible.

Exhausted as he was, Bud also felt a kind of exhilaration. He was going to get married to the most beautiful girl in the world, while Paul Carson had been taken out of the world in an exquisite kind of symmetry, proving that there was a rough kind of justice. Life just didn't get much better than this.

The police officers and FBI agents barely looked up when he walked into the apartment. They knew he was coming. He'd been in constant telephone contact and they'd kept him informed of Claire's every movement. Not that there had been much. She'd pretty much stayed in her room and read. They'd also said she hadn't eaten much, which worried Bud a little. Claire didn't have much weight to lose.

"Hey, Lieutenant." Sam Haney, cocky and stocky, one of his own, looked up from cleaning his gun. "Glad it's over. Real boring assignment. You look like shit." The other three looked up briefly, nodded, then continued with what they were doing—packing up. Messy suitcases were on the floor and the sofa. Pizza boxes, open newspapers and overflowing ashtrays were strewn everywhere. There was the funky smell of too many men in too small a space, stale food, stale smoke, gun cleaning fluid and tension.

No wonder Claire stayed in her room. She was delicately fastidious, like a little cat. Bud was sure that her room was spotless and perfumed.

Before Bud could open his mouth, Haney gestured with his thumb. "She's in there, reading. Man, that lady reads like it was a *mission*." He shook his head admiringly. "She's read more in these four days than I have this year."

That's my Claire, Bud thought. "Maybe you guys want to be out of here soon."

Haney gave a flippant salute with a forefinger to his temple. "Consider us gone." He just dumped the rest of his stuff in his bag and zipped it up. The others were doing the same.

Bud walked to Claire's room and knocked.

"Come in." God, he'd missed her voice. Bud's heart was actually racing as he opened the door. It was hard to keep a big sappy grin off his face. He was going to have to sort of…glide over why there wasn't any danger any more, but once that little hurdle was over, there was nothing but blue skies ahead for him and Claire. His car was outside. In an hour they'd be back at her house, where he didn't intend to let her up for air until tomorrow morning. After which, they'd start planning the wedding. Hell, maybe just go to City Hall and tie the knot soon as they got the blood tests done.

A lifetime with Claire. As his wife.

He loved his job. He knew he'd love his wife forever. They might even have kids. If they did, he'd definitely love them, too. Never in his wildest dreams would Bud have imagined being in this place.

There she was. The love of his life. His future wife. "Hi, honey."

Claire was sitting in an armchair, reading. Natch. Of course, this little room was an oasis of peace and neatness, sweet-smelling and orderly. He breathed in deeply, ready to collapse from fatigue, but energized at the same time. "It's all over. I've come to take you home."

She didn't smile. She put a bookmark in the book she was reading and carefully put it on a coffee table. The face she turned up to his was sober and serious. "Is Suzanne all right?"

Okay. This was where he was going to have to finesse things a little, glide a little over the harsh realities of life. "Absolutely." And in bed with John right now, he'd bet his pension on it. "She was released by the FBI. There won't be a trial because Paul Carson is dead."

Claire looked up at him, big blue eyes solemn, clear and blue as a mountain lake in summer. "Dead? Isn't that a little fortuitous? How did that happen?"

It was in the newspapers, so he couldn't lie. "He was shot and killed by a sniper. Totally unexpected, but it solved a lot of problems."

She was silent a moment. "Yes, I can see that it would solve a lot of problems. Does that mean that the danger to Suzanne is over? That's she's free?"

"Oh, yeah. And the danger to you is over, too. Come on, honey. Get your things together. We'll be back in Portland in an hour." Bud scrubbed a hand over his face, wishing he'd had time to shower and shave. But he simply couldn't wait to get to Claire. "I'll cook you a four star dinner tonight. And—oh." He pulled his hand out of his coat pocket. He held his hand out to her, her engagement ring gleaming in the palm of his hand. "You forgot this. I knew you'd want it. I'm sorry I couldn't get it to you earlier but I wasn't…in the area."

Suzanne's safe house had been in Roseburg but he couldn't tell Claire that. Safe house locations were top secret.

Claire was up and packing quietly. She glanced at his hand and shook her head without looking him in the face.

"No, Bud. I don't need the ring. And I didn't forget it. I left it because it doesn't belong to me."

He was standing, a foolish grin on his face, open palm out. "What? I don't..." He shook his head. "Of course it belongs to you, honey. This is the ring I bought for you."

Claire went into the bathroom and emerged with her toiletry articles. She put them neatly away in her beauty case. "No. That ring belongs to your fiancée. Not to me."

This wasn't funny any more. "What the fuck does that mean? To my fiancée. You *are* my fiancée."

She took a deep breath and faced him. "Not any more, I'm not." Claire's voice was quiet but firm.

"*Shit!*" Bud tried to rein in his temper, but it slipped. "What the *fuck*..." He drew in a deep breath again, trying to control his emotions. Claire had just been through an ordeal. She obviously wasn't thinking straight. "Okay, honey. Whatever. Let's get going and we can talk in the car. I can't wait to get out of here."

She snapped a suitcase shut. "I don't want to drive back with you, Bud. In fact, I don't ever want to see you again. I'll have one of the police officers drive me home."

Bud blinked, feeling as if he'd been suddenly punched in the stomach. "What the hell are you talking about?" There was something seriously wrong here, and he had no idea what it was. Then he looked down at himself. He looked like a bum and probably smelled like one, too. He'd been sleeping in his clothes and had had a chance to catch just one shower in the past four days and hadn't shaved at all. No wonder she didn't want to go in the car with him.

"I'm sorry I haven't had a chance to clean up, honey. It's been a really intense time. Just hold your nose in the car and..."

"You think I'm a snob." Claire's voice was clear and soft. She searched his eyes. "You think I'm ashamed to be seen with someone who's been working hard." A quick exhalation. "You don't know me at all if you think I'm like that. But then that isn't a surprise."

Bud was losing his footing here. "Well, if the fact that I smell like a goat and look like a bum isn't the problem, then what is? Because I'd really like to get going. We have things to do. Like planning a wedding."

"There isn't going to be a wedding."

Claire dropped that little bombshell like a stone into a pool of water. The echo of her words rippled out. It was all Bud could do to keep from grabbing her and shaking her. Exhaustion is like being drunk. Things penetrate slowly. Bud finally was grasping that Claire was quietly furious with him, and he had no idea why. He hadn't even recognized it because he'd never seen her angry. Hadn't even known she could get angry. A happy easy-going disposition was her hallmark.

He was on very shaky unfamiliar ground here. He'd never really fought with a woman before. If it ever got around to anger, harsh words, he was out the door. Why put up with any shit? But Claire was different and if he had to fight for her, even fight *her*, he would. He widened his stance and stood straight, unconsciously preparing for battle, though it would be a battle of words and not fists.

"Okay." It was going to be painful but he could do this. "Tell me what I did wrong and I'll apologize and you can forgive me and we can go. Is it that I didn't call? I swear I called the officers four, five times a day, you can ask them. I knew you were okay—I was keeping tabs on you all the time. Maybe I should have asked to talk to you but things were really intense. I can't talk about the details, you know that. But I realize now maybe I should have somehow found the time to talk to you."

"I know you were busy, Bud. I'm not a child. But that's the problem right there. You seem to think I *am* a child. A sick child, to boot. I wasn't in any way consulted about where I should be taken to be safe. Did it even occur to you that I spent 5 years essentially locked up in a compound in Switzerland with armed guards? I had an armed escort every time I left the compound for a walk. I hated every second I spent there. I felt as if I were in prison for a crime I didn't commit. I told my father repeatedly that I hated it, but he couldn't seem to hear me. Just like when I speak to you, you can't hear me. It made *him* feel better to know that I was there, so that was it."

"Goddamned *right* it made him feel better!" Bud said heatedly. Anger moved in him, hot and slick. "You were Goddamned kidnapped by a man with a Goddamned gun and a knife and your father was supposed to just let you go stay where you wanted without protecting you?" The memory of a bald-headed, sick, fragile Claire shivering in his arms made his anger blossom. "Do you even realize what Gavett could have done to you if I hadn't happened along?"

"Of course I realize what could have happened. What I'm saying is that locking me up for five years wasn't the answer. Just like locking me up for four days wasn't the answer. There are plenty of places I could have gone, where Paul Carson couldn't have found me."

"Oh, right." The anger was rising with each word she spoke. "Claire Parks, who's never lived on her own, who's spent maybe five minutes not under her father's wing, is all of a sudden this great expert at evading an international mobster. He'd have been on your tail in five seconds, tops. He was a monster, Claire. Smart and ruthless. You wouldn't have stood a chance. You have no idea what the outside world is like, what a man like Carson was capable of. No notion." He was getting all heated up at the thought of her trying to outwit someone like Carson who had immense financial and human resources at his disposal coupled with utter ruthlessness. Carson would have tortured her to death without blinking an eye. He would even have enjoyed it. Just the thought of that, of Claire at a sadistic monster's mercy, had Bud breaking out into a sweat. "Goddammit, Claire, you shouldn't even be let out loose! Look at you! First night out on the town and you fucked the first guy you met at The Warehouse! How stupid was *that?*"

It was a mistake. He knew it, could feel it was a mistake even as he said the words, but they came tumbling out in his exhaustion and anger. The words reverberated in the little room, harsh and stark. He couldn't call them back.

Claire had gone bone white. She watched his eyes for a long moment, then her slender shoulders slumped in despair.

Tears glittered in her eyes, but she didn't shed them. "I knew what I was doing. I knew who I was choosing and I didn't make a mistake. I chose you and, at the time, I was right. But in the end I did make a mistake. I thought you really loved me. But you can't love me, Bud, and have that opinion of me. That I'm a stupid, careless, spoiled child who needs looking after." She bit her lips. They'd gone bloodless. "I fought too hard and too long to be able to have the chance to live long enough to become an adult to have that taken away from me now. You don't trust me, and I don't want to have to fight for that trust. I'll ask one of the officers guarding me to take me home."

She glanced at his fist, curled around her engagement ring. "Maybe the jeweler will take that ring back," she whispered. "I won't be wearing it."

Chapter Fifteen
January 5th
The Pavilion lunchroom
Portland

∞

"So…" Claire said, and sniggered. "You're married. You were single, not even dating, last time I looked. I turn my head for one second and bam! You're married without even an engagement in between. That was quick."

Claire studied the enormous diamond wedding ring on Suzanne's left hand, a different shape and a different setting, but just as beautiful and overdone in its way as her own engagement ring had been. She ruthlessly repressed that thought. For all the good it did her. She thought of Bud about 23 hours a day. The other hour she slept. Badly.

"It *was* quick." Suzanne looked at the ring, too, in bemusement, and threw Claire a helpless *how-did-this-happen?* look. "I don't know, Claire. It's all sort of a blur. First I'm running for my life, then I'm holed up in a mountain cabin somewhere, then I'm surrounded by FBI agents and then the next thing I know I'm in the registrar's office, getting married." She looked slightly shell-shocked. "Whenever I imagined getting married, I always thought it would be after a long, calm engagement, where I got to know the man well. We'd have similar tastes. Take a trip or two together to see if we're compatible while traveling. Maybe even live together for a while. I never thought I'd find myself married to a man I've known…" Suzanne counted the days off, the wedding ring casting blinding lights as she moved her hand, "… fifteen days." She looked appalled as she met Claire's eyes. "I've only known John for *fifteen days*. And we've been married for six of them." Suzanne shook her head helplessly. "Amazing."

"Are you happy?" Claire asked bluntly. She had no business commenting on Suzanne's marrying John after only knowing him a few days. She herself had become engaged forty-eight hours after meeting Bud.

"Oh, yes." Suzanne lost that bemused look. Her beautiful face glowed. "Oh, absolutely. John's a wonderful man. A very loving husband. Very, uhm…" a light blush crept up under the glow. "…very…loving."

If John was anything like Bud, Claire had a good idea what the blush and the glow meant. She'd met John once, over dinner at their house, which doubled as headquarters for John's security business and Suzanne's office as a designer.

John didn't look like Bud but he had the look of Bud. As if both of them came from the same planet, a different one from here. One where they grew the men stronger and bigger and tougher. John even had some of Bud's mannerisms—a quiet watchfulness, a keen awareness of his surroundings, an overprotective manner.

A sigh escaped her before she could stifle it.

"How about you, honey?" Suzanne asked gently. She covered Claire's hand with hers and both of them had to look away from the intense glare of her wedding ring. "You're looking tired and sad. Is it because of Bud?"

"Absolutely not," Claire replied. "I'm fine. *Fine*."

"Because *he's* certainly looking tired and sad," Suzanne continued. "We saw him the other evening and he didn't look well at all."

"He didn't? How did he…" Claire suddenly shut up and set her mouth. "I don't care."

There was a little silence. Claire pushed around the bits of excellent fish she hadn't managed to choke down. Suzanne calmly ate her own fish with every sign of enjoyment.

"So…how sad and tired?" Claire asked finally.

Suzanne waved her fork and gave a dainty shrug. "You don't care, remember?"

There was a long silence, a tribute to Claire's complete and utter indifference to anything Bud might be doing or feeling. She pushed the fish around and around, bit her lip and finally gave in. "Okay, okay. *How* sad and tired?" she repeated in a mumble.

"Very." Suzanne leaned forward. "Oh, honey, if you could just see how miserable he is and like the lunkhead that he is, he can't even express it. He just walks around with these tight lips and red eyes and white face. Not talking." She wrinkled her nose. "Not shaving, either. He looks like a wreck."

Claire put her fork down with a clatter. "He deserves it," she said hotly. "I won't be treated like a child. A sick one, at that. It was already coming to a head before he had me carted away and locked up. I couldn't sneeze, I couldn't cough without him going into nurse mode. He was constantly checking to see if I'd eaten, asking me if I'd slept. Saying I was working too hard. It was like having a nanny instead of a lover. I'm not a child and I'm not sick. I'm *fine*."

"He loves you," Suzanne said gently. She watched Claire's face. "He wants to keep you safe and healthy. And you love him."

Claire shrugged angrily, swiped impatiently at her eyes. More tears welled. Throughout the long, painful years of her illness, she'd never cried. Not once. Crying would have spelled defeat, a weakness she couldn't afford. Here she'd cried more for Bud in the past few days than she'd cried in her whole lifetime. It seemed that she spent all her time lately with her eyes leaking. She hated that.

"Don't you?" Suzanne angled her head to meet Claire's eyes. "Don't you love him?"

Claire bit her lips to not say the words, a tear coursing slowly down her face.

"You know, John is wildly overprotective, too." Suzanne dabbed daintily at her mouth and sipped her glass of white wine. "It gets very annoying, let me tell you, particularly if you've been independent as long as I have. He won't let me drive if it's raining or snowing or even threatening bad weather. You can imagine how much fun that is in Portland, in winter. He deputizes one of his men to drive me and they are not what I'd call great conversationalists. If he's free, he insists on accompanying me anywhere I have to go. Actually, having lunch with you on my own is a minor miracle. He's in Salem for business today. It's all a little overwhelming and I'm hoping that with time, he'll tone it down. But..." she smiled, "it's because he loves me. And I guess it's a price I'll just have to pay. To tell you the truth, I pay it willingly, because I can't imagine ever loving another man the way I love him."

Claire blinked. Her eyes burned. There was a huge hot rock lodged in her throat.

"They're not easy men to love," Suzanne went on. "Bud and John are hard men who've spent their lives in dangerous jobs, with not much softness in their lives. I think perhaps they're not used to loving someone. So it's hard for them, you know? To know how to draw the line, to know when to step back. John finds it enormously difficult to find that line between being caring and being...well, obnoxious and suffocating. I find myself having to nudge him back over that line every once in a while. God knows what he'll be like as a father. Probably freaking out every ten minutes."

Claire straightened. Father. Children. Oh, God. She wanted children, but now she'd never have any because she was mad at Bud, who was the only man she could ever marry.

"Life is short," Suzanne continued. Tears suddenly appeared in her eyes, too. "Think of Todd. Think how quickly people we love can be taken away from us. Love is fragile and precious and should never be thrown away."

The two women held each other's hand tightly. Claire was crying openly. She looked at Suzanne in dismay. "What am I going to do?" she whispered. "I can't go forward and I can't go back. I can't go back to things the way they were, but I can't stand the thought of never seeing Bud again."

Suzanne squeezed her hand. "Don't worry, sweetie. I have a feeling it will all work out."

* * * * *

January 5th
437 Rose Street
Late evening

Suzanne smiled as she heard the living room door close. Her husband, John, was finally back from his business trip. She was seated at her bedroom vanity, combing her hair, in her brand new, very pretty, very sexy peach silk nightgown.

Hearing the door close was a new thing, quite an achievement for her. John was a former commando, a warrior. He'd been trained to move stealthily, without noise. It was eerie how a man as big and heavy as he was could move with such silence. He'd frightened the life out of her more than once as he suddenly appeared before her, like a big, dark, powerful wraith. He was under strict instructions now to *make a noise* when he came home or entered a room she was in.

There he was at the door and she watched his reflection in her vanity mirror, heart pounding. Everything about her husband excited her and her heart still soared whenever she saw him suddenly.

Maybe the excitement would wear down eventually, as time went on. Though she doubted it.

He met her eyes in the mirror, gaze dark and intent. Silence reigned in her pretty bedroom. John only slept here, and hadn't made his mark. Luckily, he was neat and tidy, a relic of his navy days, she supposed. The four big rooms across the hallway where he worked were bold and masculine, imprinted with his personality, but her rooms, where they lived, were pretty and feminine. John seemed to find the contrast amusing and, at times, exciting.

"Welcome back," she said softly, watching him in the mirror as he moved toward her with his lithe walk. "I missed you."

"Nice nightgown," he replied, his voice a deep growl. He had a look in his gunmetal eyes that she had come to know very, very well. "I missed you, too."

Deep inside her body she was already opening for him, already excited by his mere presence. But before he made love to her and she forgot her own name, they needed to talk.

Suzanne swiveled in her chair, rose and moved toward the window. She had to be out of his physical grasp. One touch and she'd go up in flames. She held up her hand and he stopped obediently, eyes gleaming.

"John, I need to ask a favor of you."

"You got it, darlin'." His eyelids lowered. "Anythin' you want, you can have. Jus' name it."

Oh, God. Suzanne locked her knees before they buckled. When he used that smoky tone with the faint Southern accent, she knew mind-blowing sex wasn't far behind. She usually heard that tone rumbling in her ear as he was making love to her, thrusting hard and fast and for hours. She had to concentrate here or she'd be on her back before she knew it.

"You know how miserable Bud looked the other night when we had dinner together?"

John froze. Suzanne could almost see the wheels whirring in his handsome head. Was this a trick question? Was this a trick question that involved *emotions*?

"Yeah?" he said warily.

"Well, I had lunch with Claire and she was looking just as miserable. They're both going to stay miserable on either side of the fence they've erected between them, the idiots, unless someone does something. Both of them have heads as hard as concrete and neither of them are willing to give in first, so they'll both be miserable forever. John, we have a responsibility here."

"No, we don't." John held his big hands up, palms out. "No way. Bud's having a hard time, yeah, I can see that, and I'm sorry if Claire isn't happy, but that doesn't have anything to do with us."

"Of course it does," Suzanne said sharply. John was amazingly intelligent about a lot of things, but absurdly obtuse about others. "Bud and Claire are our friends. Their happiness is absolutely our concern."

John blinked at the idea. He opened his mouth to object when Suzanne continued.

"Their paths don't cross, ever. How could they? Bud's a police officer and Claire works for an ad agency. Unless someone throws them together, they're just going to stay quietly miserable forever. And Bud's beard will reach his sternum. That won't do." She smiled persuasively at her husband. "But I've got a plan."

John wisely kept his mouth shut. Still, she recognized that mulish cast to his jaw.

Suzanne gave her husband her most winning smile. "You know the opening of the show at the Parks Foundation we're invited to on the 15th? 'The Jewels of the Czars'? The one where you keep complaining about having to wear a tux?"

"Fuck, yeah," John said, then winced. "Sorry. But I hate formal dos, you know that. Plus you insist that Kowalski and I have to attend *unarmed*." John looked aggrieved. "What's with that? I'll feel naked."

"Well, you have to attend because I designed the jewelry display cases and they're brilliant if I do say so myself. And you and Douglas will be unarmed because the idea of carrying guns into the Parks Foundation is ridiculous. Nothing violent could ever happen there."

And also, Suzanne thought, John's new partner, former Senior Chief Douglas Kowalski, looked frightening—like a dangerous thug. He'd be frisked for weapons immediately by the security company of the jewelry show.

"Can't you convince Bud to attend, too?" she asked.

John looked astounded. "Why the fuck—why the hell should *Bud* come? When he'd have to wear a tux? What does he care about Russian jewels?"

"He cares because Claire will be there." Suzanne refrained from rolling her eyes.

"Well, I sure can't force him to come to the opening. And if he's smart, he'll stay far away."

"No." Suzanne took a deep breath. "That's not good enough. We need to be certain Bud will come to the opening."

"There's no way I can promise you that," John said.

Suzanne smiled. John was a strong-minded man, with a will of iron. What saved her from being brow-beaten by her own husband was that fact that he had a very strong sense of justice and fairness. And the fact that she had a secret weapon.

She reached to her shoulders to unleash that secret weapon. Slowly, Suzanne slipped the straps of her nightgown off her shoulders and felt the gown slide silkily and sexily to her ankles. She was naked except for her kidskin mules.

John's eyes widened and his nostrils flared. He stepped forward, big hands reaching for her.

"I'll talk to Bud tomorrow," he said hoarsely.

* * * * *

January 15th
Parks Foundation
Opening ceremony of the 'Jewels of the Czars' Show

"No, I guess I missed the Tibetan Music Festival. What a pity."

Claire smiled insincerely, evaded the groping hands of Professor Smith Bogdanovich, Emeritus Professor of Musical Ethnology and drone extraordinaire, and moved on to the next stuffy blow-hard with an avid desire for a Parks Foundation study grant. She'd met them all and been on the receiving end of thousands of monomaniacal rants on their obsessions. Tibetan Music. Medieval incunabula. Etruscan tombs. 17th century Neapolitan dance. Maghrebian foodways. All interesting in and of themselves, but not in the hands of fanatics.

Boy, was Claire glad she'd quit working at the Foundation. She'd been making polite conversation with a concentration of all of Portland's bores for the past hour and a half, remembering how often she'd had dealings with them and how tedious she'd found them all. Working at the Foundation had been hell. She'd hated every minute of it.

Depressed as she was, Claire had decided to forego the gala opening tonight, though Suzanne had designed the display cases and Allegra was providing the music. Much as she loved her two friends, she had zero desire to make polite conversation when all she wanted to do was sink her head in her arms and cry with despair. Then her father had come down with a mysterious virus a few hours before the opening and she'd had to do the family honors. Which, she thought with a sigh, consisted mainly of making sure there were enough canapés and champagne for the crush and keeping from yawning.

The footmen opened the big doors behind her and another gust of gelid winter air billowed in. Claire had to work not to shiver. This dress was a big mistake. Red, strapless, form-fitting and slit to mid-thigh, it didn't offer much cover. She'd bought it in a vain attempt to cheer herself up.

It didn't work. All it did was make her feel exposed and chilled. Coupled with the red satin Gucci stiletto heels, she managed to be both cold and unsteady on her feet.

Still, she mingled and shivered and tottered until she made her way to Suzanne and heaved a sigh of relief. "Hi," she murmured. "Congratulations on the display cases. They're gorgeous. Almost as beautiful as the jewels themselves."

"Thanks, sweetie." Suzanne swirled a lock of dark blonde hair behind an ear. "I worked hard on them. It was a pleasure and a privilege. The jewels are truly exquisite."

Suzanne had been receiving compliments all evening, but she wasn't getting much of a chance to mingle with the crowd and do a little PR work for her budding designer studio. Her husband, looking handsome in a black tuxedo but with a grim off-putting scowl, seemed surgically attached to her side, never more than a hand's span from her. His expression discouraged conversation. And the man with them looked positively frightening.

No. Not frightening so much as...dangerous. Predatory. Ferocious. Claire gave up trying to describe him to herself. Huge and hard, fierce-looking and battle-scarred, he wasn't a man anyone would strike up a conversation with. Not at the Parks Foundation, anyway. Maybe on the waterfront. If you were looking for a contract killer.

Suzanne was doing her best to be sociable, though. "Claire," she said with a forced smile and a small sigh at the intractable male material she had to work with. "I'd like to introduce you to Senior Chief Douglas Kowalski. He's John's new partner."

Claire blinked. John's new partner. John's office was in the same building where Suzanne lived. Suzanne was going to have to live in the same building as *him*?

Manners had been drummed into Claire. She knew perfectly well she should offer her hand and make some polite comment. Steeling herself, she stretched her hand out gingerly, wondering if she'd get it back. "Senior Chief Kowalski." She tried to smile into the man's eyes but they were way way up high, dark and scary-looking. "N-nice to m-meet you."

Damn! She never stammered. And she was the hostess, after all. It behooved her to be gracious.

"Ma'am." The big man engulfed her hand in his for just a moment, squeezed gently, carefully, then let go. His hand was hard, callused and huge. "My pleasure. This is a very beautiful building. My compliments on the show."

What he said was perfectly ordinary, but his voice made her shiver. He had a basso profundo voice, the deepest voice she'd ever heard. Deeper even than Bud's.

Oh, God. Don't even think of Bud.

Allegra started singing and Claire nearly closed her eyes in relief. She didn't have to make polite conversation with Suzanne's husband, who was tugging at his collar and looking like he'd rather be anywhere but here, or with—God!—his dangerous-looking partner. When Allegra sang and played, people listened.

Silence fell over the room, guests turning in surprise. Allegra was on a raised dais, in a gorgeous dress of green taffeta, brilliant red hair streaming in curls down her back. She was playing her harp and looked like a fairy angel, come down to console poor mortals.

It was Allegra's first concert in public since she'd been assaulted. No signs remained of the trauma on her beautiful face, but Claire knew what it cost her in her heart to be out in public.

Allegra's voice soared, high and pure.

Everyone turned to the dais, a few voices murmuring in the crowd. Some quietly commenting on the music, some on Allegra's beauty.

Claire took the moment to gaze around and check that was all running smoothly. She froze at the look on John's partner's face. What was his name? Kowalski? He had turned stiff, huge frame still and focused on Allegra, like a hunting dog. Oh, God. She couldn't read his expression at all. She couldn't figure out what the expression was, except he was raptly fixated on her friend. He looked frightening and dangerous. Was he dangerous to Allegra? Surely Suzanne wouldn't allow a dangerously violent man in her home?

While she contemplated what the man's intense interest in Allegra might mean, another gust of chill air made her shiver and raised goosebumps.

"What the *fuck* are you doing dressed like that in sub-zero temperatures?" a deep furious voice from behind her demanded. "You're half-naked!"

Claire turned in surprise.

Bud.

Bud looking wonderful and tired and lean and angry. Handsome and tall and frowning and delicious in a tuxedo. Her heart—her treacherous treacherous heart—took a huge leap of joy in her breast before she remembered that she was angry with him. Before his words had a chance to sink in.

The first time she'd seen him in weeks and he reprimanded her. She'd cried her eyes out over him. In her heart of hearts, deep in the sleepless wee hours of the night, she'd pined for him.

And the first thing he did when he saw her again was criticize, try and make her feel like a hapless child.

She wanted to cry and scream and shout. She wanted to throw herself into his arms. He roused roiling emotions in her she couldn't begin to handle without screaming like a banshee at him. Not here. Not now.

She wanted to open her mouth to give him a gelid reply. Maybe something along the lines of—"Hello, Tyler. It's nice to see you, too." But if she opened her mouth, she'd start crying.

Claire couldn't handle it. She turned on her heel and stalked off.

A big hard hand cupped her elbow. "Oh, no, you're not running off," Bud said from between clenched teeth. "You're staying with me and we're going to talk. But first you're going to get something to cover your shoulders with. You're chilled and you look like a hooker."

Claire opened her mouth in outrage, ready to blast him, but she didn't have any breath to do it. He'd grabbed her upper arm and was propelling her through the crowd, out of the Hall of Columns and down the immense hallway leading to the back of the building. He was walking fast. With those long legs of his, she had to run to keep up with him. She wanted to wrench herself out of his grasp but it was ridiculous even trying.

"You're hurting me," she tried to say coldly, but it came out as a gasp. It was hard to speak coolly and calmly when running in stilettos.

"Am not," he ground out from clenched teeth.

There were very few people out here in the back. Bud turned right, into the high, narrow corridor that ran the length of the back of the building. There was nobody here. The kitchen and service rooms were on the left flank. Five rooms down the empty corridor, he wrenched open a door. Claire knew the building inside out. This was the library, an enormous room with bookcases stretching to the high ceiling. Propelling her in, he followed and slammed the door closed. He flipped a switch and a Murano chandelier lit up, casting a brilliant glow. More than enough light to see that Bud was furious.

Fine. So was she.

"How dare you manhandle me," she said, her voice shaking. "You have no right to touch me or tell me what to do."

"The fuck I don't," he growled. "You're *mine*."

Claire sucked in a breath to tell him off and he kissed her. One of those tongue deep in her mouth, fingers digging into her back and backside, hips grinding into her kisses. Violent and passionate and out of control.

Bud was back.

Claire could hardly breathe, Bud was holding her so tightly. His mouth moved hard over hers, sucking and biting at her lips. Hard. Everything he was doing was hard. Kissing her hard, fingers digging into her hard. His penis was rock-hard. He ground against her and it was as if he sparked off a conflagration inside her.

She was mad at him. This was her cue to tell him off, tell him he couldn't order her about, tell him she needed to be treated like a full-grown adult woman.

Though he was treating her like an adult. There wasn't a woman in the world who wouldn't go up in flames at being kissed like that.

Bud lifted his head a breath away from her mouth. "Goddammit," he breathed. "I wasn't going to do that. I was going to talk to you, reason with you, but then there you were in that fuck-me dress…"

"Shoes," Claire murmured. "Only shoes can be fuck-me."

"No, that dress is definitely a fuck-me dress." Bud leaned his forehead against hers. Claire had hooked her arms around his back. He felt leaner, as if he'd lost a lot of weight in the past two weeks. He was actually trembling. Deep down, she'd known how much he loved her, and this was the proof. Tough, combative Bud didn't tremble easily. "I missed you so much, Claire," Bud whispered.

Claire bit her lips. Her eyes filled with tears. If she moved, if she so much as breathed, they would spill down her cheeks. She clutched his back harder, hoping he would get the message.

Me, too. I missed you, too. So much.

A rasping sound and she felt air at her back. Through the teary emotions wracking her, it took her a second to realize that Bud had unzipped her dress. He stepped back just enough so that it could slide down to her ankles. His big hands moved from her back to her hips, sliding her panties down her legs and there she was—naked except for stockings and heels.

He was looking down at her, eyes golden hot. "Just like in the police station," he whispered. "I wanted to fuck you so hard that day. We couldn't do it there. Then...things happened. I've been walking around with a hard-on since then." His gaze went lower, so intense it was almost as if he were touching her with his hands. Her nipples rose to hard peaks at the expression in his face as he stared at her. One big hand slid around her hip to reach between her thighs. "Open." It was a rough command.

She obeyed and they both sighed as a big finger touched her sex. Bud didn't have to comment on how wet she was. She knew.

He raised his head, shook it, seemed to come to his senses. He looked down at her, gaze circling her face. "Can't fuck you like this," he muttered. "Make up. Hair." He glanced around. "There."

This was the Bud she'd missed. The one who got so excited he could barely speak.

He picked her up and carried her a few paces to the Empire marble-top hall table that had been a recent Foundation acquisition. He turned her around and pushed gently against her back until she was bent over the table. The marble felt icy cold against her nipples and belly, in exciting contrast to the heat coursing through her.

Bud tugged at her hands, curling them around the edges of the marble. He pressed with his hands on hers and she understood the message—*stay*.

The zip of his pants was loud in the silent room. Not a whisper of sound from the Hall of Columns or the corridor outside penetrated. It was as if they were all alone in the building. His knees opened up her thighs to him. His big hands, hot and hard, gripped her hips.

"This is what I wanted to do that day," he muttered. His penis nudged her. "God, I wanted to fuck you...*so hard*." He slid into her in one long strong stroke, touching her womb. Claire clutched the cold edges of the marble top, electrified to feel Bud in her once again, when she thought she'd be empty there for the rest of her life.

He bent over her, hands still clutching her hips, crushing her against the marble with his weight. Claire loved it. Loved the heavy feel of him against her back, his hot steely penis deep inside her. She even found it exciting that he was dressed and she was naked. The only place skin touched skin was his hands on her hips and his penis buried deep inside her. Then he licked her ear and she shivered. Her womb pulsed, a short sharp contraction.

He wasn't moving, wasn't talking. She couldn't move, either, completely immobilized by his heavy weight, his legs holding hers far apart. They were in some sharp-edged limbo, Claire shaking, so completely possessed by Bud her world was reduced to her breasts, belly and vagina.

Bud's fingers flexed and he tightened his grip. It was almost—but not quite—painful. She could feel his leg muscles move against hers as he pressed in harder, more deeply, and rotated his hips.

It was enough to set her off. With a wild cry, Claire climaxed. Bud jolted on top of her and it was as if her climax were his cue to move. His heavy thrusts moved her back and forth across the cold marble top, the movement keeping her climax going for so long she thought she'd pass out. Just when she thought she couldn't take any more, Bud gave a loud groan, swelled even further inside her and ejaculated. She could feel his semen filling her in long jets, almost in complete synchronicity with her contractions.

She came again, right at the end of her first orgasm.

It was so intense everything went black. She clung, shaking, to the table's edges.

There was a loud bang and the ground shook. Far away spitting noises.

Her head swam, her heart thundered.

Bud pulled out immediately. Claire was vaguely aware of the fact that he zipped up.

"Jesus Christ!" Bud swore in the pitch blackness. "That was a flashbang. And AK-47s. At least three. They took out the lights."

Claire was dizzy, lying prone on the marble top of the hall table. She heard Bud's words but couldn't concentrate on what he was saying. Her body was still climaxing, vagina still pulsing. She couldn't move, could barely breathe. Her body had taken over completely and she couldn't stop the pleasure coursing through her.

Dimly, she was aware of the fact that Bud had left the room after muttering something about her staying put. The door had quietly opened and closed. Only by the faint noise of the door could she tell Bud had gone. The lights in the hallway had gone out, too. The room was pitch black. Claire lay stunned in the darkness, blind and confused, rendered helpless by her body's satisfaction.

The lights came back on just as her climax finally wound down.

Claire blinked, shaking. She was spread-eagled across a table, naked. She blinked again as nerve endings sprang to life and consciousness returned. Awareness rippled out in waves. She was clinging naked to a table while something had happened in the Hall of Columns. And Bud had disappeared.

Confused, she got up and shakily made her way to where her dress was pooled on the floor, looking for all the world like a little lake of blood. She was very wet, Bud's semen trickling down her thighs. She was still so sexualized the world felt far away, the only reality the piercing sensations of her body. Her hands shook and it was hard to concentrate. She stared at her dress for a long moment, then stooped. A shake and a shimmy and her dress was up.

She looked around. Bud was still gone.

Faint noises carried from the front of the building. Cries and shouts. Claire couldn't quite make them out, but there was distress and pain in the air.

She stood up straight, finally inside herself, finally in control. Something had happened at a Parks Foundation ceremony. An accident, maybe. A fire that had taken out the electricity, or…or something. Whatever had happened, she was Claire Parks and this was her responsibility.

Moving swiftly now, she opened the door and froze.

It was like a tableau from a thriller, the kind she'd read all her life. Three protagonists at a climactic moment. Young woman dressed in red outlined against a doorway. Criminal with ski mask and submachine gun turning in her direction. And last—the action figure. Bud, who'd been sneaking up behind the criminal to knock him out.

Time speeded up, flowed tragically in the wrong direction.

Bud's eyes widened when he saw her, saw the masked man moving. He shouted, attracting the masked man's attention, rushing forward. Claire heard the gunshots, *felt* the reverberation of the gun's reports. But she wasn't the one who felt the bullets.

Bud was.

Blood bloomed on his chest and he crumpled as the stench of cordite rose sharply into the air. He lay still on his back, blood pooling bright red and running in little rivulets. The masked man moved toward him, machine gun at the ready, waiting for Bud to show a sign of life so he could get off the death shot. But Bud lay deathly still.

Afterward, Claire had no idea how she'd gotten from the doorway to the man's back. She had no clear memory of that moment and it would remain forever befogged in sorrow and rage in her mind.

Claire knew the Parks Foundation building like the back of her hand. She'd grown up there, knew every nook and cranny. Knew, particularly, where the fire extinguishers were kept. In a rush of crazed grief, she wrenched the extinguisher from the where it was hidden in a niche in the wall and ran full tilt toward the masked man standing with his back to her, ready to finish Bud off.

No. No way. As Claire had fought with all her strength to live, she would fight with every fiber of her being for Bud's life.

The intruder must have sensed her behind him. He was turning, lifting the machine gun, Bud was rising horrified on an elbow, shouting to attract the man's attention, when Claire sprayed extinguisher foam directly into the man's face.

With a cry of pain, he bent over, trying to claw at his eyes. Claire took the steel cylinder in both hands and swung it upwards into his face with all her strength.

The man fell like a slaughtered bull, without a sound.

"Bud!" Claire slid to her knees, already ripping at her long skirt. Oh, God! Bud had lost so much blood. She was kneeling in it, kneeling in his lifeblood, the color of the material she was frantically trying to wrap around his chest. He was so deathly pale her heart hammered.

"Claire." Bud's voice—normally so strong and so deep— was weak. "Go away. Get out of here."

On a sudden horrified suspicion, Claire studied his chest, searching desperately for signs that his lung had been punctured. There was no sign of bubbling blood, however. Nor was the blood pulsing out of him in spurts. He hadn't been shot in the lungs and the bullets hadn't severed an artery. There was still hope.

Bud was trying to rise, slipping slightly in his own blood.

He coughed and scrabbled on the floor until he was holding the masked man's submachine gun, lifted himself up using the unconscious man's shoulder for purchase. "Go away, Claire. Get out of here."

"Bud," Claire whispered. "What's going on?"

He glanced toward the big doors leading into the Hall of Columns. "Jewel thieves," he gasped. "At least five. Armed. They've got everybody on the ground. Got to help." By some superhuman effort, Bud started staggering toward the big doors. He was panting, face utterly white with exertion.

But his hands on the gun were steady.

In an electric moment, Claire realized he was going to go in and face at least five armed men alone and wounded.

"*No!*" She knew enough to keep her voice low. The man she'd felled was obviously a guard and who knew how many others were around. The last thing she wanted to do was attract the attention of another masked man with a submachine gun. But damned if she was going to let Bud walk to his own death. "Stop! What can you do on your own?"

He wasn't even listening. He was moving slowly, steadily towards the doors, face white, trailing blood.

Claire rushed forward, clutching his elbow.

He gritted his teeth, the jaw muscles moving. "Get out of here. *Move!* In a few minutes there'll be shooting. I want you as far away as you can get."

There was no stopping him. Claire understood that, in an electric moment of clarity. He was going to sacrifice himself in an attempt to save the hostages on the floor of the Hall of Columns. She realized that he understood he wouldn't survive the attempt. But he was going to make the attempt anyway.

She had to think fast. Bud was five feet from the doors and his own death. She had to do something to give him a chance. "Listen Bud," she said desperately. "Where's John? Do you remember what his position was?"

Suzanne's husband was a former commando. If there was anyone who could help Bud, it was him.

"Under the big mirror. On the left hand wall."

Under the ornate baroque mirror. Perfect.

"Listen to me," she said urgently. "There's a little service door not five feet from there. It's almost invisible and it's hidden behind a big palm, anyway. I'm going to go into the kitchen and get some knives and see if I can sneak through the door and get them to John. Can he throw a knife?"

A faint smile flickered across Bud's hard, pale face. "Yeah. John can throw a knife." He shook himself, obviously only just realizing what she'd said. "Are you *crazy*, woman?" he demanded, turning to look her full in the face. "I want you far away from here. As fast as you can go. You can't go into there—no, wait. *Claire!*" This in a fierce whisper.

But she was already kicking off her shoes and running. She ran straight into the kitchen, slamming open the double doors, realizing too late that there might be guards posted here. There were no guards, but there were dead bodies.

Two men in once-white-now-red jackets, toques grotesquely askew, lay on the kitchen floor, blank dead faces staring at the ceiling. Dominic and Jerry—the chef and sous-chef. Claire raised her eyes and saw four white faces through the little porthole of the meat locker. The intruders had killed the two men, and then herded the others into the locker. There was a big padlock on the door, so there was nothing she could do for them. Either she and Bud and John would be successful or not.

She didn't want to think about the 'or not'.

Moving as swiftly as she could, Claire pulled out the chef's knife set, bound in leather. The set was made of the finest Japanese steel and, she knew, kept perfectly honed to a razor-sharp edge. Keeping his knives sharp was almost a religion with Dominic.

Holding the leather bundle awkwardly, Claire exited from a side door. This part of the building was a labyrinth, a relic of the days when families had an army of servants. It was a warren of small rooms and cubby holes.

But she knew where she was going. In a minute she was at the small door set so cleverly into the wall of the Hall, it was almost invisible.

She dropped to her knees and eased the door open. Keeping a low profile, she quietly slid through. The magnificent royal palm in its huge Chinese vase hid her from view, though she knew that her red dress was highly visible through the leaves if anyone happened to be looking her way. She vowed never to wear red again. Red was danger.

Red was the color of Bud's blood...

All the guests at the ceremony were on the floor, most against the walls. There were ten women at the front of the room, watched over by an armed man. Clearly hostages in case some of the men decided to rush the thieves. Suzanne was one of the hostages. Allegra was nowhere to be seen.

Four men in masks were systematically smashing Suzanne's crystal display cases, tossing the priceless jewels into heavyweight gym bags.

Claire saw John sitting with his back to the wall, eyes glittering, gaze locked on the man holding a gun to his wife's head. Claire scooted forward, using the backs of some of the hostages as screens.

John watched her out of the corner of his eye. She remembered his ability to be aware of his surroundings at all times. He didn't betray her presence by so much as a twitch of a muscle, but she knew he was aware of her.

Claire reached him, then sat up, her back against the wall like all the others. The guard's attention was taken with the women hostages. When he turned this way again, he'd simply assume she'd been one of the people in the room surprised by the intruders. She raised her knees and slowly lowered her head, as if in despair. Moving carefully, she slithered the leather bundle over to John.

"There are knives in there," she murmured, head low so the guard couldn't see her lips moving. "Bud's outside with a machine gun he took off a guard. He's badly wounded. I don't know if he'll make it."

"If he's alive, he's coming," John answered, his voice a soundless whisper.

Claire blinked. He hadn't appeared to move, and yet the knives were now lined up next to his thigh. He also had a knife in each hand.

The seconds passed, each one an agony. Was Bud outside bleeding to death? Or was he—oh, God!—already dead? Claire pushed that thought away. Should she have…

It happened in an instant, so fast she could barely understand what was going on, though she watched it happen.

The doors to the Hall were kicked open, and a grim, white-faced Bud was through, machine gun firing. John rose and flicked the knives so quickly they were a blur as they flew through the air. The man guarding the women hostages went down instantly, frantically clutching at a knife through his throat. John's frightening-looking partner appeared out of nowhere, in a deep dive that turned into a roll. When he rose an instant later, he had the downed man's gun in his hand and was firing. All the masked intruders went down.

Women screamed and men shouted and then the firing stopped, just like that. John was clutching Suzanne tightly.

Claire didn't see anything else. She was up and running to Bud, stepping on hands, kicking anyone who got in her way.

"Bud!" He looked at her and dropped the machine gun, as if it was suddenly too heavy to hold. Then, horribly, he dropped to his knees, face utterly white.

The tuxedo jacket was glistening, the shirt front a deep red.

Claire skidded to her knees, holding Bud. "Oh, God, Bud!" she sobbed, as she tried to ease him down. "Don't die on me. You can't die!"

"No," he whispered and closed his eyes. "I can't. You won't let me."

Epilogue

** හ**

Claire wouldn't let him die.

She stayed with him in the ambulance, was there when he came out of surgery and was by his bedside as he drifted in and out of consciousness. Even when he dove down into a morphine-induced haze, he was aware of her. Knew she was constantly by his side.

On the fourth day, Bud woke up and realized he was going to live. He was hooked up to every monitor known to man. He barely had the strength to raise his head. He was weak and his mind was fuzzy but one thing was clear. He was going to live.

Claire wouldn't let him die.

Claire. His Claire.

She was sitting in a chair by his bedside, one hand on his arm, as if to reassure herself of his presence. The other was under her cheek. She was sleeping, long lashes lying against her pale cheek. She looked about twelve years old.

About the only muscles he had that didn't hurt were his cheek muscles, so he smiled.

Claire's lashes fluttered, and she opened her eyes. They stared at each other a moment.

"You're back," she whispered.

"And staying back." His hand moved on the sheet until he found hers. Their hands clasped. "Life's going to be easier for me from now on. I'm going to have this kick-ass wife by my side. She's such a toughie. If my Captain doesn't watch his step with me, I'll just sic her on him. She's a real scary lady."

Claire smiled. Her first smile, he knew, in four days.

"You betcha," she said.

Enjoy an excerpt from:
WOMAN ON THE RUN

The sky rumbled as she made her way down the corridor, and the lights flickered once. *Great,* she thought. *Just great.* She really had to hurry home now. Something in her house was leaking and she didn't want to have to try locating the source by flashlight.

She entered the classroom, with its familiar smell of chalk dust. Mr. Big leered at her from his corner perch. She'd have to remember to tell Jim to leave it on the school steps when he finished cleaning.

The lights flickered again in the shadowed room. Heavy footsteps sounded in the corridor outside the classroom, loud in the silence of the school. Someone was striding quickly, then stopping, then walking quickly again, as if—her heart started racing—as if looking for something...or someone.

Don't be silly, she told herself, but her heart continued its wild thumping, anyway. She pushed papers into her briefcase with shaking hands, cursing as one slipped to the floor. She could hear herself panting and made a conscious effort to slow her breathing. The footsteps stopped, then started again. Each teacher had his or her name taped to the door. If someone was looking for Sally Anderson...

Stop, start...

She grabbed her coat, trying to calm her trembling. Davis had spooked her, that was all. It was probably Jim...

...except that Jim was an old man and shuffled...

or one of the teachers...

...except that all the other teachers had gone home...

Closer, closer...

The footsteps stopped at her door and her gaze froze on the glass pane that covered the upper half of the door. She had to see who was out there, reassure herself that it was just one of the harmless citizens of Simpson and not...and not...

A face pressed against the window. A man. He reached inside his jacket to pull something out.

The lights went.

Julia whimpered and tried to think around the icy ball of fear that had formed in her mind. What could she use as a weapon? There was nothing in her purse but a pocket diary, keys and makeup. The kids' desks were too heavy to lift, and the chairs were of lightweight plastic. Her hand brushed something hard and round. *Mr. Big!*

Panting wildly, she hoisted the enormous pumpkin in her arms and stood at the side of the door, ready to smash the man out there over the head. Her body tensed, going into fight and flight mode.

The knob rattled.

Julia closed her eyes and saw again the face that had been revealed in the bright neon lights of the corridor.

Overlong, straight black hair, framing a series of slabs angling harshly together to form cheeks and chin, a straight slash of a mouth, black eyes.

An unfamiliar face.

An unforgettable face.

A killer's face.

Why an electronic book?

We live in the Information Age—an exciting time in the history of human civilization, in which technology rules supreme and continues to progress in leaps and bounds every minute of every day. For a multitude of reasons, more and more avid literary fans are opting to purchase e-books instead of paper books. The question from those not yet initiated into the world of electronic reading is simply: *Why?*

1. *Price.* An electronic title at Ellora's Cave Publishing and Cerridwen Press runs anywhere from 40% to 75% less than the cover price of the exact same title in paperback format. Why? Basic mathematics and cost. It is less expensive to publish an e-book (no paper and printing, no warehousing and shipping) than it is to publish a paperback, so the savings are passed along to the consumer.

2. *Space.* Running out of room in your house for your books? That is one worry you will never have with electronic books. For a low one-time cost, you can purchase a handheld device specifically designed for e-reading. Many e-readers have large, convenient screens for viewing. Better yet, hundreds of titles can be stored within your new library—on a single microchip. There are a variety of e-readers from different manufacturers. You can also read e-books on your PC or laptop computer. (Please note that Ellora's Cave does not endorse any specific brands.

You can check our websites at www.ellorascave.com or www.cerridwenpress.com for information we make available to new consumers.)

3. *Mobility.* Because your new e-library consists of only a microchip within a small, easily transportable e-reader, your entire cache of books can be taken with you wherever you go.

4. *Personal Viewing Preferences.* Are the words you are currently reading too small? Too large? Too… ANNOYING? Paperback books cannot be modified according to personal preferences, but e-books can.

5. *Instant Gratification.* Is it the middle of the night and all the bookstores near you are closed? Are you tired of waiting days, sometimes weeks, for bookstores to ship the novels you bought? Ellora's Cave Publishing sells instantaneous downloads twenty-four hours a day, seven days a week, every day of the year. Our webstore is never closed. Our e-book delivery system is 100% automated, meaning your order is filled as soon as you pay for it.

Those are a few of the top reasons why electronic books are replacing paperbacks for many avid readers.

As always, Ellora's Cave and Cerridwen Press welcome your questions and comments. We invite you to email us at Comments@ellorascave.com or write to us directly at Ellora's Cave Publishing Inc., 1056 Home Avenue, Akron, OH 44310-3502.

erridwen, the Celtic Goddess of wisdom, was the muse who brought inspiration to story-tellers and those in the creative arts. Cerridwen Press encompasses the best and most innovative stories in all genres of today's fiction. Visit our site and discover the newest titles by talented authors who still get inspired - much like the ancient storytellers did, once upon a time.

Cerridwen Press

www.cerridwenpress.com

Made in the USA
Lexington, KY
27 May 2010